BINDER

BINDER

David Vinjamuri

TABLE OF CONTENTS

For Tessa

bind•er

noun

1. a person or object that holds something together
2. a streak of impurity in a coal seam, usually difficult to remove

WEDNESDAY

John McCarthy knew they were in trouble before the hooded men boarded the bus. He saw the danger before dim headlights revealed muddy pickup trucks blocking the road, before a line of men carrying shotguns and tire irons emerged from the dark. John knew something was off the moment they hit a roadblock on Route 3 that hadn't been there the past dozen times they'd made the trip.

He'd noticed just one thing as they'd approached the detour, a single flaw that made him look for others: the man holding the yellow sign wore sneakers. He wasn't the teenager John had been the two summers he worked roads in Columbus, either. This guy was in his late thirties, and the arms poking through his reflective vest showed the kind of hard biceps that have to be worked every day to last at that age. His tan was a little light for a road guy too, but that wasn't the thing that caught John's eye. It was those white Nike crosstrainers. You don't wear shoes like that when you're working on roads because hot asphalt will burn right through the soles. And nothing white stays that way for long when you're around construction.

Then John eyed the two men standing in front of the striped barricade in the middle of the road. Both were lean and fit like the first, but younger. That was odd, too. Those jobs were the ones the union guys covet—much easier than bending over a shovel or driving a paver in the scorching sun all day. The guys who worked them usually had bellies that betrayed the beer and burgers they downed at the same pace they had in their glory days. And both of them faced the school bus. That was just wrong. Neither was watching the other direction for oncoming traffic. Road workers don't turn their backs on distracted moms in SUVs, even if there's another crew up the road responsible for stopping traffic.

But the bus driver didn't spot those warning signs; he only paid attention to the yellow diamond the guy in sneakers was waving. He swung the bus off the main road like a skipper steering a barge around a reef while John was still weighing the risks of bucking the chain of command. Tiny fingers of spiny leaves scraped the roof of the decommissioned school bus as it slipped under the low-hanging branch of a holly tree.

The detour put them onto a poorly paved road that didn't look like it would connect to anything. A half-mile on, after narrowing down to a single lane, they found two old Ford pickups blocking the roadway. A line of men in grubby clothes wearing hemp hoods with crudely cut eyeholes stood in front of the muddy trucks. Several of them carried torches, and John half expected to see a burning cross greet them as a tall man with a shotgun stepped forward and waved the bus off the road. The driver—a kid from the suburbs of Seattle—finally started to panic, but by then there was no way to escape. A white panel van had followed them through the detour and pulled up close behind them. They were boxed in. So the driver followed directions and pulled the ramshackle bus into the empty lot by the side of the road. It was a construction site of bulldozed earth. A grader sat next to a big yellow Caterpillar dump truck at the edge of the lot. *There's the construction equipment missing from the roadblock*, John thought dazedly.

The barrel of a shotgun rapped against old glass, startling the driver. Hands trembling, he leaned over and pulled the handle to open the door. Three hooded men smelling of sweat and bourbon came aboard, leaving prints of red mud on the ridged rubber mat that lined the aisle.

"Don't resist. They're just trying to scare us. They're not going to hurt us," Judy said. Judy's badge of honor was having been arrested at the G-8 summit in Glen Eagles. She was the designated leader in Roxanne's absence, but John knew she was wrong. He could smell the brittle pheromone that precedes violence on the hooded men. He badly wished Roxanne were with them. She'd have read the situation as he had but reacted sooner, perhaps even ordering the driver to run the barricade. If not, she might have cowed the hooded men into submission with words, a talent John did not possess.

But Roxanne was not on the bus and John knew that anything he might do would only make the situation worse, so he complied just like the rest. They were marched out and made to kneel down on the damp, scarred earth. A man spinning a baseball bat in rough hands approached them. His piercing blue eyes shone out from under the hood.

"We warned you. Stop interfering with our livelihood or face the consequences. Now's time for consequences." John had been sitting at the front of the bus, which put him at the front of the line. Two men dragged him forward. Throughout his life, John had always been clear in his convictions—not the type given to uncertainty. As the bat rose above him, framed for an instant by a luminescent cloud concealing the moon, he experienced a moment of doubt.

Then it began.

1

THURSDAY

It was a classic ambush, and I walked straight into it.

I saw the two of them when I kicked the screen door open. I had a duffel bag slung over my shoulder and a box in my hands. There was no room to maneuver, so I stopped dead in the doorway. I lowered the box carefully to the ground and dropped my bag before raising my hands in surrender.

"You're not leaving...are you?"

"Of course he's leaving. What else would he do?"

"That's not helping."

"He's not helping."

"That's not fair. He dropped everything to come here."

"Spare me. He's only here because you blubbered on the phone. Mom doesn't want him here."

"How do you know what Mom wants?"

"Remember what happened last time?"

"That wasn't his fault!"

"Oh that's precious! Whose fault was it then?"

"Those men."

"They were here *because* of him. Then he left, didn't he, and he hasn't been back since."

"What did you expect? You told him not to come back. Then you didn't invite him to Gabe's baptism."

"Don't you dare bring my son into this!"

"You brought him into it! Mikey is Gabe's only uncle."

"And now he's leaving Mom in the hospital so he can go back to work."

"I—" I tried to interrupt. Amelia glared at me and the sound died in my throat.

"He's been here for five days. Mom is going to be recovering for a long time. What else do you expect him to do?"

"You don't understand..." I interjected. Ginny laid a hand on my shoulder without looking at me.

"What do I expect him to do? Are you kidding? One of us needs to be with Mom around the clock. A nurse almost killed her the other night with the wrong 'scrip. They took her off the catheter last night but Mom still can't reach the buzzer when she needs a bedpan. There are test results coming in every day and Dr. Kassavian doesn't take time to call us when he gets them so I have to call the neurologist myself. Plus the shingles on the roof still need to be repaired, the washing machine is leaking and there's a mountain of laundry. And by the way, I still have a six-month-old at home."

"So Mikey's supposed to quit his job to help us?"

"He can take more than three days of vacation to help the family when there's a crisis."

"He got in the car ten minutes after I called him."

"Because you're the only one he listens to—his precious baby sister."

"Maybe if you stopped trying to boss everyone around all the time..."

"Oh don't you start with me, Virginia Herne!" Amelia knocked my shoulder as she brushed past, muttering about Ginny being a freeloader and moldy bread in the pantry. Ginny scrambled after her, still bickering even though Amelia was no longer listening.

I was standing there, speechless, when I realized my third sister Jamie, who is older than Ginny but younger than Amelia, had been watching the argument. She was standing in front of a burnt orange 1995 Honda Civic parked on the street in front of my mother's house. Every time I see that car I'm amazed that it hasn't been stolen for parts.

I grabbed the duffel and slung it back over my shoulder, then leaned down and picked up the box. As I approached, I saw that Jamie's lips were all bunched together in amusement.

"You like to stir the pot, don'tchya?" she said.

I made a face. It was the same one I'd first used when she was eight and I'd stranded her six feet up in a tree after she smashed a chocolate ice cream cone into my head.

She wrinkled her nose. "Are you really leaving today?"

"Yeah, but not for work. I have to help a friend. It's important."

She raised an eyebrow.

"For real."

"You're leaving an emergency for another emergency?"

"When you put it that way..."

"You can't fix this mess but maybe you can do something about the other one?"

I thought about that. "Maybe."

She pursed her lips and shook her head. I shrugged and turned my palms to face her and nearly dropped the box.

"So go," she said as she kissed my cheek, "and then come back."

2

Three of them came for me as I left the bar. The big one had a couple of inches on me. Worse, he was built like a bull and outweighed me by three or four sawbucks. He shoved me into the first alley we passed. The push was strong enough to lift me off the ground for an instant before I landed flat on my feet. The leader wore a Carhartt cap, a rough canvas shirt and boots that looked like they might have steel toes. He was skinny and sported an uneven beard that didn't mask his crooked teeth, broken nose and narrow, deep-set eyes. He slipped a hand into an outside pocket of his surplus Army jacket and emerged with a pair of brass knuckles.

"You done a lot of talking back there," he said. That's what I managed to translate, anyway, as his accent was two shades denser than others I'd heard so far. The third man stood behind the leader and nodded. He looked like he'd been doing that for most of his life.

"We don't 'preciate strangers, 'specially thems with a mouth full o' questions," the leader continued.

I retreated slowly to avoid being flanked. Then I reached a hand inside the breast pocket of my windbreaker while I held the other hand up, empty palm forward to try to forestall the skinny guy from throwing a punch with that brass-knuckled fist. I pulled a color photo from my breast pocket. It was oversized and printed on glossy paper that I had neatly folded in half. It was considerably bigger than the snapshot I'd flashed in the bar when I was asking if anyone had seen the girl it pictured. More importantly, she wasn't alone in this photo. The men slowed and squinted at the picture, which moved their thoughts away from beating me up.

"That's a happy family, right? The girl is the one I'm looking for. She was demonstrating at the Hobart mine. Maybe you don't like outsiders or maybe the demonstrations pissed you off? I get it. So ignore her. Look at the man standing behind her. That's her father. Do you see him? See the ribbons on his chest? That red one with the vertical blue stripe running through it? That's the Bronze Star. These two purple ones? Purple Hearts." This froze the three angry men in their boots. These days, everyone from a small town has a friend who lost a leg in Iraq or Afghanistan. The uniform means something in places where real people live.

"Before you raise a hand against me, look at one more ribbon on this man's chest. See the black one with the blue and red stripes on either end? That's a prisoner of war medal. This girl's father was chained to a wall in a North Vietnamese prison, and beaten to a bloody pulp every day for two years before any of you were born. You may think his daughter is just some pampered college kid, and you might be right. But this man deserves your respect. He deserves to know what happened to his daughter." I let a little indignation enter my voice. The men looked at each other, suddenly off-balance.

In truth, I'd never met the man in the picture and didn't know if he'd even served in Vietnam. But he was wearing an Army colonel's dress uniform with a POW medal, so I guessed at the war from his age.

"Mister, I ain't never seen that girl. And I don't 'preciate you expectin' I might've," the leader responded. The other two just kept staring at the picture.

"Do you work at the Hobart Mine?" It was a question I already knew the answer to from the black dust under his fingernails, the rheumatoid arthritis evident in his walk and his difficulty hearing. Plus the fact that I'd asked the manager at my motel which bar in Hamlin the miners frequented. His first answer was, "All of 'em," but he picked one when I pressed.

"Yessun," he answered slowly. The other two men were still trying to decipher the medals and ribbons that soldiers call "fruit salad" on the chest of the man in the photo.

"Then you've seen her. She's been protesting in front of the mine entrance since the beginning of last summer," I explained. The leader considered this for a moment, looking thoughtful but still guarded.

"Listen, guys," I continued, "you may not know much about this girl or what happened to her, but I guarantee it's more than I do. I've never set foot in this state before today. I'm just trying to help a friend find his daughter. She came here with Reclaim—the group protesting at Hobart—but the hospital has no record of her being admitted last night after the attack. The only thing I care about is finding this girl. So let me buy you a drink. Even if you don't know anything, you can pretend you do until my wallet's a little lighter." I'd been in Appalachia for less than six hours but already saw a story I recognized in the eyes of these men.

"Ain't no such thing as a bad free drink," the big man said hopefully, looking toward the leader. Silently, the question was resolved. The leader's brass knuckles disappeared into a pocket. The big guy took a step away from me then turned. I followed the three miners back into the bar. It was a shabby, intimate dive that wouldn't have felt out of place in Conestoga. Technically it wasn't even a bar, just a private drinking club, but the membership only cost a dollar and you got that same buck off the price of your first drink.

The bartender did an honest-to-God double take when I walked back in. He must have seen the men leave after me and figured I wouldn't be drinking in Hamlin much longer. There were a few raised eyebrows along the grooved oak countertop as well, but they quickly turned back to their own conversations. We sat down at a table and the leader looked at the bartender. "Four glasses a' Buffalo Trace," he said, not bothering to ask me what I wanted. So I'd be paying for the good stuff, which was okay with me; anything that put them in a better mood was worth the money. The bourbon was smooth, but it wasn't until we were on the second round that the men relaxed enough to introduce themselves.

"My name's Caleb. You can call me Cale. This big man's Seth and this'n's Braden," Caleb said as he pointed to his agreeable friend who nodded warmly to me, his suspicion having disappeared with Caleb's approval.

"My name's Michael. Michael Herne." I stuck out my hand and Cale grabbed it, squeezed it hard.

"Where y'from, Michael?" Cale asked.

"Virginia—the other one." My GTO still carried a set of the state's stark white plates with blue letters. But I was actually living in the District of Columbia. Still, "Virginia" sounded a lot closer to "West Virginia" than D.C. I'd lived there for almost a decade, so it wasn't much of an exaggeration.

"You know this girl you lookin' for?" Seth asked.

I shook my head. "Never met her. I'm doing a favor for her father."

"These hippie chicks all look the same to me," Cale said. I wondered if he was talking about the blue streak in her hair, the nose ring or just the fact that she was protesting. Staring at the photo, I had to admit she was as mysterious to me as she was to Cale, though I met a few like her in college after I left the Army. "Every one a'them thinks we're tryin' to kill the planet just 'cause we need to feed our kin. Some of the local kids are nicer, but those from up North all think we're damn stupid hillbillies here jus' 'cause we do a day's work."

"People think the same thing about my hometown," I observed. You wear the dirt under your fingernails forever.

"A mine town is a place that has domesticated despair and learned to live with it happily," Seth, the big guy, said somberly.

"Are you quoting Flannery O'Connor?"

"Paraphrasin'. We may be miners, but it don't mean we ain't readers," Seth replied, his face dead serious. He held that expression for a moment before starting to chuckle. The sound rattled in his chest and rolled around his throat until it was real laughter that shook the faded green paint on the wooden panels of the room. Braden laughed more at Seth than the joke and after a moment, Cale joined in. So did I.

We started talking for real then, trading stories of small town life. I found myself liking Cale in spite of how quick he'd been to pull a pair of brass knuckles on me. By the time we hit our fourth refill, I was starting to get hazy even though I'd been to the bathroom twice to stick a finger down my throat. It seemed like the right time to ask about the girl again.

"Cale, why did things get out of hand with these kids? Isn't it normal to have protestors at a big surface mine?"

Cale had a warm bourbon glow and I could tell he wanted to help me. He waved a hand in a dismissive gesture. "It warn't miners done that. I'm not sayin' we loved those eco-nuts. They tied up things pretty good the last coupla' months, that's for sure. Ain't been no layoffs, though, and as long as they got you clocked in, they got to pay you whether you can get to your rig or some dumbass teenager is all laid out on it. They may think we're hillbillies, but nobody hates those kids 'cept management. And no-fuckin-body likes management." They clinked glasses to that. "I'll tell you the God's honest truth: if we got a call from upstairs tellin' us to tweak up those kids, we'd'a done it. But nobody got that call or I'd'aknowed about it."

"But you were ready to rough me up for asking about one of the protestors."

"A man comes inta' my damn drinking club askin' damn stupid questions, I'm gonna tweak him up. But I'm not gonna stomp on some soft college kid just 'cause she thinks we're killin' the damn planet. You look like you'd go a round or two jus' for the fun, anyways."

I knew the truth when I heard it, but even if I hadn't, I would have taken Cale at his word. He wasn't showing the caution of a man wondering if the law was about to come down on him and his friends. I know something about company towns and I suspected that if a bunch of miners assaulted those kids, a man like Cale would have heard about it. But that left me with more questions than I had when I was sober.

"Do you know where those kids are staying?"

Cale looked stumped but Braden spoke up. "I heard they camped up in a holler 'tween here 'n' the site. Which'n was that?" he asked himself. "Stone holler?" Seth nodded agreement. Or maybe he was just drunk.

An hour later I walked carefully back to my motel, grateful that I had chosen one that I could reach by foot from the bar. I inhaled slowly to steady myself, dragging in the smell of burning wood fires. A damp wind was blowing in my face, threatening rain but delivering only a cold chill. It was that time of year when fall tips toward winter and the world feels more dead than alive.

3

FRIDAY

I was surprised how warm it was when I pulled myself out of bed the next morning. Normally I'm up before dawn—then again, normally I don't drink. It was still early when I forced myself to take a run that was more penance than exercise, but it was already well into the seventies in the last few days of October. Indian summer had always been my favorite time of year growing up—the days when you woke up expecting to wear a sweater but got to pull on a t-shirt instead.

Instead of being happy, though, I felt disjointed and out-of-place in a myriad of small ways. The cozy, dilapidated Main Street on a small grid joined by Sycamore, Walnut, Elm and Oak Streets, the view of hills in the distance and the battered pickup trucks that crowded the church across the way could all have been ripped from my childhood, but the reproduction was imperfect. To an outsider, my Catskills town would be unlovely in its details. There, an overgrown lawn with an old Plymouth up on four cinderblocks is easier to spot than a flowerbed. The cement mill, tens of abandoned lots and miles of flecking paint and failing shingles all testify to our condition. But a sense of order persists. Our town center has its limits; we separate our commercial and residential despair.

Hamlin had an advantage to start. The mill that loomed over Conestoga was absent, replaced by a coal mine somewhere over the horizon. But instead of a town built by settlers before a mill overtook it, Hamlin was unambiguously a mine town. Driving in the previous evening on Route 3, I'd been greeted by a row of modest houses on half-acre lots on one side of the road faced off against an industrial yard filled with monstrous steel pipes on the other. Hundred-year-old houses with rocking-chair porches were pushed up against cinderblock office buildings and small warehouses. It was hard to imagine sustaining the bucolic disbelief of childhood on those streets. But most people would say that about my town, too.

I showered and found a diner a block from my motel. The eggs were good, and the sausage had a smoky flavor I've never tasted further north. I persuaded a waitress to part with the location of Stone Holler after confirming she had heard the "hippie kids" were camping there. I was tempted to check out of my motel but didn't. Instead I left my single duffle bag on the bed but grabbed the large manila envelope I'd found propped inside the door when I returned from breakfast. My old boss hadn't changed.

I'd spent seven hours the day before driving from Conestoga to see the man in an office building just outside of the District of Columbia, and then another six and a half hours straight from there to a hospital in Charleston, only to be told the girl whose name I gave them had never been admitted. A triage nurse with thin lips and the faint stink of tobacco on her scrubs refused me access to any of the other protestors who'd been assaulted. With more than a dozen hysterical and grieving parents in the ER, I didn't press the point. I'd been told as much before I started the trip but wanted to confirm it myself; nothing makes you look so much like an idiot as not checking your basic facts. I was eager to locate the Reclaim campsite because, truth be told, I wasn't sure the girl I was looking for was actually missing.

It was just one thing among many that had bothered me when I'd met my old Army commander. His office sits on the top floor of a nondescript building in the Rosslyn section of Arlington, Virginia. I hadn't been inside the building in almost five years and felt an involuntary shiver run down my spine when I crossed the threshold.

We call him Alpha. I know his real name—I learned it some years ago by accident—but it was never used around the Activity. That's what they call his unit, as the actual designation is classified. Alpha had phoned me at 5:30 on Thursday morning. He's an important man, the kind who briefs senators and presidents. He's not the kind of man you say "no" to, not without careful consideration. I did that once. This time I agreed to meet with him when he asked me to come see him at lunchtime that day, even though a long drive and two angry sisters stood in my way.

Alpha was somber that afternoon. It was a relative thing as the man never smiles, but I saw something in his eyes that told me to tread carefully.

"I understand your mother is not well?" he asked. It was the closest he'd come to an apology for disrupting my family visit.

"She had a stroke on Saturday."

"I'm sorry to hear that."

"Thank you, sir."

"I need to ask a personal favor," Alpha said, using neither my given name nor the old code name he'd have trotted out if he wanted me to run an errand for the Activity. This told me something in itself. Alpha is the kind of man who stockpiles favors while scrupulously avoiding owing them, a sort of Polonius in the government service.

I was in Alpha's debt because of some trouble I'd run into the year before in Conestoga. Alpha ran interference with the FBI and kept me out of custody long enough for me to resolve things on my own. It ended up working out in his favor, but the man took a risk on me. It was the kind of obligation I would have honored even if it cost me my job. He knew that, too.

"Of course, sir," I replied, my back rigidly straight in a leather chair with arms. I'd rarely sat in his presence before.

Alpha handed me a red folder from his desk. I flipped it open and saw the face of a girl at her high school graduation. Her dark hair had a streak of purple running through it that matched her robes, and she sported a nose ring.

The folder also had news clippings from the morning papers. I'd already heard the story on the radio as I drove to Arlington. A group of protestors got beaten up in West Virginia and one of them had died.

"Who's the girl, sir?" I asked the obvious question.

"Her name is Heather Hernandez. She's the daughter of a friend. The picture is several years old, but I understand her appearance was the same when her parents last saw her. She left home at the beginning of the summer with a group called 'Reclaim' to protest the activities of the Transnational Coal Company in West Virginia. The parents' only contact with her after she left was by e-mail. Her mother also saw some of her Facebook posts through a family friend. After the incident last night, Heather's parents were unable to reach her and neither the police nor any West Virginia hospital has a record of Miss Hernandez being transported or admitted."

"Can we confirm she was on the bus last night?"

"We cannot."

"Do you have any background on the other protestors?" I asked, thumbing through the documents in the folder.

"There are some profiles at the end of your file," Alpha answered, pulling on a pair of reading glasses and flipping open his copy. "Reclaim has a fairly typical composition for a radical environmental group: somewhere between thirty and fifty members, mostly young, almost all white or Asian and largely from the Northeast, California and the Pacific Northwest. A number of them took part in the Occupy Wall Street protests. Some have criminal records, but nothing unusual—one shoplifting conviction, some minor drug charges—but primarily a large number of arrests for disorderly conduct, vandalism and similar crimes. Three of Reclaim's older protestors have the majority of the disorderly conduct citations and other misdemeanors consistent with protesting, but no criminal backgrounds."

"Do you have a complete profile of the leaders?" The folder only had photos, basic information and the police records.

"No, but we can run that," Alpha replied, making a note on a blank white pad sitting inside a leather portfolio on his desk.

"Sir, I'm not a licensed investigator. That could create some problems, particularly with all the media attention on this story," I pointed out.

With a curt nod, Alpha pulled a sheet of paper from his file and handed it to me. "This letter from the governor of West Virginia welcomes you to the state to investigate Miss Hernandez's whereabouts as a private citizen on behalf of the family. It may not carry any force of law, but it should suffice for your purposes. The governor has already called the Sheriff for Lincoln County and the Mayor of Hamlin, West Virginia to ensure you receive their cooperation. If you need any other help, please let me know."

"Could you get me a meeting with the head of the mining company? I'd like to get a look at the mine site where these kids were protesting without getting knocked on the head myself."

"I'm sure that can be arranged. There *is* one more thing," he said. I looked up from the file, knowing he was about to share the case's most important detail. Nothing he'd told me so far justified the urgency of his request. He pulled a sheet of paper from his folder and handed it to me. It was the printout of an e-mail.

Mommy I miss you. I'm going to run out of insulin and gas for my car on Monday and I wont be able to get more. Can you please help me? Sorry about things. Tell Dad I miss him. Love you. H

"Heather's mother received this yesterday morning?" I asked, looking at the date.

"Yes."

"That's an odd note."

"It is."

"Heather's diabetic?"

"Type 1, the kind that requires insulin."

"How often does she dose?"

"She has an insulin pump she needs to use once a week with a medicine called Novalog. I'll send some along with you in a cooler."

"And if she doesn't get the medicine by Monday?"

"Difficult to say, but hyperglycemia is the most likely consequence. For a Type 1 diabetic, that can lead to diabetic ketoacidosis, which can be life-threatening."

"Immediately?"

"No, but she could become ill quickly."

"Isn't that kind of diabetes pretty common? Shouldn't it be easy for her to get insulin?"

"Yes."

"Then this is an even stranger note."

"Exactly."

"Does Heather have health insurance?"

"Yes, through her parents."

"So we're talking about a gallon of gas and a ten dollar co-pay? That's what's preventing her from saving her own life? Is this just a plea for money?"

"According to Miss Hernandez's parents, that would be very unusual. She's hard working, self-sufficient and very independent. She paid most of her own college expenses with jobs and a scholarship. Her mother suggested that if Heather needed to ask for money, she would have done it in another way."

"Does Heather have a cell phone?"

"Yes, but it hasn't connected to a cell network since yesterday afternoon. Her phone contract is with AT&T, though, so it would be roaming through most of that area. That mode causes heavy battery drain, so phones are often powered down when they are not being used. So we can't draw conclusions from that alone."

"A car?"

"A 1998 Toyota Tercel. Details are in the folder."

"And what do her parents think she's really asking for in the note? Assuming it's not about money?"

"Some kind of help. They suggested that writing this note would have been extremely difficult for Miss Hernandez."

"Why? Pride?"

"Possibly. I don't know."

I hesitated for a moment, wary of territory I'd never trodden. I didn't learn anything about Alpha's personal life in the years I served under him.

"Sir, you're obviously willing to use government resources on this project, in addition to my time. Why is this particular family so important to you?"

That's when Alpha pulled out the glossy photo of the three of them. It was another graduation photo—this one with the girl's parents. Her father was a Colonel, with the medals that proved he was the real deal and not just some paper tiger. The girl's mother was a beauty: raven-haired with almost translucent skin. When I saw the uniform, things slipped into place. Colonel Hernandez looked to be of an age with Alpha.

"I owe a great debt," he said, "one that I cannot hope to repay. But if I can help them find Heather, I will." He spoke slowly and evenly, but his voice was brittle. I understood the kind of obligation a battlefield creates. I noticed Colonel Hernandez's POW ribbon then and knew Alpha didn't wear one on his dress uniform. I wondered if that was part of the story.

"Sir, I can't promise you what I'll find, or how quickly."

Alpha regarded me for a minute and I couldn't tell if the ice in his cold blue eyes was hardening or thawing until he spoke. "Michael, I can't think of a more qualified person for this task."

Alpha had never used my given name before, and I found myself dazed as he offered his hand, another unexpected acknowledgement from him that I was no longer his to command.

4

"My name's Roxanne. Grab that pail and you can walk with me," a sturdy, handsome woman about two decades my senior said to me, then carried on as if I'd already agreed. She'd intercepted me as I entered the meadow that housed the protestor's camp in Stone Holler on foot. The tents were pitched in orderly rows behind a cluster of screened rooms allotted to the tasks of food preparation and consumption. A row of four portable potties sat twenty yards behind the camp. If I hadn't known better I might have thought I'd stumbled onto a Boy Scout jamboree site. Roxanne Chalmers was solidly built and of middle height with salt and pepper hair that was cut short for practicality. She was in shirtsleeves, as the warm morning dictated. I knew in an instant that she was responsible for the order in the campsite. I picked up a pail and trailed behind her, struggling to keep up with her brisk pace without breaking into a jog, though my legs were longer than hers.

"You look like a reporter but walk like a cop," she observed. "Which is it?" I couldn't imagine that she saw either thing in me. I'm an even six feet with black hair, an average face and a Mediterranean complexion. I'm the kind of guy you forget ten seconds after you meet him. My walk had been painstakingly scrubbed of telltales years before.

"Neither," I replied as we threaded our way between blooming clumps of yellow foxglove and box huckleberry shrubs toward a stream that I'd seen from the road. Finding the holler proved to be more difficult than I'd anticipated. My phone-based GPS took me off Route 3, through a series of increasingly narrow, winding roads thrust between rolling mountains. The mountains in West Virginia look much like the Catskills, but wilder and closer together. "Hollers" were the local name for the valleys formed between the ridges of the Appalachian Plateau, but they were tricky to navigate. My GPS signal got weaker and weaker as the hills closed in and eventually gave up the ghost. I ended up navigating with a U.S. Geological Survey map of the county that I'd found in the package propped up against the wall just inside my motel room door when I returned from breakfast that morning. Eventually I found the camp. It consisted of a simple clearing of perhaps five or six acres pressed up between a mountain and a stream at the side of a dirt trail. Two police cruisers blocked the entrance. The cops let me pass after they decided I wasn't a reporter.

I followed Roxanne's example and put one foot onto a sturdy boulder in the stream before downing my bucket in the flowing water to fill it. She filled two buckets before unfolding a padded aluminum frame and positioning it astride her shoulders. The buckets clipped onto either end of the yoke. It looked like a tricky job to balance them but she was able to shoulder twice the water I carried with less effort.

"I'm from Maine," she said as we walked slowly away from the stream, "and when I'm there I live in a camp without electricity or running water. In Maine a camp is a house you build with your own hands—I guess you'd call it a cabin. The thing about living from the land is how it connects you to your needs. You develop a real sensitivity to day and night, where your water and food comes from, how hard it is to heat a house if you're relying on cutting your own wood with a crosscut saw and an axe. You get very conservative. Once you've hauled a five-gallon bucket of water for a quarter mile a few times, you don't just slop it around. You wash your vegetables and yourself and then the floor with it. You have to think about things that way, or else you'll find yourself spending so much time hauling water that you'll want to get the heck out of there."

"How well does this kind of work go over with them?" I asked, nodding toward the gaggle of activity around the breakfast tent. Environmental activism and upper-middle-class entitlement seemed like a lethal combination in a working camp.

"Some of them take to it, others don't. Those that don't... well, they don't last long. But that's the way of it. We're trying to change something important here and it's not easy work."

"Fighting mining in West Virginia seems a little like tilting at windmills," I observed. The comment did not faze Roxanne.

"We're not fighting mining, just mountaintop removal. It's a horrible practice for the environment. They're relocating entire communities, poisoning the water and changing the face of the earth forever. But it doesn't look like I'd be able to convince you of that." She smiled and I returned it reflexively.

"I'm not political. I grew up near mountains like these and wouldn't want to see them changed. But I'd worry about the people first—how they were going to survive without work. And I'm not sure how I'd feel about of bunch of strangers telling me what to do." I was pushing a little to see how she would react.

She smiled again and it was genuine. "That's exactly what they say here, but it's a myth. An economy based on mineral wealth never prospers. The only people who make money are the investors. You might not want to put a miner out of work, but they have some of the most dangerous and debilitating jobs on the planet. And unlike underground mining, most of the men working on surface mining projects aren't unionized.

They have the worst deal imaginable. Every change involves pain, but this one has to happen."

"It's easy to say if the job that disappears isn't yours."

"Fair enough," she said, ending the discussion. "So I gather you're not here to join Reclaim?"

"No, I'm here on behalf of the Hernandez family. Their daughter came down here to protest but they weren't able to reach her after Wednesday night." Roxanne's expression shifted slightly when I mentioned the family name, but she was hard to read.

"There are a lot of worried families right now. We're going to head back to the hospital after breakfast. But Heather hasn't been with us for...well, more than a month now."

"She left a month ago?" I was caught off-guard.

"Maybe six weeks, even."

"Do you know where she went?"

"I don't know where she ended up, but some of the younger members here were closer to her. They might be able to tell you something more. I'll introduce you as soon as I drop my burden," she said as she dumped her pails of water into a cistern. After I poured my water in, she covered it tightly with a tarp.

* * *

"Heather left in September, right after..." The girl named Chloe hesitated and looked at Adam, having swiftly stumbled onto a taboo topic. The two of them formed the kind of couple that mirrors each other rather than contrasts. Chloe was tall and freckled, her long red hair flowing from under a bandanna. Adam had a trimmed beard and glasses and looked like he might have stepped directly from a Patagonia catalogue.

"There was a shakeup here around that time," Adam explained, taking up the story. "Reclaim was founded on communalist principles, but that didn't work for too long when we actually had to survive. The meadow got to be a mess and we attracted raccoons and lost a bunch of food. The county threatened to evict us if we didn't deal with our waste better. Funny for environmentalists, right?" I didn't smile. Adam shrugged and continued. "Anyway, it ended up that Roxanne, Josh and Amy took charge and things improved by the middle of the summer. The camp was cleaner, we ate better and we didn't have any more trouble with the locals. We were even able to shut the Hobart site down for a day in July."

"But then the three of them started having problems getting along," Chloe interjected. "And we lost some donors and there were a lot of issues about how we were going to be able to afford to keep renting this site and feeding everyone. And finally we had a meeting and Roxanne gave this big speech and she asked for a vote and she won. Then Josh and Amy left and maybe ten or twenty others followed. Heather went with them."

"You were friends with Heather?" I asked Chloe.

"Yes, the three of us were pretty close. She was special. Quiet but really sweet. I don't think I ever saw her angry. And she did her share, worked really hard. Everyone liked her." Adam looked up at Chloe and I realized that there was something they weren't telling me. I had the strong feeling that I'd get nothing if I pressed, so I moved on.

"Do you know where she went?"

"Amy and Josh went back North to work on some project on natural gas fracking in Pennsylvania. But Heather wanted to stay in the state. Peggy was going to the CC Farm—it's a pretty well known commune about an hour from here. Heather and a few others went with her. CC has buildings, running water and electricity, so it's not quite the same thing as our situation here..."

Chloe and Adam went on for a little while longer, but I didn't learn anything else helpful. I was unhappy ending the conversation with the sense that they were holding out on me, but I didn't have a good lever to open them up, and I knew where I had to go next anyway. I'd done what I came to do, and I knew why Heather was not on the bus. I knew where she'd gone. Now it was just a matter of tracking her down at the CC Farm.

I stopped to say goodbye to Roxanne before I left the camp. I wondered how long the Reclaim folks were going to hold out at the campsite. In the heat of the day, it was easy to forget how soon the cold would come. West Virginia weather would be milder than where I grew up in New York, but mountains are never forgiving in winter. Roxanne would be fine of course, but I wondered about the rest of them.

5

It's not easy to follow someone unnoticed on deserted country roads, so I spotted the big Dodge Ram pickup with the blacked-out extended cab behind me four miles before he made his move. The pickup was idling on the side of the road less than a mile from the Reclaim camp, and it pulled onto the pavement spraying gravel from its rear tires. It stayed a quarter of a mile back as I wound through the ridges and hollers of rural West Virginia, even when I varied my speed.

I was still several miles outside of Hamlin when the big Ram started to reel me in. I was relieved. Getting tailed was the first piece of luck I'd had since arriving in West Virginia. While I knew where Heather had gone, something was missing. Some of the stories I'd been told didn't hang together. Nobody had lied to my face, but I had the sense I was getting a very incomplete picture of events at the camp and the mine. The pickup tailing me told me my instincts were correct.

The Dodge was saving me some trouble by making a move. West Virginia doesn't require front license plates and the big pickup didn't have one. I needed to get a peek at the back end of the truck to identify the owner. Overtaking me wasn't what the Ram's driver had in mind, though. He pulled out as if he was going to pass and then, just as he nosed beyond the edge of my rear bumper, the pickup's driver attempted a PIT maneuver. If you've ever watched one of those high-speed chases that happen with disconcerting regularity in southern California, you'll know what I'm talking about. The police cruiser turns into one of the rear wheels of the fugitive's car, nudging it off-axis; the car spins, maybe stalls and the chase is over.

The secret of the PIT maneuver is that it's not a disabling move. All it does is put you into a spin. There are better techniques to disable a car but the police won't use them because they don't want anyone getting hurt. I learned to drive—really learned to drive—on a decommissioned runway in North Carolina. Safety wasn't the biggest concern in that particular course.

So when the big Dodge moved in to PIT me, I made a quick decision. I had a split second in which I could have pulled away from him. There was no way the Ram could have kept up with my GTO if I started running. But I saw an opportunity and followed my instincts. With a glance ahead to ensure that there was no oncoming traffic, I gritted my teeth, kept my line and tried not to think about the inevitable body damage to my midnight-black GTO. As the Dodge plowed into my left rear quarter panel and the GTO started to spin in a counterclockwise circle, I gradually turned the front wheels into the spin. As the nose of my car swapped ends with the tail, the Ram passed me on the left. I gained control of the GTO just as it finished a full 360-degree spin and, like the Red Baron completing an Immelmann turn, I found myself behind the big pickup in full control of my vehicle. Then it was my turn.

I got a good look at the Dodge's West Virginia license plate and committed it to memory. Then I downshifted to third gear and hit the accelerator, pushing the GTO forward past the pickup's bumper on my right side. I used the same PIT maneuver to nudge the Dodge into a spin. As soon as the Ram started to turn, though, I hit my brakes and hovered just far enough behind the pickup to avoid getting hit. When the Ram completed 240 degrees of spin and was perpendicular to my car, I mashed the throttle. My GTO is the kind of garage project that a lot of teenage boys from small towns fool around with in their spare time; the only difference is that when I was doing the modifying, I had access to the knowledge and tool shop of some very specialized mechanics and armorers. Along with a few other mods, my GTO puts out over 400hp and has a reinforced front bumper.

I t-boned the big pickup, arresting its centripetal momentum. I got a pretty good look at the driver, a bearded fellow who overflowed his side of the cab, and a brief glimpse at an average-sized male passenger with a pasty white face in a hoodie who had his mouth wide open and his eyes closed. Then I pulled my wheel to the right and the Dodge started spinning again, sliding off the side of the road. There was no guardrail, only a dirt apron without a lip or drop-off and some scrub brush after the pavement ended, so I was pretty sure I wasn't going to kill anyone, although you never can tell. I was tempted for a moment to stop and question my attackers. But there was a good chance guns might be drawn and I've learned the hard way that things can get out of hand very quickly if you let them. I hoped I'd be able to find the men in the Ram with their license plate number and confront them on my own terms. I was determined to find Heather and get her home without leaving a trail of destruction in my wake.

That was the theory, anyway.

* * *

My cell phone rang nearly as soon as I got back into Hamlin. I saw as I answered that I had five missed calls. My youngest sister Ginny had been trying to reach me all morning.

"You left without saying goodbye!"

I'd opened the door of my GTO to get out but sat down again instead. I left the door open.

"You and Amelia didn't really give me a chance."

"I'm sorry, Mikey. She's just so infuriating sometimes. She still thinks I'm six years old."

"I assume she's mad I left?"

"Livid. Jamie told us you were off somewhere for some other emergency and Amelia blew up all over again."

"I'm sorry I missed that."

"Yeah, right. Why didn't you call yesterday?"

"I was driving the whole day."

"Where are you?"

"In West Virginia."

"West Virginia?"

"Did you hear about those protestors who were beaten at a mine the other night?"

"It was on the news."

"Well, the daughter of a friend was with that group. She's diabetic, and now she's disappeared. I'm trying to find her."

"Oh...that sounds serious."

"Maybe, but I hope not. How's Mom?"

"I don't know. They still have her on a lot of medication. She's barely conscious and we're having trouble reaching the neurologist. He does his rounds at six a.m. or something like that and we keep missing him."

"That's frustrating."

"I think that's what's getting to Amelia. We don't know if Mom can recover, if she'll be able to talk and walk, anything. Doctor McGee says she's had ministrokes over the past few days. He said we won't know how this will turn out until she stabilizes."

"My cell phone doesn't work half the places I've gone around here, but could you keep me up to date? I want to know what's going on."

"I can do that. I love you, Mikey," Ginny said as she hung up.

I sat there in my car with the heat gradually increasing inside the cabin. It was eighty-two degrees outside but it felt at least twenty degrees warmer inside the GTO. It was just starting to hit me that my mother was going to die. Soon or perhaps later, but sometime. And when she did I was going to have to live through losing a parent. Again.

6

"An hour ago, a second protestor died. That makes this a double homicide and the worst incident this county has seen in a decade. I have a list of names here, including the two homicide victims," Sheriff Jim Casto said, handing me a thin sheet of paper that looked as if it had come from a manual typewriter rather than a printer.

"None of those folks are the girl you're looking for. She's also not on the list of witnesses we interviewed at the scene. I mean the ones who didn't leave in an ambulance. That was a pretty small group, though." Casto handed me another list with just seven names on it. The Sheriff for Lincoln County, West Virginia was a heavyset man in his early sixties whose beard was three shades grayer than the hair on his head. He spoke slowly and had the kind of deep voice naturally made for opera or the radio.

I thought I'd have to produce the governor's letter to get any help in the Sheriff's office. Instead, merely mentioning my name in the county courthouse set off a flurry of activity. The Sheriff bounced out of his office to the front desk in under a minute, treating me like a visiting dignitary for the better part of an hour.

"This seems like a bad way to discourage protesters," I said, scanning the lists and committing those names I hadn't already seen to memory. "Two days ago the mine was just dealing with a group of small-time activists. Now they've got the whole national press corps."

"That's right. Half my deputies are tied up running crowd control. It doesn't make a lick of sense. Those kids weren't gonna shut down the Hobart mine. We arrested a bunch of them in July when they managed to get on a few excavators and articulated trucks. They interrupted mine operations for a day. Hobart decided to play hardball and a few dozen spent time in the county lockup. They've repeated the stunt since then but each time they try, the mine gets rid of them quicker. They haven't even attracted a television crew in months. But Wednesday night changed things. It's stirred up the controversy over the mine and along with the press, there are protestors from half a dozen new groups at the site."

"So why the attack?" I asked.

"I'd guess that a few miners got upset with these kids and decided to scare them, and things got out of hand. Management at the mine isn't afraid to use intimidation, but they'd never pull a stunt like this."

"I talked to a couple of the miners last night who were convinced that nobody from Hobart did this. I think they were telling the truth."

"I'm surprised you got miners to say anything," Casto smiled, "but if you and a few friends planned to scare some activists and things got out of hand, you'd probably keep quiet too, wouldn't't'cha?"

"Secrets like that don't keep for long. This wasn't a simple beating. There was a fake detour and a road block. They had to know where the bus was going and when it was leaving for the plan to work. Whatever the reason, it wasn't just a few miners blowing off steam. Plus there were at least twenty people involved and like I said—secrets like that don't keep." If a mine town was anything like a cement town, the conspiracy wouldn't have survived the night.

"Those are good points. My deputies said some of the same things, but I'm glad to hear them from an outside expert. I had the FBI in my office this morning threatening to take this case over. Which I'd'a welcomed but they didn't do it. It's a grade-A mess. That's why I was glad when the Governor told me I was getting some help."

"Pardon me?" I said, caught off-guard.

"Help. That's what you're here for, isn't it?"

"I'm trying to find Heather Hernandez. It turns out she left Reclaim in September. So she doesn't have anything to do with what happened the other night."

"Well, according to my deputies, you've already met with Ms. Chalmers, the Reclaim leader, and you just said you've spoken with some miners. It seems to me you've already done as much investigating as we have."

"Sheriff, I'm an outsider. I can't imagine that I'll be able to get more information than your detectives."

Casto stood up slowly, betraying some arthritis in his hip. I noticed he didn't wear a gun on his belt. He walked around the desk and leaned back against it, crossed his arms with his left elbow resting on his right hand, and propped his chin up on his fist. He regarded me for a moment with hazel eyes. Then he tipped his head forward and spoke so softly that I had to lean in to hear him.

"I don't think you appreciate the situation here, Mr. Herne. I'm the third sheriff here since February. The man who served Lincoln County for twenty years pled guilty to federal charges of voter fraud. He's going to be sentenced for up to five years in federal jail in a few weeks. The second sheriff was never even sworn in; he was a lawyer who turned out to have a conflict of interest before he could assume the office. I'm the Pastor of the largest church in Hamlin. I have no background in law enforcement, but I was the only man in town that anyone trusted. They'll pick my successor next Tuesday on Election Day, and I'll be out of this office by year-end. My deputies—those who've stayed—are experienced, but given the lack of confidence that folks around here have in this office, a case that involves one of the biggest corporations operating in the state is about the worst thing that could have happened. With the media attention on these murders, I have to lead this investigation myself. I want to wrap it up before the new sheriff takes over to give him a chance to clean up the reputation of this department. You're the only person within a hundred miles who doesn't have a dog in this hunt."

I thought about that for a moment. I'd visited the Sheriff's office because I knew firsthand how uncomfortable things could get in a small town if the Sheriff felt you were sticking your nose into his business. I hadn't planned to ask for help tracing the license plate from the Dodge Ram pickup; but the moment I sat down with Casto, he asked me if I was running into any trouble with my investigation, so I told him about being followed and he offered to get the information. I neglected to tell him that I'd run the truck off the road and hoped to find the girl before I'd be compelled to actually track down the owner of the Dodge. Since I knew where Heather went after leaving the Reclaim camp, my plan was to go there and find her, to call Alpha then leave the state as quickly as possible.

"Sheriff Casto, I'm taking unpaid leave from my job to find Heather Hernandez. I'm doing this as a favor to a friend. I am in no way qualified to do what you're asking of me."

Casto looked down at his feet for a moment. When he looked up, he was smiling. He stood up and walked around the desk, then lowered himself back into the chair.

"Modesty is a virtue, son, but if the governor has faith in you, so do I. Pardon me for being out of line, but I hope you can understand my desperation. All I'm asking is that if in the course of looking for Miss Hernandez, you find anything that'd help us figure out who terrorized and killed these innocent people, you let me know." Casto pulled a card from his pocket, turned it over and scrawled a phone number on the back. "That's my cell number. You can reach me day or night."

"Of course, sir." I realized that whatever I did, I was going to feel guilty. If I found Heather without shedding any light on his case, I'd feel complicit in letting killers go unpunished. But Casto didn't realize what he was asking. Sending a man like me to investigate a murder is like opening a can of beans with an axe. You'll get the can open, but all you'll end up with is a big mess and a fistful of regrets.

A deputy knocked once on Casto's door before entering to hand the Sheriff another manila folder. Casto pulled a pair of reading glasses from a flapped breast pocket on his uniform, flipped them open and slid them onto his nose before examining the file.

"The truck that followed you is registered to Ethan Wright."

I read the tone of his voice and the set of his jaw. "I take it you know him?"

"Not him, but the family if I'm not mistaken," Casto said as he flipped to another page in the folder. "Let me just see here first. It's taking me some time to get the knack of reading these records. The department has its own language." Casto turned another page and read for a moment before taking off his glasses and rubbing the bridge of nose as he looked up toward the ceiling. "The family is actually from Boone County, but we see plenty of them here. Pretty much anything bad that happens in this part of West Virginia involves the Wrights in one way or another."

"How is Ethan related?"

"He's one of Jethro's nephews. Goes by 'Little Boy,'" the Sheriff flipped a page, "which he's not. He's 6'3" and 275, or was the last time he was arrested."

"What was he arrested for?"

"Auto theft, but it didn't stick. The witness recanted. I remember it. It was all anyone talked about around town for weeks. That kinda thing happens a lot with the Wrights. Little Boy served five years in Lakin for assault, though."

"Where could I find Mr. Wright?"

"It might be better if I came with you, to calm things down. The Wrights are legendarily short-tempered."

I shook my head. "He might not talk to me, but he's definitely not going to talk to you. I may not even visit him, but I'd like to have the option. Maybe there's a place I could approach him other than his home? Does he have a regular job?"

"He's still on probation. I have his last report here. Let me see...looks like Little Boy works at a body shop in Spurlockville. That's in the south part of the county near the Big Ugly, a wildlife conservation area. Which seems appropriate."

7

"Ahem, everybody, attention! Willow has something to share," a solidly built woman in her late forties named Miriam announced. Heads popped up from bowls of quinoa laced with sweet potatoes, walnuts and raisins. A slender blonde with flyaway hair stood up and fidgeted nervously before starting to talk.

"I'm having a date with Jesse tonight. I'm gonna have sex with him. I want to get pregnant," she proclaimed. She sat down abruptly. Thirty heads swiveled toward a shy kid with a dark ponytail and wisps of a beard who turned cherry-red as he tried to avoid detection by remaining absolutely still. A long dialogue ensued about Willow's motives until the girl eventually revealed that she'd been having sex with a number of the men in recent weeks, trying to get pregnant. There were some uncomfortable coughs around the room. Willow was questioned intently about her motives for seeking motherhood. After twenty minutes of discussion, Willow finally admitted to the group that getting pregnant might not be her best choice. Jesse exhaled loudly, stirring up some laughs. Then Willow announced she was still going to have sex on the date, and Jesse colored again.

"The only way to succeed in a communal situation like this is not to have any secrets. We do the Telling at lunch so if anybody's feelings get hurt, they get an afternoon of labor to work them through," my host, the man they call Bear, whispered to me after Jesse's ordeal ended. The Telling sounded more like a New Age version of *The Real Housewives* than group therapy to me, consisting on that day of a complaint about missed duties, a confession of jealousy, a prolonged dispute over the menu for the upcoming weekend and half a dozen personal dramas along the lines of Willow's news. The lunch, which I joined in progress, went on like that for an hour while I waited for my turn to speak. Finally, when I had long since given up on the quinoa, Bear cleared his throat.

"Hi, CCs! We have a visitor named Michael here today!"

"Hi, Michael!" The response came simultaneously from the assembled residents of the Creative Collective Farm. I felt like the new kid in a first grade class. Bear gestured to me and I stood slowly. I don't like public speaking.

"I'm a friend of the Hernandez family. They're trying to find their daughter, Heather. She was a protester at the Hobart Mine, but I understand she left last month to come here. I'm wondering if you can help me find her." I held up the picture and saw heads nodding.

"She was such a sweet girl, never had anything bad to say about anyone."

"Real peach that one. Always finished her chores lickety-split and helped somebody else out."

"She helped me with my knitting. She'd finish off all my loose threads at the end of a sweater."

"Real good cook, too. Did amazing things with kale."

I could see where this was headed. I interrupted. "Can I speak to Heather?"

"She left a few weeks ago...When was it, Betty?"

"It hasn't been that long, Frank—it was just over two weeks ago, when we finished with the apples. It was after that."

"I can't believe she left with him."

"He never helped anyone. I don't think he even understood the Principles."

"What did she see in that Anton?"

"Don't you call him 'that Anton'!"

"I don't think we should say bad things about anyone!"

"He wasn't kind, Florence, you know it! That boy was a taker."

"Anton was a sweet boy, Nathaniel, just misunderstood."

"He was no boy! I'd bet he was nearly forty—just looked younger because he had all his hair. And he only sweet-talked you to get you to sneak him extra food!"

"Nathaniel James Butler!"

I cleared my throat. "Heather Hernandez left?" Heads nodded. "Around two weeks ago?" More nods. "Where did she go?" Lots of blank looks and a head shake. "What's Anton's last name?" There was some grumbling. Nobody seemed to know.

Bear leaned forward. Sitting, his lips almost reached my ear as I stood. "We have some records," he whispered. "I can get you the name after lunch."

"Okay, one more question: was anybody here very close to Heather?" Nobody answered, but I watched faces. Several eyes involuntarily flicked toward a redheaded girl with freckles who looked as if she'd just reached adolescence.

* * *

"She was sweet. Really, really nice. But she was also fragile," Christina, the redheaded girl, told me. Her voice was a half-octave lower than I expected and I gathered she was a good deal older, too. It took some coaxing, mostly from Bear, to get her to talk to me. When she agreed, she made a cup of hot tea while I poured some black coffee from a dented urn into a faded ceramic mug. We sat outside on a bench in the damp autumn air. Bear left us to speak alone, possibly because there was no room for him on the bench.

"How do you mean?" I asked, watching Christina closely for a moment before looking up. It was clearing a little, the cloud cover having separated into tufted cotton clouds. Bits of blue sky were visible.

"You could tell that she felt things very intensely. I remember one day we were harvesting cauliflower and one of the biddies—" Christina said, then rephrased when I raised an eyebrow, "—older ladies didn't like how she was soaking it to get the cabbageworms out. Thought she was using too much salt or something. Heather must have mentioned that about a dozen times the next day. She was really sensitive to criticism, like it was some kind of punishment she'd earned and had to work off."

"She was conscientious?"

"It wasn't just that. She needed approval. She didn't do well without it." Christina was starting to relax. She didn't sound as guarded as she had when Bear was around.

"I was a little like that, too," I confided. "My dad always made me feel like I didn't measure up. So I looked for approval in other people." One day in my freshman year of high school, after a game where I'd sacked the opposing quarterback three times, the new linebacker coach took me aside and told me I had a real gift and that he'd work with me to develop it. After the game, my father grunted at me and said, "Boy, you blew your zone in the cover 2 in the second quarter and missed an interception." I could smell the beer on his breath.

Christina regarded me with her pale blue eyes. "I think Heather has some issues with her dad, too, but I don't know what they are. I got a sense that coming to West Virginia was more like running away for her than venturing out."

"How did you get to know her?"

"We were roommates. Everyone shares rooms here, so there's no privacy. You get to know people pretty well. I'm pretty lucky because I've been in a double since we moved the commune to West Virginia last year. It's a tiny room with bunk beds, but having just one other person in the room is nice. Heather was the second roommate I've had since we got here." Bear had already mentioned the relocation to me, explaining that the Creative Collective Farm moved whenever land values rose and taxes increased. The commune was founded during the seventies in California, then moved to Texas and North Carolina before settling in West Virginia.

"So you weren't at the Hobart Mine with Heather?"

She shook her head. "No, I joined CC in North Carolina."

"Did Heather talk about why she left Reclaim?"

"There was some kind of disagreement and a whole bunch of them left. Some of them came to stay here, but most left after a week or two. There was too much real work for them, I guess. But Heather fit in pretty well."

"So why did she leave?"

"She was in love."

"With Anton?" Christina nodded again as she chewed her lip. Her arms moved to pull a hand-knit shawl around her shoulders. "So what was the deal with him?"

"He wasn't a good person. I know that's judgmental, and it's against the Principles, but it's true."

"In what way?" I asked, taking a sip from my mug. The coffee was easier to stomach than the quinoa.

"He knew how to charm. He was a lot older than Heather—at least ten years, maybe more. He wouldn't talk about his age. He understood people, knew what they wanted to hear if you know what I mean. But sometimes he slipped up and you'd see what he really thought. He was a control nut and a racist. He had tattoos. He covered them up pretty well around here but I saw him once with his shirt off..."

"What kind of tattoos?"

"A swastika on his stomach and lightning bolts on his shoulders. And a lot of writing on his chest. I heard Ellie ask him about them. He said that he'd been a stupid kid and was getting them taken off, but that it was expensive. I didn't believe him."

"He doesn't sound like the kind of guy Heather would go for," I suggested. Then again, there's no telling what type of guy a nice girl will go for.

"In a weird way, I could see it. He was constantly complimenting her on little, very specific things. She was really pretty and you know I'm sure she's had dozens of guys tell her how good she looked. But he would notice that she held the door for Esther or how she put an extra piece of bread on Bear's plate, that kind of thing, and specifically mention it back to her. It was just so clear to me that he figured out exactly what she needed and he was feeding it to her."

"She wasn't here for very long, though. How did he convince her to leave with him?"

"They didn't meet here. He came with her from the Reclaim camp. They were already dating there. She told me that after they'd dated for a couple of months she wasn't sure how she felt. Then he left for a week and when he came back, she knew she was in love. So she let him follow her here. When I saw what kind of guy he was I tried to talk to her about him. It was just once, early on, but she shut down and walked away, you know?"

"And she left here with him?"

"Yes, she asked me to forward any mail she got to the Premier Bank in Beckley. I think she had an account there."

"Where did she go?"

"I don't know, not exactly anyway. She said Anton was moving on to join another group and that she was going with him. I didn't get the feeling she was going very far, but I think he wanted to keep it very hush-hush. I don't think there's another commune near here, so I don't know what he had in mind."

"How long ago was this?"

"Two weeks ago. On a Wednesday night."

8

I heard a little crunch of gravel and a whistle of air a split second before I saw the cherry-red cro-moly pedal wrench speeding toward my forehead.

It shouldn't have surprised me, but it almost did. I'd driven for over an hour to make the dozen-mile trip from the CC Farm in Boone County to the Big Ugly Body Shop in Spurlockville. At one point I could have sworn the British lady on my GPS app said "You can't get there from here." The Big Ugly wilderness area was between the body shop and the CC Farm, so I had to skirt around both it and the Hobart Mine site to get back north before cutting west.

I hit a brick wall with the grizzled owner of the body shop, who claimed there was no Ethan Wright on payroll. In spite of his vehement denial, I'd already spotted the banged-up red Dodge dangling unceremoniously from a tow truck in the corner of the parking lot. Wright must have hit something going off the road, because it looked like the Ram's rear axle was broken, and one of the wheels bent inward at an extreme angle. I thanked the owner and walked out the glass door to take a look around back.

As I stepped around the side of the building, that wrench flew at my head from nowhere. I ducked and it hit the brick façade of the body shop building. Little Boy Wright's chubby, oversized fingers were wrapped around the wrench. He was wearing a Pennzoil cap and green coveralls, and was exactly the size Sheriff Casto described. Unless the body shop had some sort of NFL internship program, I'd found my man.

As chips of red brick dusted my head, I pinned the wrist holding the heavy wrench with my right hand before Little Boy could pull back to take another swing. I pivoted to the left, bringing my left hand up under the big man's elbow. Then I yanked his arm away from the wall, twisting Little Boy's wrist as I turned. His whole body followed, stumbling as he tried to keep his wrist from breaking. He took two awkward steps before running smack into the side of the building. His nose broke against the red brick and blood started flowing. Before he could recover, I raised my left leg and stomped down heavily on the outside of his right knee. Big guys put a lot of strain on their joints, so that's where they're weakest. Little Boy screamed when my boot drove through the side of his knee. I didn't know if I'd done any permanent damage, but he wasn't getting up.

A second man, shorter and leaner than Little Boy, came flying around the corner. He was pulling a gun from his pocket, an old police model Smith & Wesson .38 caliber revolver with a long barrel. I grabbed the wrench from Little Boy's limp hand and swung it quickly, bringing it down hard on the second man's wrist before he could level the gun at me. He screamed in pain and the revolver dropped but did not discharge. I grabbed the broken wrist, and the thin man screamed again. While he was distracted, I pulled him forward by that wrist and slammed my fist into his solar plexus. He doubled over, gagging. Then I hit him hard at the base of the skull with the side of my fist and he dropped.

I waited for a few seconds to see if anyone else would join Little Boy and his friend, but nobody came. I picked up the .38, swung out the cylinder, ejected five rounds into my palm and tossed them into a bush, then dropped it.

"Let's start again," I said as I turned back to Ethan. "I know you're Little Boy Wright."

"So?"

"So why did you try to put me in a ditch this morning?" I asked, kneeling over him. He was holding a greasy rag to his nose, stemming the flow of bright red blood. His head was tilted back against the brick wall and his leg was extended out stiffly away from him.

"Come a little closer and I'll tell you," he said, clenching his free hand. Little Boy had seen his share of fights. He was the kind of guy who clocks you with a beer bottle before you notice he's getting angry. Even if I'd broken his nose and hobbled him, he was not defeated. He was no more likely to talk to me than he had been a minute earlier. Sometimes with amateurs, you can put them down hard and they'll open up while they're still in shock. Not true for Little Boy.

I did lean in toward him, but as he raised his fist, I tapped it with the cro-moly wrench and it dropped. Then I pressed the wrench against his knee and he moaned, tried to stand up and failed.

"Who told you to follow me?"

"I don't know."

I pressed harder with the wrench and smacked Little Boy's fist with the flat of my left hand as he lashed out at me. He shook the injured hand as if it had been stung.

"That fucking hurts," he said.

"Not nearly as much as getting run off the road," I pointed out.

"You ran me off the road, dipshit."

"Only because you're not a very good driver, Little Boy. Who sent you?" I poked him again.

"I don't know. Fuck off."

I saw that I wouldn't get anything out of him. I patted him on the chest gently and straightened the lapel of his quilted jacket.

"Maybe you should stick to body work," I suggested.

* * *

I pulled the GTO over on the shoulder of the road, under the bony limbs of a beech tree a quarter mile from the body shop. I stopped just around the first bend, just out of sight of the brick building. I opened the glove box and pulled out a small AM/FM radio, the kind that can be hand-cranked if the batteries are gone. This particular radio received an extra channel. I popped open the battery case to toggle an unmarked switch, then fooled with the antenna a bit and suddenly I was listening to Little Boy as he swore while trying to revive his friend. The device I planted on him did not record and only broadcast a short distance, but it looked exactly like the type of RFID security tag that retail stores place inside clothing. When he discovered the bug, Little Boy probably wouldn't know it for what it was.

Three minutes later, Little Boy made the call I'd been waiting for. I heard him flip open his cell phone, dial and wait. He spoke and I knew immediately that he was talking to an answering machine or a voicemail box. "It's me. We tried to do what you asked, but you didn't tell us the guy was some kind of stunt driver. He totaled my fucking truck. Then he found my shop and broke my fucking knee. So I'm keeping your damn money and I'm damn well done now. Don't fucking call me again."

* * *

"Someone down here is nervous about what I might uncover, but I have no idea if it has anything to do with Heather Hernandez," I said to Alpha.

"Yes?"

I filled him in on my visit to the Reclaim camp and CC Farm, ending with a description of my encounter with Little Boy Wright.

"I trust you left him alive?"

"Yes, but he won't be walking soon. I don't think he or his friend will cause a fuss, though. Wright made a call from his mobile phone to the person who hired him at 21:17 Zulu. Do you want me to work through the Sheriff to get the number?" There's a fairly significant federal law called *posse comitatus* that prevents the military from acting on U.S. soil, but there are also ways to get around it.

"We'll handle it on this end," he replied without hesitation.

"Could you also see if you can find any information on Anton Harmon?"

"The boyfriend?"

"Yes, sir."

"Very well. Why do you think you were interfered with?"

"Someone wants me to stop poking around, but I don't know if it has to do with Heather or the mine protest. I was leaving the Reclaim camp when I picked up the tail. On the other hand, I'd bet there were a lot of angry parents visiting that camp today and it's hard to imagine all of them getting the same treatment. So it's possible that whoever set this up drew a bead on me yesterday—at the hospital or when I was drinking with the miners."

"I was under the impression that you don't drink," Alpha observed. The barest hint of amusement colored his tone.

"Not much, sir. I wanted to see if I could get an idea of why the Reclaim activists were attacked. It hasn't done the mine any good at all. My initial thought was that some of the miners took their own initiative, but I'm not so sure."

"And now you wonder why someone would try to discourage your efforts?"

"Right. The Sheriff asked me for help with his investigation, by the way," I added.

"He did?" Alpha sounded surprised, and he had a great deal of experience dealing with local authorities.

"He's a little out of his depth."

"Given what you've seen so far, it might be a good idea to assist the Sheriff, to ensure his cooperation if nothing else. We'll arrange an appointment for you to meet with Mr. Paul, the director of the mine, tomorrow." I imagined Alpha with his reading glasses again and found myself torn. Part of me wanted to discover why someone would beat up a bunch of naïve kids, but another part of me just needed to find the girl and get the hell out of West Virginia.

"Right. I asked for that, didn't I? Let's see if we can get a bead on Anton Harmon first, though, sir. If we can't locate Heather through him, I'll visit the mine."

9

"Shouldn't you be a vegetarian?" I asked Roxanne as she bit into a hot dog with unconcealed glee.

"Ha!" She slammed her hand down on a cornucopia of fruit illustrated on the vinyl tablecloth. We sat in a booth at the M&R restaurant on the outskirts of Hamlin. "The environment may be worth saving, Mr. Herne, but this cow was a fair sacrifice." She chuckled again at her own joke, repeating it under her breath before turning serious. "We do try to eat organic and locally grown foods at Reclaim, but it's difficult. The staple of the West Virginia diet is junk food. Diabetes in this part of the state is rampant. This is a guilty pleasure, but it's justified. The West Virginia hotdog is as valuable a contribution to our national gastronomy as Po Boys or Baltimore Crabs with Old Bay."

I e-mailed Roxanne after stopping back at Sheriff Casto's office to ask him for information on Anton Harmon. I was still trying to solidify a picture of Heather in my mind. On the drive to West Virginia, I'd imagined a sheltered suburban girl looking to rebel and find meaning in a noble struggle. But the real woman I was learning about was more practical and sturdier than my caricature. She took to the routine of both the camp and the commune, and had no problem with hard work, though there was also a flaw, a weakness. I believed Christina at CC Farms when she talked about the character of Anton Harmon. The fact that Heather's two friends and Roxanne had left Harmon out of the conversation when we'd discussed Heather had to be significant.

Roxanne may not have known Harmon well, but in so small a camp she surely knew something useful. And as it was looking more likely that I was going to need to visit the mine, I thought I would ask her about that, too.

"You've been demonstrating in front of this mine for months now," I said. "Have you ever met the guy who runs it?"

Roxanne smiled. "Jason Paul is an interesting fellow. He has red hair and freckles, and he'll look like he's eighteen until his hair is grey. He's not from around here, you know," she continued. "He grew up in Ohio and went to the Colorado School of Mines. Then he worked on a big mine site in Wyoming—North Antelope I think—and skip-hopped his way up the corporate ladder out west. When Transnational Coal bought Hobart, they brought him in to run things. He was a dark horse pick. Hobart is the largest mountaintop removal site in West Virginia and it's the first complete operation he's ever managed."

"You know an awful lot about him," I remarked, surprised.

"Determine the enemy's plans and you will know which strategy will be successful and which will not," Roxanne intoned.

"Many intelligence reports are contradictory; even more are false, and most are uncertain," I countered.

Roxanne laughed. "Mine was from Sun Tzu—what about yours?"

"Carl von Clausewitz." I smiled.

"The problem with environmentalists," Roxanne observed, "is that we don't think like generals."

"I'm going to guess you haven't met very many generals."

"Ha. True, true. My point is that most of us spend a lot of time thinking about the things these conglomerates are doing and how we can thwart them. We're not very good at anticipating how they'll respond to our actions. I made that mistake with Jason Paul."

"How so?"

"Well he was very gallant at first. The day after we set up in front of the mine entrance, I got a note with an invitation to have lunch with him in the company dining room. He was exceptionally polite, almost courtly," she said.

"That's interesting. Why did he ask you to lunch?"

"It was a show of power. He wanted me to see his expensive suit, his Caribbean tan and the china he eats off every day. When a barracuda flashes its teeth, you don't mistake that for a smile. Paul flattered me. Then he asked a lot of questions and acted very interested and compassionate. He fed me a bunch of platitudes, half-truths and outright lies about mining. Told me that we were an important part of the democratic process and that he'd defend our right to express our opinion."

"And then?"

"As he was escorting me out, he asked me very carefully not to break the law. He said that he had a fiduciary duty to the company's shareholders and as long as we didn't stage any illegal protests, he'd make sure we were treated well."

"Was there an implied threat?"

"I didn't think so right then. He said it regretfully, as if it was something he had to put out there because of his position. As if he'd never act on it." Roxanne stopped and turned her gaze to a mural on the wall by our booth. It showed a kitchen counter jammed with cooking tools.

"But there was some trouble this summer, wasn't there?" I prompted.

Roxanne nodded. "We arrived here not long before Paul, so we'd barely gotten established before he started running things. I have pretty good media contacts, so I figured I could get some press down here. I knew once they got a look at the mine, we'd get coverage. But nobody came. A friend told me some high-level pressure was being applied. So we changed tactics and planned a passive resistance event for July. We blocked the path for those enormous dump trucks they use to haul away the backfill from the mountaintops. When they stopped, we took over two of them. We held work up for about a half day at the site until they arrested us and hauled us off."

"Isn't it normal for protestors to be arrested in that situation?" I asked.

"Arrested yes, but the companies don't often press charges. Local cops usually let protesters plea bargain for nominal fines. This time, though, they pressured the locals to go full bore. They targeted the college kids. A bunch of our volunteers spent the last month of their summer vacation in jail."

"That seems pretty harsh."

"You betcha. After the sentences were handed down, Paul brought me in again. This time it was to his office and he didn't offer me a seat. He was still all smiles, but he asked me not to interrupt 'the important work of our enterprise again.' Then he turned his back and two security people escorted me out. He brought me in there to show me who was boss. It was a typical male power thing," she said, shaking her head. "No offense."

"None taken. Did you stage an event like that again?"

"Several. But we got very little press—just a single national article—and the toll on morale was high. Some quit. It's normal to have some turnover at the end of the summer because of the college schedule. But we lost more than we expected and it shook a lot of people up."

"Is that why Josh and Amy quit Reclaim?" I asked, remembering that Heather left when they did.

"Partly," she replied. "There were some other issues among us. But the biggest thing was that we had different ideas about how to stop the mine."

"How's that?"

"I'm an environmentalist. They're protesters. There's a difference. That's all I'll say."

"So what did you do when your co-founders quit?"

Roxanne's shoulders dropped. "Whatever I could to keep the movement from folding," she said with a trace of sadness.

"If you weren't hurting the mine, why do you think your people were attacked?"

She shook her head. "It was a senseless, terrible thing to do. I spent most of the day yesterday and today in a hospital in Charleston talking to angry family members. I feel like I've let my people down. So many of them are so young. And John and Marcus—they were two of the brightest." Her hand formed a fist and she banged it on the table in slow motion. Then she composed herself.

I changed the subject. "I went to the Creative Collective Farm commune this afternoon," I said. This made her smile.

"They're a hoot, aren't they? I always wonder how many of them are related."

"They were...enthusiastic. It seems like Heather left there a couple of weeks ago with a guy she was dating."

"Harmon." Roxanne said the name with distaste.

"Everyone seems to have that reaction," I observed.

"No doubt. I think it's because he makes such a strong first impression. You meet this guy and you think: holy buckets, could he be *this* nice? I mean he's a tall, blond sweet-talker with great manners. Half the girls in our camp were swooning the day he arrived. But it didn't take long to find him out. You can't keep up an act like that for long in a working camp. People get cold and hungry and then you see what they're really made of. Anton got mean when he got tired. He nearly put one of the other volunteers in the hospital because of an argument over chores. I put him on notice and I'd likely have kicked him out if he hadn't left first."

"So why was Heather with him?"

"I don't know. Some gals think they can fix the bad ones. Some look for the wounded birds. She latched onto Anton right away. He was old enough to like 'em young. And she would have believed him if he told her the moon was made of cotton candy."

"Can you think of anything that might help me find him?"

Roxanne shook her head. "Just don't turn your back on him when you do."

10

Four men were waiting for me in the parking lot of my motel. They sat in an old Jeep Cherokee with a bad paint job and a rusted out panel on the driver's side. I spotted them from half a block away as I approached the motel in my GTO. I drove past them without looking, so I could plausibly feign surprise when they jumped me, and parked in the middle of the lot rather than directly in front of my room door. I might have done that anyway, out of habit, but it seemed prudent as the four men piled out of the Cherokee.

I popped open the glove box and pulled out a small metal rod. Then I stepped out of the GTO and marched straight toward the door to the motel room next to mine, showing my back to the men emerging from the Cherokee. My eyes darted toward the picture window of the room I was approaching. The blinds were closed and the window reflected enough light from a street lamppost to make it a full-sized mirror. The four men moved awkwardly, more like nervous schoolboys than professionals. I saw chains wrapped around a fist, a base-ball bat and a heavy length of pipe. Then the fourth man—the biggest, fittest looking one of them—slid an enormous Bowie knife from a sheath and tossed the sheath back into the Cherokee. Without hesitating, he started trotting toward me well ahead of the other three men, moving as silently as he could manage.

It was a blitz attack of the kind that a serial killer might use to abduct a teenage girl. It might even have worked on a soccer mom or a jet-lagged tourist, but I wasn't either of those. I didn't turn as the man crossed the parking lot, pretending instead to fumble with keys as I stood in front of my neighbor's door. I got a clearer look at my attacker from his reflection as he drew closer. He was an inch or two taller than me, with straight, spiky brown hair and a short, uneven beard. His nose was too large for his face and it looked like he'd grown the beard to compensate. He was wearing thick, black-framed glasses that might have been manufactured in the 1950s.

As he got within three strides of me, the bearded man pulled back his knife arm like a rattlesnake preparing to strike. I think he planned to skewer me to the door with that Bowie knife. He sprinted the last two steps to give himself some momentum.

I waited until the last possible moment, until he was leaning forward and fully committed. Then I spun right, moving out of the path of the knife. I hit the middle of his forearm, blocking the blade away from me and toward the door. Then I tripped him. He went flying into the door, and the knife buried itself in the cheap wood. Before he could stop himself, I drove my forearm and shoulder into his back. He hit the motel room door flat on and I heard the hinges break and the frame splinter an instant before the door gave way. He fell with it, landing flat on his face in the middle of the motel room. There was a high-pitched scream and an angry baritone voice from within. I turned to deal with the other three men.

I flicked open the 16" Leverloc extendable baton I'd been gripping as I stepped forward and juked left toward the fastest of the three men. He was thin and chalk white, but he jabbed at me like a flyweight boxer; I could see that he was setting me up for a roundhouse with his other, chain-wrapped fist. I ducked back from the jab. Then as his ironclad punch powered forward, I brought up the knife-edge of my hand in a circular motion and bobbed to the side. The blow whispered past my ear. I grabbed his extended arm at the wrist with my blocking hand and pulled him off balance. Then I brought the baton in my other hand down hard on the side of his elbow.

As I felt the joint wrench, I turned again, wrapping my arm around the back of his neck as he staggered forward. I spun him around full circle like a matador with a bull, just in time to meet the tip of the baseball bat a bald man was swinging hard at me. It smacked the thin guy solidly on the top of his skull and I heard a crunch of bone as his skull fractured. He dropped flat to the ground when I released him.

I leapt forward before the bald man could take another swing with the bat. I swept my forearm straight up, catching him under the chin and pulled him backwards off his feet. I wrapped my arm around his neck, pressing hard on his carotid arteries. With my free hand, I raised the Leverloc to parry a blow from the last man standing, who wore an Army surplus jacket and a brown hunter's cap with the earflaps pulled down. He swung again hard with the pipe, bringing it down like a hammer. I blocked the blow with the Leverloc raised horizontally and kicked his shin with the reinforced toe of my boot. He swore.

I felt the bald man go limp in my grasp as he lost consciousness and I dropped him. The guy in front of me thrust his pipe forward like a sword, and I parried with the baton. Then I lunged forward, driving the tip of the baton into the soft spot two inches below his Adam's apple. He started to choke and dropped the pipe, his hands moving instinctively to his throat. I sprang forward and to his side as I dropped to one knee. With my arm extended straight out beside me, I drove the side of my balled fist into his solar plexus. He crumpled to the ground.

I heard a heavy step behind me and rolled as a big black boot swung through the space where I'd been kneeling a second before. The big guy had extracted himself from my neighbor's motel room. He turned and tried to kick me again while I was still on my knees. I caught his boot with my hands and twisted, then spun to kick the other foot out from underneath him. He fell flat on his back and I made it to my feet while he was still struggling to get up. Stepping in behind him, I drove three fingers into a spot just below his armpit. The human nervous system works like an electrical circuit, and you can short it with training.

Only it didn't work. He twisted around as he stood and grabbed me by the throat instead. The big man pulled me toward him with a surprising amount of strength. The guy's mouth opened and I realized in a terrifying moment that he was going to bite me. His breath was foul and his pupils were dilated enormously. I tried to ignore the fact that I couldn't breathe and managed to get an arm in front of me, pressing it under his jaw before he could tear into my face. Then I kneed him hard in the groin. He didn't flinch. He clawed at my face with dirty, ragged fingernails, so I dropped the baton and slipped my hand from his grasp. Without warning, I pulled back the arm I had under his jaw and brought my forehead down on the bridge of his nose, breaking it. Then I knocked the inside of his elbow with mine and managed to pry his hand off of my throat.

The guy was insanely strong, but not terribly quick. I stepped behind him and tripped him as he turned to confront me. When he stumbled, I grabbed him by the elbow and the back of his collar and slammed him into the window of a Chrysler 300. It shattered and he howled madly, then bulled himself straight backwards, trying to knock me over. I got an arm around his neck and locked it in. I ducked my head down between his shoulder blades to keep him from butting me with the back of his skull.

I rode the big guy like a bronco as he yelled, struggling and staggering around the parking lot. He backed me into a car, whipped me around, even knocked me into a lamp pole, but I kept hanging on. After an eternity that probably lasted no more than ten seconds, the man went limp as he passed out. I lowered him to the ground and, seeing that the other men were still immobile, slid down against the black 20-inch rims of the Chrysler to catch my breath.

* * *

"You've had quite a day," Sheriff Casto said as I held a chemical ice pack to my neck. The first police cruiser rolled into the motel lot less than two minutes after I finally got the big guy down, while I was tightening a tuff-tie I'd slid from my forearm down around his wrists. The quick response wasn't surprising—we were within walking distance of the county courthouse, after all. The ambulance arrived a moment later and quickly sped off with the two men who'd suffered head trauma.

"Yes, sir, I have," I replied. One of Casto's Deputies, Mark Collins, was standing with us. He had the bearing of a professional lawman and wore a Stetson hat with his uniform.

"You took down four guys single-handed?" Collins asked.

"They were a little clumsy. Most of the damage came from them running into each other."

"Bullshit. I've seen guys like you before. Which branch?"

I eyed him again. He had the look, so I didn't dodge the question. "Army," I admitted.

"I was Navy. Shore patrol," he said. "What unit?"

"Fifth Special Forces."

"Yeah, that'll do. That's why the couple in Room 8 back there said it looked like someone was filming a Chuck Norris movie in the parking lot." Collins smiled.

"I can promise you that it was nothing like that. Just a little self-defense."

"I hope we don't see a *lot* of self-defense around here, then," Casto muttered.

Me either. "Someone really doesn't want me around, that's for sure. What's the deal with that one?" I looked over at the big guy, who'd just regained consciousness. Four deputies were struggling to subdue him. Even flexi-cuffed, he was shaking them off. One of the deputies pulled out a Taser.

"My money's on Bath Salts," Collins says.

"Bath salts?" Sheriff Casto asked.

"New drug," Collins explained. "It has synthetic cathinones, and it's supposed to give a high like cocaine or methamphetamine but with different side effects. Started showing up last year. It was originally imported from Asia but now they're manufacturing it in meth labs in the hollers. Until this summer they sold it in packets labeled 'not for human consumption,' and it wasn't even illegal here. But now it's against federal law. They're calling it the 'Zombie drug' because an addict chewed off some guy's face in Miami."

We watched a deputy Tase the giant a second time.

"He tried taking a bite out of me," I observed while I checked my ribcage. I would have some bruises but nothing was broken.

"I don't know whether this is happening everywhere, but the local blend is driving people crazy. We've seen a big spike in violence over the last few months. It's started to hit the rave scene, so we're finding high school kids amped up on it. When they get really worked up on Bath Salts, they don't feel pain." Collins nodded over to where the big man was still struggling. "How'd you get the flexi-cuffs on him, anyway?"

"I stopped the flow of blood to his brain first."

"Yeah, that's what my wife does with me. Looks like a bunch of it landed on you, though," Collins observed, gesturing to my face.

I realized that the man had probably bled on me. I lifted fingers to my chin and felt a familiar stickiness over the day's stubble.

"Do you mind if I wash up?" I asked.

"Not at all. I called the District Attorney's office. They're sending someone over to talk to you, but it'll take a spell. Just come on back out when you're done," Sheriff Casto said. He opened up his notebook and turned to Collins.

I had my hand on the doorknob to my room and the key in the lock when I froze. Something was missing. Something important. Two little pieces of cork I'd left wedged in the hinges of the door were gone. It's a little bit of tradecraft that tells you if someone has been in your room. Not so useful in a high-end hotel, where you can count on a maid or minibar checker to eventually violate the 'Do Not Disturb' sign on the door, and pros can generally spot the telltales if they're looking for them, but in a little motel, the odds of someone having entered my room for a legitimate reason after it had been cleaned for the day were miniscule. I carefully withdrew the key from the lock and backed away from the door, toward Casto and Collins.

"Someone's been in my room," I said.

"Housekeeper?" Casto asks.

I shook my head. "I was in the room right before dinner. I'm pretty sure they don't have turndown service here." Collins chuckled at that. "Maybe one of these thugs broke in, but I'm not going to bet on that. None of them looks smart enough to pick a lock."

"I'll call Charleston," Casto said. I looked at Collins quizzically.

"With all the attention we're getting right now, we need to play it safe. There are only two bomb squads in West Virginia," he explained. "One for the Kanawha County Sheriff's Office—they cover the capitol—and one for the State Police, also based in Charleston. It may take them a little while to get here."

"If there's actually something behind the door, I'd really like to get a peek at it before the bomb squad carts it off," I told Collins.

"What do you think the odds are that anyone who set an explosive charge would have set a trigger on the window?" Collins asks.

"Anything's possible. But it would surprise me. Someone who's smart enough not to open the door isn't going to break a window to get inside his motel room. And rigging a device with a vibration sensor in a busy motel is tricky." I answered the question reflexively. The look on Collins's face told me I'd displayed a little too much expertise on the subject of bomb making.

"Well let's hope the staties think I'm dumb enough to not bother trying to get me fired for this," Collins replied. He turned and walked over to the window, sliding his baton from his belt as he did. He covered his face with his jacket sleeve and hit the corner of the window hard with the end of the baton. The lower portion of the glass shattered and I ducked, instinctively covering my eyes. Nothing happened. I let out a breath that I hadn't realized I'd been holding. Collins raised the baton higher and hit the section of window above the jagged gap. He cleared the glass from the sill, then pushed back the curtain and shone his flashlight inside the room. After a second he whistled. He turned to me slowly.

"When's the last time you saw an IED?"

11

"The FBI investigates street fights?" I asked the brunette in the expensive suit.

"That was hardly a brawl, Mr. Herne. The injuries were one-sided." She was distractingly attractive, with eyes just greener than hazel, high cheekbones and an angular, exotic face that suggested a bit of Native American ancestry in her ethnic mix. Her name was Nichols. Special Agent Harper Nichols.

"You do realize there were four of them, Agent Nichols? And that they jumped me? I defended myself. There were witnesses." Federal employees play "Whose Turf Is It?" I was bound to lose because I wasn't in West Virginia on government business. But backing down too quickly would have invited Agent Nichols to come down even harder on me.

"You made sure of that, didn't you?"

Deputy Collins stifled a laugh and turned away quickly when Nichols glared at him. She obviously hadn't been told that the witnesses were the couple whose door I'd wrecked. They'd been *in flagrante delicto* when I pushed the big guy through the door to their room. Apparently they were married—but not to each other. "And if you'd defended yourself any more vigorously," Nichols continued, "we might be investigating a murder."

"Which would still be a state matter."

"When a federal employee with a Top Secret security clearance from a department of the Executive Branch with no domestic jurisdiction arrives in our state and starts asking questions that relate to an ongoing federal criminal investigation, we notice," Nichols countered. "When this federal employee continues to cross our investigative path, we pay special attention." She was fairly tall, only a couple of inches shorter than me. Her straight hair fell near to her shoulders. I wondered if she pulled it back at the office. The suit she was wearing fit her well enough to mark her an athlete. She fit that part of the profile, anyway.

"And when my SSA is in a meeting with the Governor and they're interrupted so the commanding Colonel of the State Police can report an explosive device has been discovered in this federal employee's motel room, then it becomes the business of the FBI," Nichols concluded.

"Your SSA was in a meeting with the Governor of West Virginia at 10 p.m. on a Friday night? I hope he wasn't losing too much money," I said dryly. Deputy Collins snorted loudly and started coughing into his fist. Nichols glared at him for a second, then grabbed my arm and pulled me a few feet further away.

"Does it matter?" Nichols asked. Her response confirmed what I suspected. FBI agents are among the most territorial creatures on earth. After needling this young, aggressive agent, I had just taken a shot at her boss. I gave Nichols an ideal opportunity to threaten me, but she hadn't; I knew she'd been ordered to play nice. Since my job with the State Department is at roughly the same level and pay grade as a municipal dogcatcher, Alpha must have already reached out to the FBI. It also hadn't escaped me that they'd sent an attractive young female agent instead of a couple of surly, seasoned old pros to question me.

"So how did you draw the short straw?" I asked.

A small smile pulled tightly across her lips. "This is my case, Mr. Herne."

"Then I'm sorry to have ruined your evening, ma'am."

"Perhaps you could fill me in?" she suggested.

"Is there any place we can get coffee at this hour?"

* * *

I sat across from Special Agent Nichols in a booth at a truck stop a mile out of town. I had my hands full following her Suburban on the wet roads from Hamlin. The woman could drive a truck. She projected a highly specific brand of self-confidence. It was one I recognized.

"Naval aviator?" I asked.

Her smile reached her eyes for a moment. "That's right. Annapolis, then wings plus eight." So she had fulfilled her eight-year service commitment after finishing at the Naval Academy and completing flight school.

"What did you fly?" I asked. There weren't many women in the Tier One Special Ops community when I served, but women have flown combat in jets for years.

"The F/A-18F Super Hornet."

I let out a low whistle. Flying a fighter for the Navy is about as easy as making the starting roster on an NFL team. "That's a serious job. When did you get out?"

"Two years ago. I applied to the FBI when I made Lieutenant Commander. I started at the Academy three weeks after my discharge."

"I thought you needed a law degree to become a special agent." Every D.C.-based agent I'd met through a friend at the FBI—who holds a J.D. himself—was a lawyer by training.

"No, but having a law degree or a law enforcement or accounting background is useful." I heard an edge in her voice. Her looks were undoubtedly a double-edged sword. She'd have had to work twice as hard as an average-looking woman to prove her competence in a conservative outfit like the FBI. And carrier pilots are a very specific breed. You have to have a lot of nerve to land a jet plane on a runway that pitches and rolls while you're trying to set down.

"I know what you mean. I'm an intelligence analyst without a master's degree working in a department full of PhDs. I take it you're not from around here?"

She shook her head. "Arizona. But the FBI is like the Navy. You go where they send you. You?"

"New York State, south of Albany. But I haven't lived there since I was eighteen."

"And where did you serve?"

"Special Agent Nichols, I think you've already seen my service record." I smiled.

"I scanned the file," she admitted without hesitation, "but I don't believe that you sat behind a desk for half your time in the Army." Our waitress ambled over with two cups of black coffee. I'd suspected all along but the confirmation shook me all the same: I'd been in West Virginia for just over twenty-four hours and the FBI had already pulled my service record.

That file, even the one the FBI can access, is intentionally incomplete. It correctly notes the time I spent as a Ranger and in the Special Forces, as well as some of the things I did in Afghanistan. But it lists me as having been partly disabled, finishing my enlistment as a Master Sergeant in a logistics support unit based in Arlington, Virginia. The fake logistics unit was the operational cover for the Activity.

"You know how it goes," I responded, because while I couldn't tell her the truth, a lie would have insulted her intelligence.

"Yeah, I've met your type before." Her tone was clipped.

"Well I'm just a civilian now. Or a civil servant, anyway."

"Perhaps you can tell me what you're doing in West Virginia, then?" She was suddenly all business. I realized she was following good interrogation technique. She'd established rapport by sharing something personal. Then she started the interview with a question whose answer she already knew.

"It's all about a girl," I responded. The corners of her mouth twitched before the impassive mien returned. "A friend asked me to find her. She came here over the summer to protest the Hobart Mine, but her parents weren't able to reach her after the incident."

Nichols pulled out a notebook and, after slipping the black elastic band off the cover, withdrew a silver pen from a worn-looking soft leather briefcase and started to jot down notes as I spoke.

"When I arrived at the hospital in Charleston last night, I learned that the girl—Heather Hernandez—was never admitted. Then this morning I went to visit the protesters and found that she'd parted ways with them six weeks ago." Nichols glanced up from her notes momentarily to stare at me with green eyes.

"So you're not investigating the murders?"

"No, I'm just trying to find this particular girl," I answered, watching Nichols closely as I did. She scribbled for a second and met my eyes again.

"Then why is someone trying so hard to kill you?" she asked slowly. I had to stop myself from giving her a flip answer because it was the same question that had been eating me.

"I don't know. I picked up a tail this morning after I visited the meadow where the Reclaim activists are camping. It was two guys in a pickup truck—amateur thugs like the bunch I ran into tonight. They didn't just follow me; they tried to run me off the road. From what I can tell, they were blind-hired to do the job. It could be someone was worried I was investigating the attack, but since the police and fifty journalists are doing the same thing I don't know why they'd pick on me. On the other hand, nobody but me is looking for this girl, although it's hard to imagine why anyone would care. The cheap muscle who attacked me tonight nearly made me miss the signs that someone had been in my room, which makes the whole job look more professional in my book."

"Do you have any insights you'd like to share on that?" Nichols asked carefully.

"Off the record?" I hadn't been able to call Alpha yet, and I was reluctant to tell an FBI agent something I hadn't told him. On the other hand, they'd track the signature of the device sooner or later, and telling Nichols directly would establish trust that I might need down the line. I wondered whether

Nichols's job description really gave her the latitude to protect a source. I was counting more on the uniform she'd once worn than the suit she had on at the moment.

She put down her pen. "Fine."

"The man who built that device was trained by the U.S. Army, probably at Fort Bragg."

Nichols nodded and I knew that she understood what I meant. "You're certain?"

"Pretty sure. The signature's distinct."

"That puts things in a different light," she said, drumming her fingers on the linoleum tabletop. Her nails were unpolished and cut nearly to the quick, but they still looked manicured.

"Yes it does. I was lucky I didn't open that door."

"Why didn't you?"

"I'm a careful guy."

"That's good, because your actions are being watched. I'd ask that you keep me personally apprised of your progress."

"Happy to. I'd value your opinion," I said and meant it. She moved on, asking me an increasingly specific set of questions about what I'd seen and heard since I'd started looking for Heather Hernandez.

12

Deputy Collins approached me as I stepped out of my car, back in the motel parking lot. The state's bomb squad had departed, but a few police cruisers and the Sheriff's SUV lingered in the parking lot.

"I forgot to tell you. We ran the name of the boyfriend— the one who took your girl away from that commune." Collins fished a small notepad out of his uniform shirt pocket. "Harmon. Anton Harmon."

"You found him?" I asked, feeling a ray of sunshine break through the clouds hanging over my head.

"There was nothing in our records or the state databases. But we put the query through CODIS and the National Sex Offender Registry and we got a hit. I should have told you earlier," he admitted.

"Bombs are distracting."

"Harmon served time for a sexual battery charge in Illinois. He's been in this state for about three years," Collins said, withdrawing a booking photo from a second envelope. Anton Harmon had straight brown hair and a piercing stare.

"If he's in the registry, you must have an address for him, right?"

"Yes, and that's where it gets tricky. His residence since 2009 has been in a compound outside of Fayetteville in Fayette County. That's not too far from Beckley." Beckley— where Heather had her mail forwarded after leaving CC Farm.

"A compound? He's from another commune?"

Collins shook his head. "No, different story. This compound is the headquarters of the National Front. It's a white supremacist group."

"What? Are you sure this is the same guy?"

"No, I'm not. We only had the name to work with. But it's not a common surname locally, so I wouldn't bet that it's wrong, either." Collins scratched his chin. "It would explain why the Feds are involved. The National Front has been linked to hate crimes, illegal guns and drugs. They're dangerous people and if this girl you're looking for is with them, I'll tell you that you're out of luck. There's no way they'd let anyone in there without a warrant and a SWAT team." Collins handed me both photos and the envelope as he spoke.

My head was spinning. How could a girl who came to West Virginia to protest mining and moved to a commune end up with white supremacists? More importantly, why would a white supremacist join an environmental group?

* * *

"Are you certain, Orion?" Alpha asked, using my old call sign. I phoned him after changing motels. When Sheriff Casto and Deputy Collins finally left the parking lot in front of my motel room in Hamlin, I grabbed my bag and checked out, then left town. I drove the kind of route you use when you need to see if someone is following you, but nobody was. Then I headed north, got on the interstate and drove a few miles east before exiting to a chain motel just off the highway. I paid cash and parked around back, wedging my GTO between two SUVs where it would be harder to spot if much easier to dent. Not that a door ding was going to compare to the work I'd need to do on the rear quarter-panel since Little Boy Wright's pickup spun it around.

"Sir, you'd recognize the signature," I said in response to Alpha's question about the explosive device in my motel room. "Whoever built that device was definitely trained in the community. I got a good look at it. There was a tilt fuse with a mercury switch, triggered by a tension wire attached to the doorknob. It was double-primed. The explosive wasn't mil-spec but the signature was clear. Whoever planted it came pretty close to getting me, too." In fact, if I'd had one ounce less fieldcraft pounded into me in the Activity, I would have yanked the door to my motel room open without checking the telltales.

"Unfortunately, this fits with some other information we've gathered," Alpha said. "It appears you may have crossed paths with a group called the National Front. Anton Harmon is a member."

"The Sheriff's office traced the name on this end as well, but I haven't confirmed it's the same Anton Harmon. It's hard to imagine a neo-Nazi suddenly joining an environmental group. It's even harder to imagine one dating a girl named 'Hernandez.' I got a picture of him, though, so I'll run it by someone who knew him on this end," I replied. I remembered the girl at CC Farms mentioning the tattoo of the swastika she'd seen on Harmon and my skepticism weakened.

"Please do, but you should know we've established a second connection to this group. We were able to get the details on the phone conversation you overheard," Alpha continued, obliquely referring to the call I'd intercepted on the listening device I'd planted on Little Boy Wright. "The call was made to the voicemail box of a prepaid phone. This particular phone falls under a monitoring warrant being run by another agency. The phone in question is one of a lot that was bulk-purchased at a warehouse club by a member of the National Front."

"Oh," I said, frowning. "That complicates things."

"There's more. Harmon has a military background. He was with the 26th Infantry Regiment of the Big Red One during the first Gulf War. After his discharge, he completed a degree in civil engineering, then reenlisted after 9/11. He went in under the X-ray program and served with the Third Special Forces Group as an engineer sergeant. He was DD in 2008. That file was sealed, though we're trying to get a copy of it."

"He's an explosives specialist?"

"Yes."

"So he could be the one hiring these men to keep me from finding Heather?"

"It's possible," Alpha conceded. "At the very least, it suggests that Miss Hernandez may be in some real danger. And that someone doesn't want you to connect the dots."

I cleared my throat gently and took a breath.

"Sir, if we step back for a second, you'd have to agree that this trip has taken a serious turn down the rabbit hole, wouldn't you? Last night I started asking questions about a girl who was protesting with an environmental group. In the span of twenty-four hours I've been sideswiped, attacked and nearly bombed."

"You'd like to withdraw?"

"Not at all, sir. But if I keep playing by the same rules, I won't make it through another day. Which makes me wonder..."

"Yes, Orion?"

"While I was driving here I wondered why you would send me on a job that a real private investigator could finish in half a day. Unless you already knew more than you shared with me."

The line was silent for a few seconds.

"When Miss Hernandez's mother forwarded her note, I made some inquiries. I got a strong reaction from my federal sources. The FBI was very interested in the attack on the protestors, but their motives were unclear. Given that, I wasn't confident a private detective would be able to operate effectively."

"Sir, why didn't you just tell me this yesterday morning?"

"If I'd told you there was an FBI investigation, where would you have gone first?"

"To the FBI," I said, thinking about the next call I wanted to make.

"Exactly. And had you approached them first, they might have gone all the way to the National Security Council to force me to recall you."

"I very nearly got myself killed, sir."

"Perhaps not so nearly, Orion. And now you've gained the FBI's attention by getting the National Front to make an overt move against you. This opens a door to cooperate with them."

"Cooperate?"

"As you said, we need a different approach. Groups like this mistrust outsiders in general and the government in particular. The National Front may be worse. It's a very serious criminal organization."

"What do you have in mind, sir?"

"We're looking for a way to get you inside the compound."

"Infiltration?"

"No, something more circumspect. We think we have a viable approach, but we need to do some work overnight. I'll have more information for you later. In the meantime, call the TOC and give them your current location and any other information they request. We'll bring you under operational control in the morning."

"Yes, sir," I responded crisply as the call ended. I realized that I'd been pacing back and forth in front of the two full-size beds in my Spartan roadside motel room for over an hour. Suddenly exhausted, I sat down. As I'd told Alpha, I didn't like the direction things were headed. More to the point, I didn't like the way he'd used me as bait to tease out the FBI's interest in the Reclaim killings. Now he wanted to put me inside the National Front compound. That would be a real trick, as I would be in the midst of the same people who'd tried very hard to kill me. All for the daughter of my ex-boss's friend.

Don't get me wrong—I understand loyalty. It's what brought me to West Virginia. But it surprised me that Alpha would devote government resources to a private project. A single misstep could end his career. It seemed like a big risk to take to find a missing girl. I decided I needed to know more about the girl's father and Alpha's connection to him. Some of the things I'd heard about Heather suggested the man might not have been the best parent, and I couldn't let that lie, either.

BINDER

As I pulled another phone from my bag and dialed the number for the tactical operations center at the Activity, I wondered how I managed to get myself into another mess. But I knew the answer. When you're a hammer, they always find you a nail.

13

SATURDAY

"Another hundred yards and you can stop bitching," Roxanne said as we trudged up a muddy trail.

"I wasn't complaining. I was pointing out that it's polite to tell someone when you invite them for coffee that they'll be climbing a mountain to get to it."

"I'm not sure I see the difference," Roxanne replied without looking back at me. "Besides, you're barely sweating!"

"I'm at least six months younger than you. And I grew up in the mountains."

"I'd peg it closer to a quarter century. And the Catskills aren't mountains, they're foothills—just like the hill we're on right now. Maine has mountains."

"That's probably why you're not puffing too much, either."

Roxanne snorted. I'd sent her a note before I collapsed into bed the previous night, asking her to meet me in the morning if she was available. When I awoke at 5:30 there was a reply waiting for me, suggesting that we meet at 8 for coffee with a view. Attached were driving directions that had me navigating a narrow dirt road winding through the Big Ugly Wildlife Management Area.

Roxanne found me sitting on the hood of my GTO, playing with a ruggedized tablet computer. I'd arrived almost forty-five minutes before she pulled off the road in her twenty-year-old Land Rover Defender exactly at our scheduled meeting time. The small dirt parking lot off the side of the road looked like it was primarily used as an offloading point for an ATV trail, and the satellite maps I'd scanned of the Big Ugly showed a pretty extensive network lacing the mountains— or rather, foothills. Roxanne stepped out of the Defender as I snapped the case to the tablet shut and slid it into a sage-colored backpack. Roxanne was wearing ancient gray hiking boots, thick wool socks with green wool pants blousing out from them and a sturdy wool coat over a cable-knit sweater. It was in the forties, a full thirty degrees colder than it had been the same time on Friday. I'd grown up thinking that Hudson Valley weather was unpredictable. Apparently it wasn't alone.

Roxanne greeted me with a smile and a wave. "Early bird?"

"You bet."

"Well let's go," she said, pulling an embroidered Norwegian cross-country ski hat with a small black pompom down over her ears. I donned a pair of gloves and slung the pack over my shoulders as she grabbed a pair of hiking poles and led the way.

In the Catskills, the mountains are low enough to lie completely below the tree line, so you sometimes don't see anything but woods until you reach a vista, like the top of a ridge. It was the same on this trail, as we switch-backed up the hill to a ridgeline and then followed it along a narrow, muddy path for two miles before briefly heading downhill and then ascending again. The woods were old growth, a dense mixture of deciduous varieties from white oak to holly, clinging to their leaves weeks past the time they'd have dropped them up north. The crunch, crunch, crunch of Roxanne's thick, practical leather hiking boots brought back weekends trailing behind my sister Amelia and her friends as we went to gather blackberries in the springtime in a field up on the side of a mountain just outside Conestoga. Amelia wore hand-me-down oversized leather boots that year that seemed destined to snap her skinny ankles.

We reached the end of the trail. "Well, here you go," Roxanne said. "Here's something I guarantee you've never seen before." Then she pulled back a tree branch and we stepped out into a clearing on a ridge in the middle of the Big Ugly. Up at that level, all you see of southern West Virginia is hilltops—the houses and towns in the hollers recede from sight. It was a pristine view.

"Gorgeous," I said.

"You're looking the wrong way," Roxanne said sharply. Gently grasping my shoulders, she turned me ninety degrees to the east. The Hobart Mine site spread out below us, a raw wound on the face of the earth. It looked like someone had erased a complete ridge of mountaintop—just rubbed it out with an eraser. The entire site was chalk white and it seemed to go on for miles. The hills were gone and so were the valleys. In their place were broad, flat plains of dust studded with geometrically unnatural plateaus and a great deal of heavy equipment.

It should not have come as a surprise. I knew Roxanne was planning to show me the Hobart site. It was the obvious destination. I'd checked the geological survey map before we started the climb and she'd picked the highest hill overlooking the site that was still on state land. I'd been ready for it as we snaked our way up the trail. But some time during the hike I had succumbed to the rhythm of the walk and forgotten her purpose for bringing me up the hill. So the view took me as unsuspectingly as if I'd been someone navigating the network of roads around the mine for years without ever catching site of the entirety of it.

"This area is part of the Appalachian Plateau. These ridges and valleys were formed nearly 500 million years ago, during the Ordovician Period." Roxanne pointed in the direction I'd looked first, where the hills were packed so closely that they seemed to squeeze the hollers between them. "The mineable coal in this region was deposited at least 300 million years ago, during the Pennsylvanian period. So you can say that the view here didn't change for about 300 million years, give or take." She held up three fingers as though she was lecturing to an audience and not just to me.

"Then in the nineteen seventies, American Coal started strip-mining the plateau. They're the ones who sold Hobart to Transnational. The Hobart site is nearly ten miles across. To get a single ton of coal, they have to remove sixteen tons of soil. To work the seam, they blast the top off a mountain and deposit the overfill in valleys." That explained why the site looked so flat. I'd assumed the mine was just the product of digging. It hadn't occurred to me that all the dirt had to go somewhere. "Mines like this cover 1200 miles of Appalachian headwater streams. Two years ago a team of researchers from Duke University came here and collected 15,000 water samples. They published their data last year. They found significant water pollution, high concentrations of selenium and mutations in the fish."

"Poor fish," I said. Roxanne scrunched her nose at me.

"Transnational Coal isn't a West Virginia company. The profits don't flow to this state. There are only 15,000 miners left in West Virginia. Big business came and stripped the land

and when they're done they'll leave, but the land won't ever be the same. This is why I'm here." Roxanne delivered her words like a political stump speech, but the power of the view in front of me was undeniable.

"The scale is...unbelievable."

"This is one of the biggest mountaintop removal sites in the state, but there are over a hundred others that are large enough to see from outer space. Five hundred mountains are gone forever."

I nodded, still looking down at the chalk-white stain on the landscape. I was perhaps a thousand feet above the mine site, which seemed to stretch on for miles. Dump trucks whose wheels must have been twice my height looked like toys.

"I dragged you up here to see this because you'll never see it from down there." Roxanne pointed back to the highways. "The site is designed so that the hills block the view unless you're inside the site. There are children playing a few hundred yards from the edges of the mine who've never seen it."

"This is not what I imagined," I conceded. "The scale is so...vast. I'm not saying I'm ready to lay down in front of an earthmover, but...it's disturbing. But you know I'm here for a different reason, so why would you take the time to show this to me?"

"Because you've got enough of a head on your shoulders to understand what you're seeing. Some don't. I also wanted you to understand the impact of this single mine will still endure after everyone living now is long gone," she said.

"So it's high stakes poker?"

"But they're playing with the future. It can't be undone." She paused, surveying the scene for what I imagined was the hundredth time. "You said you had something to show me?"

"Yes I do." Unzipping my jacket, I withdrew the photo of Anton Harmon from an inside pocket. "Do you recognize him?"

Her face clouded. "That's Anton."

"Did you know he was a registered sex offender?"

Roxanne shook her head. "I'm not sure that surprises me, but no."

"Or that he was living in the National Front compound earlier this year?"

That did surprise her. "What? The neo-Nazis? Really?"

"Yes. And I don't know why a supremacist sex offender would suddenly decide to defend the planet. It's more likely that someone planted him to keep tabs on you."

"For Pete's sake, why on earth would anyone do that? I can't imagine why those people would care about us."

"Do you think Anton could be connected to the incident on Wednesday?"

"How could he? Anton left weeks ago."

"I don't know. But I do know that he had no conceivable reason to join Reclaim unless he was sent to you. And I know that half your group was dragged off a bus and beaten three nights ago. That seems like too much of a coincidence."

"You don't have to look past the mine for that. They had plenty of reason to want to scare us."

"Maybe, but attacking a bunch of defenseless kids was guaranteed to backfire. How many special reports on mountaintop removal have there been in the past couple of days? How many reporters are flying helicopters over the mine now?" I didn't know the answer to either question but I could see that Roxanne did.

"It's hurt them," Roxanne admitted.

"The other theory was that some of the miners beat up your people on their own. But miners haven't been hurt by the work interruptions, so they wouldn't have much of a reason to care, would they?"

"Folks around here are touchy about outsiders," Roxanne countered, crossing her arms in front of her.

"They should be! But miners didn't assault your people on their own. If four or five guys beat up a few of your kids in a bar, I'd say it was miners. But a fake detour? Twenty armed, hooded men? I don't buy that, not unless Hobart management was involved, which would make no sense."

"Unless they didn't figure on the reaction."

"I'll judge that when I meet Jason Paul, but you told me he's no fool. Which leaves us with a white supremacist undercover in your group to explain."

Roxanne didn't have any more thoughts on that, so we stood there silently, looking at the mine and thinking our own thoughts. Then we started back down the trail.

"You grew up in the Catskills?" she asked.

"Yup."

"There's some nice hiking there. But my favorite is the restaurant that serves those enormous pancakes."

"I know the one. My town's a ways from there, not so much in the tourist zone."

"Do you get back home often?"

"I didn't for a long time, but I actually came here from there," I admitted.

"Apple picking?"

"No." I hesitated, realizing that I'd stumbled into a topic I'd have preferred to avoid. I decided honesty would make it easier to lie when I needed to. "My mother had a stroke."

Roxanne stopped so suddenly that I almost ran into her.

"That's awful! When did it happen?"

"Last weekend."

"And you still came here to help Heather's parents? It seems like you'd have your hands full at home."

"That's probably true."

"So why would you leave your poor mother?" I was beginning to understand that Roxanne wasn't prone to subtlety. But it was a good question.

"I spent most of my life being trained to do one thing. What I'm doing right now feels a lot more useful than what I was doing at home. When I was at home, it was more like... like being in everybody's way all the time."

"I remember the feeling. I may be as old as these hills, but I had a family once, too."

Roxanne lost herself in reflection for a moment, so I changed the subject. "Did you know Heather was diabetic?"

Roxanne nodded. "We always had to have ice for the cooler she stored her injections in."

"She sent a note to her mother on Wednesday saying that she was going to run out of insulin on Monday and that she didn't have access to more."

"Why couldn't she find insulin? She got her insulin with no skip-de-doo in Hamlin when she was with us."

"That's the question. Before I got here, I imagined the mine site might be so remote that she'd somehow gotten cut off from civilization..."

"It's West Virginia, not the Gobi Desert." Roxanne snorted.

"Right. So that suggests she's being denied access to the outside. Which makes more sense when I think of her having wandered into a compound of white supremacists without knowing what she'd gotten herself into."

"Do you think she's with them? The National Front?"

I shrugged. "It's the best lead I have, so I'll have to run it down."

* * *

I stopped abruptly before we crested the last ridge. We were still a good twenty minutes from the trailhead, about to start switch-backing down. We'd walked in silence as my thoughts flitted between Reclaim, the National Front and my mother. I called softly to Roxanne, who was still hiking up the hill.

"Hold up, Roxanne."

"What's wrong?" she asked, reluctant to surrender her upward momentum.

"Trouble ahead," I said. I wasn't going to say more, but her body language told me that she wasn't going to stop without a good reason. "You were followed from your camp by two men. I need to make sure it's not a problem. Wait here, keep this turned on and I'll call you when it's safe to come down," I said, withdrawing a small Motorola walkie-talkie from the side pouch on my pack. I switched it on and adjusted the channel, then handed it to her.

"You can't be serious."

"Yesterday someone tried to run me off the road. Then later, more men attacked me in the parking lot of my motel."

"Good grief! Why didn't you tell me?"

"I didn't want to worry you, but I made it to the parking area at the trailhead before you left your campsite so I could watch you drive here to see if you were followed."

"How could you possibly see me driving from down there? It's in the middle of a holler."

"I used a drone. It's like a model airplane with a camera on it. I controlled it with the little computer I was working on when you drove up."

Roxanne ground the heel of her palm against the side of her forehead. "Sometimes I feel so old. I didn't even know such a thing existed. But why on earth did you think someone would follow me?"

"The first time I was tailed, I was leaving your campsite. The second time was after we met for dinner."

"And you think these folks who followed me are dangerous?"

"I don't know. But wait here and I'll make sure things are okay before we go back to our cars, okay?"

She nodded abruptly, still in disbelief. But she stayed put.

I walked off the path, parallel to the ridge, and didn't stop for a quarter mile, well out of earshot. Then I pulled an earpiece out from under the collar of my shell, pushed it into my ear and fixed a microphone to my cheekbone. It would transmit my voice clearly at a whisper. I slipped my hand into another pocket and pushed a button on a satellite phone. The call went through immediately and after a brief identification ritual, I was passed through to the tactical operations center at the Activity. A young Indian-American specialist whose call sign was Mongoose answered. I'd met him once, just before I left the Activity for college, but I'd never worked with him. He had come to us from MIT, Cal-Tech and the Jet Propulsion Labs. He was the newest boy genius at the TOC when I left.

"Mongoose, thanks for the help. Did I manage the handoff correctly?"

"Roger, Orion, we have your bird under control."

"Did you see what I saw?"

"Yes, we were streaming your video feed from launch. We observed two vehicles driving from the campsite you identified last night. From your description, we identified the first vehicle as Queen Bee's. The second vehicle was parked off the road a few hundred yards from the entrance to the campsite and followed at a distance of one klick. It pulled off of the road before Queen Bee did—and out of visual sight. This suggests that the driver knew her destination."

I wondered how Roxanne would react if she knew the operations center for one of the U.S. government's most clandestine military agencies had nicknamed her Queen Bee. "I think there's a good chance someone has hacked Queen Bee's e-mail," I said. That would also explain how they knew I'd be out of my room last night.

"Two men exited the second vehicle and ascended the hill just west of your location. They are in place about ten meters from the ridgeline and have a good line of sight over the road and your parking area."

"You were able to track them under the tree cover?"

"We have them on infrared. Based on their movements I would say that there's a good chance you're looking at a two-man shooter-spotter team. They've picked a good spot for sniping."

"I didn't know the little drones had infrared," I said. I'd launched the four-foot unmanned aerial vehicle like a paper plane, tossing it from my hands more than a half-hour before Roxanne arrived. Using a joystick rigged inside the case to the ruggedized tablet computer, I'd guided the mini-drone to Roxanne's camp less than five miles from the trailhead as the crow flies, though much farther by road. When she left, I locked the drone on her Defender and it guided itself. The ops center took over before Roxanne arrived.

"Your discharge was four years ago, correct?"

"Four and a half."

"You're probably more familiar with the Puma AE. The model you launched this morning is three generations newer. In addition to very robust infrared, it has a five-hour flight window, can lock on targets and follow them autonomously, and has a satellite uplink, which is how we can control it from this end."

"You mean it's not on a wireless data plan?"

"Luddite."

"Why don't you guys just switch over to a satellite now, anyway?"

"And how many geosynchronous satellites do you imagine the Department of Defense has tasked on West Virginia?"

"Ah, good point. Can you give me coordinates on these guys?"

"We can do better if you open your tablet."

"Gotcha," I said. Taking a knee, I slid off my pack and withdrew the tablet. When I opened it, the screen showed an aerial infrared view of the holler with lots of shades of blue between the two ridges where the cars were parked. As I watched, it zoomed out to include both ridges.

"I'll mark your position in green, your vehicle in blue and the sniper team in red," Mongoose said, and like Chris Collinsworth on Sunday Night Football, he did just that.

"Can I zoom in on them?"

"Yes, with two fingers, like an iPad. You *have* used an iPad?"

"Yes, thank you, I recently experimented with a microwave oven, too. Did you know you can make popcorn in there?" Using two fingers I manipulated the view and zoomed in on the shooters. They were little blobs of orange on the side of the hill in the infrared-enhanced view. "Can you turn the infrared off on my screen but keep their position marked so I can see the terrain?"

"Roger, there you go," Mongoose said. Suddenly I was looking at a Google Earth-type map again.

"Did they take this trail just to the south of their position up toward the ridge and step off it or did they bushwhack?"

"They hiked up the trail, Orion."

"They're not using any infrared shielding, either, right?" There are several ways to block your heat signature from drones or handheld infrared scanners. But I'd easily spotted the two men on the infrared view, and that suggested they weren't under a thermal blanket or wearing thermal-blocking gilly suits.

"Roger that."

"Did they scout exfil before they hunkered down?"

"Negative."

Together, these little pieces of data painted a clearer picture. These guys were laying in wait, but they were expecting the man they'd seen yesterday: the ex-special ops veteran who could still drive a car, take down a few locals in a brawl and avoid walking into a room rigged with an IED. That guy might notice if someone was following him but he wouldn't be expecting a trained sniper team under cover on a hillside. So they had deployed as hunters rather than snipers. There's an important difference. When you're a hunter, you're not expecting the game to fight back. In combat, though, snipers are prime targets. So they stay off trails, plan emergency escape routes and generally go to great lengths to remain undetected after they shoot. This ambush was set up without those precautions. They only needed one clean shot.

"I have an idea," I said to Mongoose after studying the map for a few more minutes. "Let me see if I have what I need." I dug through my backpack for three things I was pretty sure I'd stuck inside while it was still dark that morning. "Ah, gotcha, all set. I'm going to have to do some quick maneuvering here, but I think I can flush these guys." I stopped to think for a moment. "Listen, Mongoose, I'll need some kind of extraction for these hitters and an interrogation team. Hopefully my action will be non-lethal. I suggest the FBI—can you confirm with Alpha? I'm assuming he won't want to let them know until it's a done deal, though."

"Roger that—hold on." I started moving in the direction I knew I needed to go, not wanting to lose any more time. He came back on the line ten minutes later. "Your pickup is approved. Let us know when you have the package."

"Thanks. I'll keep the line open but I'm going to make another call."

"Roger, Orion. Good luck."

I started to move again and then thought better of it. Instead, I slid my wallet from a Velcro side pocket on my pants and fished out a business card. I hit the hold button on the satellite phone and manually dialed another number. The line answered on the second ring.

"Nichols."

"This is Michael Herne. Do you remember me?"

"It's only been twelve hours, Mr. Herne. Where are you? My caller ID screen is blank."

"It's a work phone."

"Ah."

"Yes, exactly. Right now I'm near the edge of the Hobart Mine site on a hill in the Big Ugly. There are two guys waiting to take a shot at me from the opposite ridge when I get back to my car."

"You know this how?"

"I'm a professional, Agent Nichols."

"And you need rescuing?"

"No, this is a courtesy call. The Charleston office of the FBI is going to field a request to clean this up some time in the next hour. These guys are trained, definitely ex-military. I think they may be National Front. You'll want to get a look at them."

"Oh. Thanks. I appreciate that. I'll make sure I'm there. Be careful."

14

A voice crackled in my ear just as I saw the smoke rising from the ridge.

"Orion, targets on the move, heading north. They're moving on a trail and closing on your position." I clicked my earbud to acknowledge. I focused on my breathing, slowing it, calming myself and bringing my heart rate down. I'd set a small brush fire downhill to the north of the snipers. It took a little while to get going, but by the time they noticed it, there was enough smoke to obscure their view of the parking lot where my GTO was tucked in beside the old Land Rover. The fire was spreading up the hill, still small but growing. In a drier season it could have turned into a wildfire, but I wasn't giving it odds in the damp. It was hard enough to start. The smoke gave the shooters two clear choices: head straight down the hill and back to their car or climb up to the ridge, loop around the fire and find another spot with eyes on their target. Either way, I figured I'd accomplished the most important goal of not getting shot. I'd gambled that these guys wouldn't be easily put off their target, and I was right.

I crouched behind a hundred-foot oak as the two men flew by me, moving quickly to keep me from escaping under the cover of smoke. The spotter came first, wearing a heavy red plaid wool shirt over jeans. He had a gun in one hand and a pair of binoculars with a folded tripod still attached in another. Three steps behind him was the sniper, clad in black with his rifle in both hands.

I stepped onto the trail just as the spotter tripped over the 550 paracord I'd strung at ankle length across the trail, anchored between two trees. He went sprawling forward, one forearm coming up reflexively to protect his face and the other splayed out to the side, trying to keep a Kahr Arms .45 out of the mud. He dropped the binoculars on his way down.

The sniper jumped the cord and spun, spotting me as he turned and firing his M24 rifle from the hip. I moved as I saw the weapon come around and the slug missed me. It was jarringly close, though, and chips of bark hit my cheek. Then I placed the dot of the laser sight back on my target and squeezed the trigger on the Heckler & Koch 416. It bucked twice against my shoulder and the sniper's arm jerked back, his rifle dropping to the ground. I'd hit him in the shoulder and the upper arm, more or less where I was aiming. It was the kind of Hollywood stunt I'd never attempted before.

In my old line of work, I only shot a guy to put him down. Rifles aren't scalpels, especially when the target is moving. If you're trying to disable someone without killing them, you use other means. But I didn't have a Taser or a shotgun with beanbag rounds in the bag of tricks the Activity had delivered to my new motel room early that morning. And I was trying to avoid killing these guys, because that would complicate my dealings with the FBI. So I took the chance. It wasn't a crazy bet, mind you. I'd fired over 100,000 rounds from an HK 416 in the last decade, which made it less than a winning-the-lottery kind of proposition. I hoped that I'd missed the axial artery, or all of that risk would be in vain.

"Drop the weapon, hands on the ground," I barked as I saw the spotter start to roll over, the .45 still in his hands. I put three rounds in the ground next to him. "Last warning," I said. He dropped the gun. "Hands away from your bodies and both of you step away from the weapons." They spread their hands and backed away slowly. The sniper was bleeding profusely from the wound in his arm. I pulled a black Velcro band from a pocket and tossed it to the spotter.

"Sit him down by that tree." The man complied. Without any prompting, he looped the tourniquet around the sniper's arm above the wound and tightened it. That told me all I needed to know about these two men. I had the spotter slip on flexicuffs and lay flat on the ground, then I pulled the slack from them as I knelt with my 1911 Kimber Custom .45

pressed into his neck. Then I duct-taped the sniper to the tree. I took a Glock and a fixed-blade knife off him while he regarded me with dead eyes, then I treated his wound. One of the slugs was still inside his arm, but it wasn't for me to remove. I stopped the bleeding, covered and taped the wound and adjusted the tourniquet high and wide around his arm.

I'd been lucky and I knew it. You can't play games with veterans these days. When I first made Special Forces in 2000, the U.S. had been at peace for a decade. Outside of the special ops community and a few other guys who'd been deployed to Somalia, almost nobody in the Army under the age of thirty had seen combat. Our regular infantry was well trained but inexperienced. Rangers were fitter and had a much better understanding of small unit tactics, but all of it was theoretical. Only the guys in the elite units like CAG (which replaced Delta Force) and DevGru (the successor to Seal Team Six) were combat veterans.

By the time I left the Army, as the war was winding down in Iraq, it was a different story. There were National Guardsmen who'd spent more time under fire than virtually any enlisted man who'd ever served in Vietnam. They were as competent as the Special Forces guys I trained with before 9/11. The Tier One guys, like those I worked with in the Activity, were at another level. Most had deployed on and off for the duration of two wars. Afghanistan and Iraq produced the best generation of warriors the world has seen since Julius Caesar took a professional army on an eight-year tour of Gaul two thousand years ago.

All that experience matters. The first time you get shot at, everything seems to happen at once. Your adrenaline pumps, rounds seem to come from everywhere and depending on your personal body chemistry, you either want to dive into a hole or run screaming with your M4 blazing toward the source of the gunfire. You don't consider that the woman holding a child in the room you've entered might be wearing a suicide vest or clutching the trigger of an AK under the bed sheet. You give the man who doesn't slow his vehicle at a checkpoint an extra second's grace before you shoot him. Those are the mistakes that get you killed. If you survive it's because you saw someone else make them before you had the chance.

The sniper and spotter hadn't expected an ambush, but they reacted like veterans when things went south. Retreating along the trail was a mistake, but as soon as the spotter tripped, the sniper turned backward with his rifle raised, covering their vulnerable point and trusting that his teammate would manage to cover his back. His hip shot with a rifle was better than ninety percent of civilian shooters could manage with a pistol at a range from that distance.

So I knew before the FBI arrived that these guys wouldn't be carrying identification and that they weren't going to talk. While I was waiting, I took pictures of them with my smartphone, paying special attention to their faces and the tattoos on their neck and chests. I used the same phone to take their fingerprints before transmitting everything to the Activity. The rifle worried me the most. It was an M-24, and not the civilian Remington 700. All of the other equipment the two men were carrying was mil-spec. It meant that the National Front employed some serious men. And Alpha and I both knew the only way to find Heather would be to walk straight into their lair.

15

"Mr. Herne, you have a fascinating background. High school football and track star, turned down a Michigan football scholarship to enlist in the Army. Won the Best Ranger competition at age 18, Special Forces by 21 and then the Silver Star and a Purple Heart in Afghanistan. Six more years with a logistics unit and an honorable discharge as a Master Sergeant, followed by undergraduate studies at Georgetown where you graduated *cum laude* in three years. And now you're an intelligence analyst with the State Department. Very impressive." Jason Paul looked up from the folder and pulled the vintage horn-rimmed reading glasses off of his face, folding them with care and sliding them back into a velvet case sitting on his desk.

Paul's office was as elegant as Roxanne had promised. The oriental carpet on the floor was silk, with a level of workmanship I recognized from my time in Afghanistan. His desk was solid walnut, buffed to a high sheen. The whole setup looked oddly out of place in the ramshackle pile of pre-fabricated buildings that made up the offices for Transnational Coal. I was dubious about the wisdom of going ahead with the meeting, but Alpha had insisted. The office building stood just inside the entrance to the mine, at a spot where you couldn't get much of a glimpse of the rest of the operation aside from the top of a horseshoe-shaped canyon that formed the boundaries of the active mining area.

"It's nice to know that Google works on your computer, Mr. Paul," I said, not flinching from Paul's blue eyes as they turned a shade cooler. Paul was just as Roxanne had described him. Telling me the story of my life was an attempt to put me off balance. I couldn't play along; if Paul thought he'd intimidated me, I wouldn't get anything useful from him.

"I'm told you're looking for a young woman with the protest group. I'm not sure how I can help you," Paul continued, ignoring the insult. He poured a cup of coffee from a silver pot into a bone china cup sitting on a sterling tray on his desk. He put down the pot, then raised the cup and slid a saucer underneath it. He handed both to me.

"Heather Hernandez stopped protesting in September. There was an internal rift in Reclaim at that time, and understanding what happened may help me find her."

"I'm still not sure how I can help. I don't know anything about the internal workings of those groups," Paul said. He'd just lied to me for the first time.

"I know that Reclaim staged a protest in July. Can you tell me about that?"

"About two dozen activists marched to the mine entrance. They ignored the guard's warnings and held the gate open while a private vehicle was admitted. Then they continued into the mine. Some of them lay down in front of haulers and loaders. When the vehicles stopped, the protestors climbed on them and put banners on the windshields. We called the police and they were arrested."

"Did this happen again?"

"They came again in subsequent months but we've continued to update our security procedures and they didn't cause that level of disruption again."

"I'd like to know what else they might have done that affected your operation."

"Nothing, Mr. Herne. And miners didn't attack the activists if that's what you're implying."

"So you're saying it's sheer incompetence that's responsible for your dismal performance here? The output of this mine was down 15% in August and over 30% in September. Bad enough to bring the CEO of Transnational here on the corporate jet three times between July and the end of September. That's two more trips than he made in the previous three years."

"And how do you know all of this?" Paul remained composed, but ropy tendons in his neck contracted.

"You know my background, Mr. Paul," I said gesturing to the folder he'd been reading my history from. "Why don't you tell me?" The speed with which the Activity had unearthed these details didn't surprise me; it was just another sign that the private errand I'd been sent on had become a government matter.

Paul coughed and stood abruptly. He walked over to the mahogany sideboard against the wall.

"This is a very complex surface mining operation," Paul said as he poured scalding water into a cup before dumping the liquid into a small silver basin. "We operate twenty-four hours a day, 365 days a year. We have some of the most expensive mining equipment in the country on this site and it's constantly in use. The cost of this operation is so high that any drop in production can swing the entire operation to a loss."

Paul poured more water from a different kettle into the cup then opened a small stainless steel canister. He scooped loose tealeaves and gently tapped them into an infuser, then dunked it into the water in the cup.

"Something disrupted your business. And if I'm not mistaken, it's something the activists did that you didn't report to the police." I said this with as much conviction as I could muster, looking flatly into Paul's eyes.

"With an operation this large, small events can have a cascading effect," Paul answered. I noticed that he'd scrupulously avoided talking directly about money. After a moment he took the infuser out of the tea, added a teaspoonful of raw sugar to the cup and stirred it. After the sugar dissolved, he added a dash of cream. He walked back over to his desk and sat down, putting the teacup and saucer delicately down on his leather blotter.

"Mr. Paul, the FBI has two men in custody who tried to kill me with a sniper rifle this morning. There are another two men in the Lincoln County jail and two more in a hospital in Charleston who tried to attack me last night. In less than an hour, I'll be leaving this state to deal with more urgent matters back home. But before I do I'll advise the FBI on whether the girl I've come looking for has been kidnapped and whether they should treat this mine as a crime scene. The violence used by my attackers has persuaded federal authorities to take my investigation seriously. So if you think a bunch of college kids and ex-hippies can hurt your profitability, just wait and see what happens when a hundred federal agents shut down every piece of machinery on this site."

Paul adjusted his cuffs one by one, ensuring I could see the pearl cufflinks through the functional buttons of his hand-tailored suit. When he was done, he leaned forward with a half-smile on his face. "I'm not someone you should be threatening, Mr. Herne."

Then Paul leaned back and continued, "But there's no harm in sharing this with you. During August and September, some of the activists infiltrated this site several times at night.

The first few times, they targeted smaller trucks and other minor equipment. The last time, early in September, they set a charge that badly damaged the engine of our dragline. We call it Big Jack, and it can lift almost 100 cubic yards at a time. It was out of operation for over a week. That's what caused the production shortfalls. I called the Reclaim leaders in here and showed them evidence of what they'd done and told them if they didn't stop, I'd hand it over to the police."

"You called Roxanne, Josh and Amy into your office?" I asked.

"Yes, I did. And I know that you're friendly with Ms. Chalmers. Please remember that she could go to jail for ten to fifteen years. That's what will happen if I turn the evidence over to the authorities. And I will certainly do so if there's any more disruption to this operation from the FBI or anyone else. You can think about that on your way out," he said as a guard appeared at the door.

But Roxanne's potential prison bid wasn't what I pondered as I left the mine site. Instead, I was wondering why Paul didn't have the Reclaim leaders locked up when he had the chance.

16

I engaged the clutch lever, downshifted into third gear with a flick of my left foot, let out the clutch and twisted the throttle. I hadn't perfectly rev-matched my downshift, but the big bike surged forward without a lurch. It always amazes me how power that would be insignificant in a car—in this case, 125 brake horsepower—can make a motorcycle feel like an absolute monster. The bike I was riding is not the one you picture in your mind when you hear the name Harley Davidson. It didn't have high handlebars or a backward-leaning seat. This bike was the Night Rod Special, a black-on-black design exercise that mostly served to showcase a gorgeous engine.

I have pretty specific tastes in bikes—I own both Japanese and German motorcycles for different reasons. The Night Rod is not in a performance league with the machines I keep in my garage, but it's a lot prettier. It's also American-built, which was part of the reason I was riding it. And it was plenty fast. It wallowed a little in the corners, though, which reminded me that I had borrowed it for serious purposes. The mercury was above 50 degrees, a marked improvement from the morning. As the roar of the bike echoed off the low mountains, I thought about my mother. This part of the country reminded me of home, but the mountains seemed closer together, as if someone had needed to get more of them into the state and ended up rushing the job. It was the peak of the foliage season in Appalachia and though the colors weren't as impressive to my northern eye as those I'd grown up with, they were memorable.

I'd driven the GTO from Paul's office onto Route 119, straight through Charleston and onto Interstate 79, which was the way back to D.C. I stopped at a truck stop about ten miles east of Charleston to refuel. I walked into the bathroom with my Blackhawk shell, a black baseball cap and sunglasses on. A few minutes later, a man of my size and general complexion wearing the same items left, but it wasn't me. He pulled the GTO out of the truck stop and onto the highway, back to D.C. The plan was that he wouldn't stop until he reached Activity headquarters in Rosslyn. I watched my car leave without me from inside the diner of the truck stop. The BMW X5 with blacked out windows that had been trailing me since I'd left the Hobart mine followed the GTO.

Wearing work coveralls and a different cap, I got into a panel van with two men I recognized. We drove a few miles before exiting the highway and pulling up to a semi in the parking lot of a defunct warehouse. They escorted me to the back of the trailer, where a team of specialists started to work on me. As the makeup artist applied temporary tattoos designed to look permanent, I winced. I never believe those things will come off. My hair was cut and dyed to a light brown, contact lenses gave me blue eyes and small prosthetics subtly changed the contours of my nose.

While the work was underway I received briefings from an Activity armorer and one of the electronic surveillance specialists who form the core of the Activity.

Then agent Nichols walked in. She whistled.

"So this is what it's like to have a secret budget."

"Careful or you're next," I warned her.

"They did a good job with you. You look...different." She picked a bit of fluff off of the shoulder of the black motorcycle jacket.

"Thanks for helping me out up there on the ridge," I said as she pulled a chair to face me. The senior responding FBI agent had handcuffed me and was about to arrest me alongside the shooters when Nichols intervened. Three cruisers from the Lincoln County Sheriff's office arrived at the same time as the FBI, and the senior agent had his hands full debating who should take the suspects into custody. One of the Sheriff's people was Deputy Collins, who was apoplectic to see me in handcuffs. In the end, Collins and Nichols made an impression on the older agent: he removed the handcuffs and let me go with a stern warning. I wondered if Nichols would pay a price for not backing her senior man.

"You'd think the hardest part would be not getting killed, wouldn't you? Sheldon was more upset that you started a fire than he was that you'd shot someone."

"He might be right about that. So what brings you to my tractor-trailer?"

"I'm here to brief you on the National Front. I've been following them since I came to the Charleston office. We've never gotten someone inside the compound, but I can fill you in on some background that might help."

"Thanks."

"The most important thing to understand is that these guys are not skinheads or Klansmen. You're going to a music festival in the National Front compound, but it won't feel like a hate-fest."

"They're not supremacists?"

"They are. They have the same racist beliefs, but they've evolved on the outside. They've got the tattoos, but not where you can see them. They don't shave their heads; they wear their hair short and neat. They couch their racism in coded language an outsider wouldn't recognize. Even the music is different. You might mistake it for Top 40 pop—and that's intentional. Only the lyrics are different."

"These groups have been around for decades, haven't they? When did they change?"

"The National Front is the only supremacist group like this. It's unique—and that's part of the reason we're watching them so closely. Dr. James Madison Pace, the guy who founded the National Front, died almost a decade ago. He had no family, and he left the compound and his personal fortune to the organization. Without the money to fight over, the National Front would probably have fallen apart. Ulrick Gleich was the designated successor, but he was nearly Pace's age when he took over. There were five lieutenants—apostles they called them—who fought behind the scenes for control. In the end, Eric Price, a man who ran a spinoff group of the National Front called the Popular Alliance, won."

"The National Front had a tribute band?"

"Not exactly. The PA never operated like the rest of the organization. Price was a soldier decorated in Operation Desert Storm. When he got out of the service, he went to work in pharmaceutical sales and marketing. He met Dr. Pace in the mid-nineties and pitched him on setting up a clandestine version of the National Front—the Popular Alliance. The PA was intended to influence public policy to favor the goals of the National Front."

"I can't imagine them getting very broad support."

"It was an underground organization. Price formed it like a resistance movement, in cells so that the entire membership wouldn't be visible to anyone but him.

"Within five years, the PA eclipsed the National Front in funding and influence. First Price found a few wealthy patrons who supported his goals. Then he hired lobbyists and started backing political candidates for offices in very small races at the state and municipal level. The PA became the go-to guys for local money for both Democrats and Republicans."

"How did that work? I can't imagine there were many politicians willing to align themselves with white supremacists."

"Price kept a very low profile. If anybody suspected his real motives, they weren't talking. He also used his influence carefully. He focused on smaller elections, everything from school boards and planning commissions to state representatives."

"And the politicians taking this money never said 'Wow, this Eric Price guy wants me to segregate the lunch counter, that could be a problem'?"

"He was smarter than that. The issues he backed were incredibly specific and very technical. In New Mexico, Price identified an upscale housing development that was becoming popular with mixed-race couples. So he got a water conservation bill passed through the Democratic legislature that made it impossible for the development to expand. In another state he got Republicans to back a repeal of some state highway taxes that ended up defunding a school busing program."

"Did little stuff like that have any kind of effect?"

"More than anyone thought it would. The first six states they got into had measurable increases in racial violence and saw declines in intermarriage. None of the states was known to be racially intolerant and they were equally split between Democratic and Republican-controlled legislatures."

"So how have I never heard of Eric Price before?" I asked.

"Because he kept his own name, and the names of the few men he recruited to the PA, hidden. The PA formed fifty-three political action committees over the past eight years. These committees are the source of the funds. They act anonymously."

"So why would Price want to run the National Front? It sounds like he had all the power and influence he could want with the PA."

"He'd always wanted the PA to be the vanguard of a broader revolution. He needed a true grassroots organization to go along with it. Not just a few wealthy donors filtering money through PACs to a bunch of local legislators with no idea what cause they were actually supporting. He wanted to lead a national group of like-minded believers. When he got control of the National Front, he started changing it immediately. He severed ties with the skinhead movement and changed the recruiting target. They started recruiting middle and upper-middle-class suburbanites. No more swastikas or shaved heads, because he said they made enemies of natural allies. That's why you've got the twin lightning bolts here," she said, tugging aside my collar to reveal the new tattoo just below my collarbone.

"That's the symbol of the Nazi S.S. but it's not as recognizable to most people as a swastika. And it disappears under work clothes. It's the equivalent of a twelve-year-old girl getting a heart tattoo on her butt. It carries the thrill of defiance without the risk of discovery."

"Can you tell me anything about the rally I'm crashing?"

"Once a year they have a festival for Lawful Records; that's the four-year-old record label of the National Front. The first year they held it in Wisconsin, then Oregon, and last year in Texas. This is the first year they're experimenting with West Virginia. They're holding it on the grounds of the National Front compound. They seem to think this weekend will be a big draw because the compound is not far from Fayetteville, and there are a bunch of whitewater rafting events this weekend on the Gauley and the New River. Tomorrow is Bridge Day and the last dam release for the Gauley."

"So why are they opening their compound now? And why aren't you sending someone in yourself?"

Nichols smiled. "Why would you think we aren't? As for why they're having the event on the grounds of their compound? Hard to say. It's taken this long for the National Front to clean up its image and be a big enough draw to get a good size crowd to travel to West Virginia. As for getting inside the compound? It's a matter of degree. They've set up tents in a meadow in front of the compound buildings. I'm sure your own people will show you aerial photos before you go in. We don't think the rest of the compound will be open to the public. It will certainly be guarded if that's the case, so be careful. But if this girl you're looking for is with the National Front, she may be at the concert."

"I hope so. Heather wrote a note to her mother on Wednesday afternoon, saying she was going to run out of insulin on Monday. She's a type 1 diabetic."

"I didn't know that. Her mother must be worried."

"Yes, but the note made more sense when I thought she was camping in the wilderness somewhere cut off from civilization. There's no reason she couldn't make a run into Fayetteville or Beckley from the National Front compound to get insulin."

"Do you think she's in trouble?"

"If she's on that compound, she's in danger one way or another. She might have followed a guy there, not understanding what he was really into. His name is Anton Harmon. He's a Gulf War veteran like Price, but then he went on to join the Special Forces. He's also a convicted sex offender. He followed Heather from the Reclaim Camp to a commune called CC Farms. Then she left with him, maybe to the National Front compound. I think it's unlikely she knew what she was getting into. So I can't imagine how she reacted when she figured things out. If she's there and she's unhappy, they might not let her go to the concert," I said. "But this is best shot I have of finding her."

"Does it strike you as odd that a white supremacist would be dating a Hispanic girl?"

"Yes, but she looks Caucasian."

"Even so, racial purity is a very big issue for these guys."

"I agree with you, but I met a woman who had seen Harmon without his shirt on. He had the tattoos. Including a swastika. And he is definitely a National Front member and she definitely left Reclaim with him."

"I've put together a briefing book that has the language you need to use," Nichols said, handing me a binder. "I hope your cover is good. This festival is invitation only. It's a tight-knit community."

"I'm going in as a small business owner from Wyoming. He was intercepted on his way here. He served in the infantry in Afghanistan, and we knew some of the same people. I gather that he lives in a small town and there isn't anyone else coming from his neck of the woods."

"Does that sound a little thin to you?"

"Yeah, probably. But I've run out of leads. This is the only way I can think of to find Heather."

Nichols pursed her lips, then turned to the Activity people who were still working on my appearance and my gear. "Can we have a moment?"

Without a word, three men and two women stopped what they were doing and shuffled out of the semi.

"I want to share something, but if it gets out my career is over. Do you understand?"

I nodded.

"I don't know how this connects to Heather, but I think you should understand something. The reason the FBI jumped on the murder of the protestors has nothing to do with hate crimes. It's an internal issue for the Bureau. One of the two protestors killed was an undercover FBI agent. His cover name was John McCarthy."

"That changes things."

"Yes it does. We think there's a chance that someone staged the attack to remove our agent. The second victim died because he had an undiagnosed heart condition. Nobody else was beaten as badly as McCarthy."

"Why would you have someone undercover with Reclaim?" I asked.

"I don't know. All I know is that for the entire time I've been working on the National Front, I've been bumping up against agents working on Reclaim and Transnational Coal. But everything is walled off from me, so I don't know who or what they're investigating."

"Jason Paul, the head of the Hobart mine, told me some of the protestors were sabotaging his equipment. He got incriminating video on them and confronted one of the Reclaim leaders, Roxanne Chalmers, with it. That's when the group splintered. Some of them left the state and others, including Heather and Anton, went to the CC Farm commune."

"But you think there's more?"

"If Paul had video linking the protestors to sabotage, why didn't he just have them arrested? He didn't show much restraint over the summer when they shut down his operation, and sabotaging the loader was much more serious and costly. So it makes me think he was using the video as leverage to get something else he wanted."

"What would that be?" Nichols asked.

"I don't know. But Roxanne acts as if she's been holding onto her guilt for a lot longer than the three days since the school bus attack. And the mine hasn't returned to full production even though the equipment has come back online. Paul's job has to be hanging by a thread. Which suggests that he's got some bigger plan."

"You think he's blackmailing Roxanne but he still hasn't gotten the mine back running?"

"I don't think you could blackmail Roxanne with a threat of jail. She's the type who would probably be happy to serve time if she could stop the mine. And after her split with the other Reclaim leaders, it's hard to imagine blackmailing her for their actions. There would have to be a carrot, too."

"Ensuring that the mine fails slowly?"

"That's what I was thinking. So the question is what's in it for Paul? What could he possibly accomplish by ruining his own career?"

"And whether the National Front is connected. The men who've tried to hurt you and that explosive device last night... Anton Harmon could have arranged all of that on his own, right? Maybe he's just trying to keep the family away from his girlfriend," Nichols suggested.

"It could be, but if so it's like waving a red flag in front of a bull. He couldn't possibly think he'd scare me off if he knew my background, and if he killed me it would just attract more attention. It also seems like too many unconnected coincidences when you look at it that way. Imagine the odds of a tiny camp of protestors having both an FBI agent and a National Front member undercover at the same time. That can't be a coincidence. This has to be about something else."

Nichols put two fingers over her lips and rested her thumb beneath her chin. "You might be right. The problem is that the kind of scheme you're describing covers at least three separate task force investigations in our office and Pittsburgh. Which makes it hard to put together the pieces. Until we can connect the dots with evidence, that is. And we haven't gotten there yet."

"You're sticking your neck out more than a little just to be here, aren't you?" I asked.

"No, just the opposite. The order to brief you came down the line from Washington. The head of our office was livid. I'm at the bottom of the food chain, so I get the scut work." The FBI is driven by seniority, like many federal bureaucracies including the one I work for. An agent with less than two years on the job would be very junior, especially in a small field office.

"Well I appreciate it. I don't know if I'm going to help move your investigation forward, but this is the last thing I can think to do before I leave the state."

"Then you're lucky they didn't cancel the festival."

"Why would they cancel it?"

"Haven't you been listening to the news for the past three days?"

I shook my head, uncomprehending.

"There's a hurricane headed up the coast. A big one. We're supposed to get some snow by Monday, which is pretty unusual for October in West Virginia. They think it might hit D.C. or New York. This morning they started talking about it combining with some other weather system and turning into some kind of crazy Frankenstorm."

"A hurricane?"

"That's right. They're calling it Sandy. Hurricane Sandy."

17

I slowed the Night Rod to a roll as I approached a wrought iron gate. The barrier continued up the hill on either side of the road as a nine-foot chain link fence topped with barbed wire. There was an observation post visible on top of the ridge just east of me. I came to a stop about ten yards from the guardhouse as a clean-shaven man in a brown uniform with a Sig-Sauer on his hip signaled me to stop and approached me with a clipboard. His partner was inside a guardhouse with reinforced 6-inch-thick plexiglass and a gun port.

"Are you here for the event, sir?"

"Yes. My name is Ray Larney," I replied. This guard was no rent-a-cop. He stood just beyond arms' reach and gave the bike a careful look with one hand on his weapon before looking down to his clipboard. He would have done fine in an outpost in Afghanistan.

"Thank you, sir, you're on the list. If you follow this road up a half mile, you'll see the white tents. Parking is on the left. Please stay on the main road."

He nodded to his partner and the gate slid open on rollers. I eased the bike through and kept it under thirty as I wound through the last stretch of road. The two-lane blacktop plunged into the woods for a stretch and then veered east. I was surprised to see that it cut right through the hill—they'd blasted the road as they might have an interstate. Looking up I realized that I wouldn't want to go through this pass uninvited. With both ends blocked, it would be a killing box. As soon as I made it through the hill I found a holler that rolled on unimpeded to the horizon. It might count for a modest spread in Montana, but it was enormous in West Virginia.

The tents were set up in a large field off to the side of the road about a quarter-mile into the holler. There were two of them; pristine white and billowing like sheets in the breeze. They might have been cheerful on a sunny day but in the blustery autumn weather they looked menacing, more like Klan hoods than wedding whites. Even more jarring was the main building of the compound, which towered above the rest of the landscape. I'd seen a satellite image, but it didn't do justice to the enormous structure. I'd been mentally prepared for a newer version of the CC Farm compound, which was something like the lovechild of two colonials and a barn. This was something else.

In front of the building, a reflecting pool the size of five Olympic swimming pools was festooned with three fountains spraying green water into the cool air. Behind the pool and a carefully tended flower garden was a building with a vaulted roof at least four stories high, which looked something like the mega-churches of middle America. The drab taupe masonry of an enormous, plain-sided church was accessorized with a two-story structure wrapped around the main building like an anaconda. The wraparound was an architectural jumble, with a dual-pitched gambrel roof running into turrets at each corner of the building. The entire structure was devoid of windows. I knew from satellite pictures that a whole compound of buildings sat behind this monstrosity, at least one of which we'd pegged as residential.

A man in a black turtleneck waved me into a field that had been pressed into duty as a parking lot. I parked the Night Rod next to a dozen other bikes—a good number of which were Harleys. There were virtually no cars to be found, just bikes, pickups and SUVs, along with a few ATVs clustered in a far corner of the field. The ATVs all bore the National Front logo I'd seen in the FBI file.

They'd gated off the festival, putting it behind a three-foot-high white picket fence like a suburban lawn party. Two young men manned the entrance. They wore Beretta 92s in a way that suggested long familiarity. One checked my name against his clipboard list while the other patted me down. He carefully slid the holster securing a Kahr Arms PM-45 from inside my belt. Nonplussed, he handed me a claim check and pointed over to a stand at the other end of the tent where I could retrieve the gun on my way out. He didn't ask me to relinquish my folding Spyderco knife.

The music was loud, but just as Nichols predicted, it sounded more like Coachella than Hellfest. I stepped inside the tent and saw the truth behind Nichols's assessment of the National Front. There was hardly a bare head to be seen except those crowning middle-aged men. There were a smattering of couples, a fair number of men dressed in bike leathers and a few teenagers. I even saw one couple toting a baby in one of those front carriers that mimic a kangaroo pouch.

The first tent was set up for a barbeque. Burgers, bratwurst, ribs and chicken with fries and coleslaw, along with beer and soft drinks, sat along a buffet line that chefs in white coats and toques replenished in real-time from a line of grills that stood just outside the open-air tent. The grills were upscale, stainless steel rigs that would have looked appropriate outside a McMansion in the suburbs, only bigger. Sunlight reflected from them in the couple of spots where it poked through the clouds.

It struck me that October was odd timing for an outdoor concert, even as far south as West Virginia. The mercury was barely into the fifties and shivering undoubtedly caused some of the nervous energy in the tent. The corner of West Virginia

I'd explored for two days was beautiful, but I couldn't imagine the attraction of river rafting in ice-cold water. Then again, my only experiences with whitewater have been involuntary and without the benefit of a raft.

I hadn't moved far into the tent before another young man with a clipboard approached me. The tag on his chest said Mark and told me he was 'Here to Help!' Mark was one of a dozen or so men and women in their teens or early twenties milling about in identical khaki pants and white oxford shirts with the National Front logo embroidered on the chest pocket.

"Can I have your name please, sir?"

"Ray Larney, and I work for a living so call me Ray, not 'sir,'" I said. Mark smiled as he located my name and checked me off. I felt like an evidence bag going through the chain of custody. He handed me a blank nametag and a marker.

"Just put your first name on that if you would please, sir—er, Ray," he corrected himself. "Help yourself to lunch and enjoy the music. There are two more tours left for the day if you'd like to try one—at two and three p.m."

"Sure would. Two sounds great. How do I sign up?"

"I'll put your name on the list for two o'clock, Ray. The tour will meet right over there and leave promptly on the hour." He pointed toward the entrance to the tent, flashed symmetric rows of teeth and walked away.

I skipped the buffet line and meandered into the second tent. This looked more like a trade show, with booths scattered around the periphery. The signs were specific and hard to decode, with names like "Zoning laws and community growth" and "educational advantages of cultural unity." Only a small display tucked in the corner of the tent with the bland title "The History of National Socialism" betrayed the movement's origins. The National Front wasn't skimping on the budget, either. The booths were trade-show quality, with professionally produced signs and graphics. There were sign-up boards for more information and a schedule of weekend informational events following the music festival. Each booth also had stacks of books supporting the position it was advocating, along with custom-produced instructional manuals that helped attendees understand how to enact change at the local level. Everything was glossy and everything was free. It looked like a show they could take on the road.

All of it made sense to me. From a distance, the festival looked like it could be a college alumni reunion. Taking away the overt racism allowed the National Front to navigate in the cultural mainstream while quietly peeling off those sympathetic to its cause. Belonging to the Klan or some skinhead organization wouldn't do for a small business owner or a company man. But belonging to a group promoting stronger communities through zoning, environmental laws and education reforms would be just fine.

I helped myself to a canvas tote bag with the National Front logo on it and quickly filled it with literature as I moved through the tent. The staffers in this area were older than the kids minding the barbeque, but they were dressed identically. I wondered if the National Front had hired a brand consultant.

I stepped out of the second tent onto a wide grassy lawn that was nominally separated from the grounds of the compound by interlocking plastic crowd control barriers. The lawn was set up to hold perhaps a thousand people and was already half full in the middle of the day. People were sprawled on blankets or folding camp chairs, talking animatedly while a new band set up on stage. The ratio of single white men to families and couples was reversed from the crowd inside the tent and the whole gathering had the air of a Sunday at the park, albeit a brisk one. The wind was whipping up in gusts and I could see a dense layer of clouds moving in from the distance. We might be hundreds of miles inland, but it looked as if the hurricane that was threatening the east coast might be fixing to take a piece of West Virginia with it, too.

The lawn also afforded a splendid view of the reflecting pond, with its three fountains and the National Front Headquarters building rising behind it. Kentucky bluegrass was manicured to the height of the fairway on a golf course. The National Front building still looked like a church to me, but I wasn't noticing the architecture at this distance. Instead

I saw armed guards patrolling with dogs, motion and infrared sensors, a fairly sophisticated radar array on the roof and that distinct lack of windows. The group was going to significant trouble to ensure that whatever was happening in the compound stayed inside. Which made me more confident that I was finally in the right place.

I took a walk around the entire lawn, stepping awkwardly like a sightseer while my eyes moved quickly behind sunglasses. I exhaled as I completed the full circuit. There were more women at the festival than I'd expected, but none of them was the one I was looking for. She might have left briefly or she might not be attending at all, but I let go of the unreasonable hope that I'd spot her. I craved a bratwurst but knew it would be a bad idea if I ended up having to leave the party in a hurry.

"It's a hell of a show, isn't it?" a man with curly brown hair and a salt-and-pepper mustache a decade or two older than me asked, nodding toward the bandstand where "One Nation" was doing a sound check. He was leaning against a barricade on the compound side of the great lawn, puffing on a cigarette.

"It's impressive. I've never been here before," I told the man who introduced himself as Dennis.

"Almost nobody has. This is the first time they've held one of these things at headquarters. You had to be Founder's Circle to have been invited here until now."

"Founder's Circle?"

"Newbie?"

"Pretty much. I live in a small town outside Laramie in Wyoming. I've been to a couple of meetings in Cheyenne, but that's about it. This isn't what I expected at all. I thought there would be a lot of angry teenagers."

"Nah, that's the old way." He took a sip from a can of Budweiser. "Skinheads made us look like radicals. The fact is, most decent folks in this country agree with us, they just can't say it if people get distracted by swastikas. It's like Eric Price says—nobody ignores a white man in a suit. Now we're the man."

"It's amazing it took someone this long to figure that out."

"It's all marketing. After the sixties you couldn't belong to the Klan if you didn't want trouble. They should have just gone underground and changed their name, but it didn't happen. The old guard held on way too long, then they just withered away. You had the skinheads in the eighties but they looked pretty outdated by the nineties. Price was a genius to turn this into a real people's movement instead of a freak show. Every week in Dayton I bring my family to the Saturday lunch and we see lots of people we know. The public face is all about communities now, and that's a very mainstream topic."

"I have to confess, I don't understand half the brochures I picked up." I'm about as interested in politics as I am in basket weaving, but I hoped I sounded like a believer.

Dennis took another swig of Budweiser and brushed the side of his mustache with a calloused fingertip. "That's the point. We don't put anything in writing that the media could get hold of and use to paint us bad. But you can count your bottom dollar that every single issue the cause gets behind helps preserve white culture in this country."

"That makes me feel better. Have you been inside the big building?"

"Yup, sure have. This morning. Are you doing a tour?"

"Yes, in about a half hour," I replied, using the excuse to check the watch on my wrist.

"It's impressive. They've got a fully outfitted conference center, a library, study rooms, a cafeteria, all that."

"Do people live here? Or do they commute?"

"I dunno. It could be that some live here. There's plenty of housing for conferences anyway. The old Pace family mansion is somewhere around here, too."

"This is all a much bigger operation than I realized." This at least was the truth.

"You don't know half of it. There's like a 7,000 foot runway, a helipad, every damn thing. It's a thousand miles from where this movement was ten years ago. We finally hit the big time."

"It sure does look like that."

18

"The National Front was founded in 1968 by Dr. James Madison Pace, a physicist who taught at Bob Jones University in Greenville, South Carolina. Dr. Pace became concerned about the effects of changing cultural patterns in America and founded the National Front to promote traditional American values." That was a nice way of saying that the end of Jim Crow laws and the breakdown of the Klan had led him to form a successor organization. Our tour guide, Valerie, who was responsible for shepherding two-dozen aspiring supremacists was herself white, blond, Viking-tall and well spoken. She delivered the tour information while walking backwards around the reflecting pool and gesturing with her hands like a flight attendant.

"From its founding, the National Front has worked to preserve the traditional culture of the Anglo-Saxon and Aryan heritage that founded America." I tried to remember which of our forefathers might have been Aryan, but couldn't. Jefferson had red hair, so not him. Washington? Definitely not a blond.

"You are standing on the ancestral estate of the Pace family, who settled here in 1769. An ancestor of Dr. Pace fought in the Chickamauga Wars against the Cherokee Indians and in the American Revolutionary war. The family continued to prosper in this place in the timber and mining industries for over two hundred years. In 2003, Dr. Pace passed away without heirs, ending the line of the Pace family in this state. However he left the property to the National Front foundation, which continues to run it today."

We'd made it around the pond and were approaching the main building. The entrance was on the side of the building—on the narrow end where you'd enter a church. I'd noticed a plainer entrance on the other side before we'd started winding our way around the reflecting pool.

"The National Front Headquarters building you're looking at today is just three years old. Until 2009, the organization was run from the family house, which is on the other end of this 940-acre property. This building was commissioned by former National Front President Ulrick Gleich and completed by our current leader, Eric Price."

We were around to the front entrance now and it looked less like a church from that angle. True, there were two enormous wooden doors at the top of a half-dozen Carrera marble steps. But it looked as if another entire structure, an office building made of stone, had been attached to the far side of the church. Carved above the great wooden doors in stone were the words "Church of National Unification." The tour guide noticed me reading the inscription.

"This may look like a place of religious worship, but it's not. Dr. Pace founded The Church of National Unification in 1968 to heal the wounds of race warfare in this country, but the church only operated for three years. This engraving serves as a memorial to Dr. Pace's aspirations, which have been fulfilled in the political philosophy of the National Front."

Valerie mounted the marble steps in front of the great wooden doors backwards, in heels. The doors swung outward as we approached, not from mechanical imperative, but with the assistance of two guards wearing earpieces. They weren't armed, but they had the look of men who habitually carried weapons. One of them instinctively tucked his thumb down by his waist, where you'd pull on the strap of a machine pistol slung over your back to take the slack out and keep it from swinging around. We stepped inside a large auditorium that was church-quiet.

"The Grace Auditorium is dedicated to Dr. Pace's wife, who died in childbirth three decades before him. This modern facility features full multi-media capabilities and serves as the heart of the conference center in this building. The National Front hosts over thirty conferences a year and welcomes visitors from around the world." Grace Pace? Poor woman.

We entered the auditorium. The ceilings were vaulted to a full six stories, and the floor descended from the entrance about another story or so before it reached the stage. This allowed for stadium-style seating in comfortable-looking swivel chairs. Each row had a long table in front of it, and there were two aisles separating the space into three parts, like a theater. Or a church. We walked out a side entrance to the auditorium and found ourselves in a break area with beverage machines serving everything from fountain soda to single-cup shots of coffee and espresso.

"There are twelve conference rooms on this level, and another six on the second level of the building, along with our administrative offices," Valerie noted, gesturing toward a bank of elevators. "The cafeteria, which sits just beyond this refreshment area, can serve up to a thousand guests. The glass doors to your right lead out into the reflection court-yard, where we will visit the founder's library as well as the Museum of the Study of Race." I followed Valerie's manicured nails as she pointed to a colossal clash of architectural styles. The neat lawns and stone buildings looked like nothing so much as a quad on a Northeastern campus, while an enor-mous round fountain with elaborate carvings dead center in the quad looked like a Rococo take on a Spanish courtyard. The library and the museum each stood at one corner of the square but there were two other buildings opposite the conference center. One of them, a four-story structure with about a dozen small balconies, was the building Nichols told me was probably residential.

"If anyone would like coffee or a bathroom break, we'll stop for about five minutes here. I'm sure some of you would prefer to use these restrooms to the portable potties outside." Valerie smiled and got a sympathetic burst of laughter from the dozen members of the tour group. Half of them moved immediately toward the espresso machines while the rest headed for the restroom. I noted that straying into the office area was not an option, as there were able-bodied men in tight black turtlenecks posted at the entrance to the interior corridor and in front of the elevators.

I'd taken a step to approach Valerie to ask a question when a young man with slicked-back black hair and intense blue eyes in a pinstriped blue suit stepped out of the elevator and strode directly over to me, interposing himself between me and the tour guide. The two black-turtlenecked guards who had shared the elevator with him kept pace a few steps behind him, just far enough to look like bodyguards rather than a military escort. As the man approached me, two more men fell in behind me. I was suddenly boxed in.

"Mr. Larney?" he asked, inclining his head toward me.

"Yes?"

"My name is Jay Ventura. Mr. Price would like to have a word with you privately. Would you please follow us?" He gestured toward the elevator bank.

* * *

"Mr. Herne, your reputation precedes you. Or would you prefer 'Orion'? Please have a seat." I froze as Eric Price gestured to a leather sofa that sat in front of an enormous plate-glass window in the corner of the office. He took an Eames chair opposite me. Ventura and the guards withdrew from the office. I didn't doubt they were within earshot, though.

"You're well informed, Mr. Price." Unnervingly so. Price had the look of a professional politician, or a game show host. He was mid-to-late forties, tall and handsome, with a strong jaw, prominent cheekbones and wide-set blue eyes only a shade or two darker than a wolf's.

"I've always admired the Activity. Better than CAG or DevGru if you ask me. And much more versatile."

"There are a lot of good soldiers in the Army."

"Nonsense. Men like you are worth a hundred regular infantry, twenty Rangers or ten Green Berets."

"I didn't know there was a fantasy league, sir."

His laugh was clipped, precise. "There should be, I think. I can tell you that you'd be drafted early. I heard the stories even before you came to our attention here."

"I've heard some of them, too. I'd love to meet the guy who inspired them, but it wasn't me." I shifted uncomfortably on the leather sofa. Late in my career with the Activity, a bunch of folktales that nominally featured me made their way around the special ops community. They were absurd, exaggerated and intensely embarrassing, like Chuck Norris jokes without the punch line.

Price waved his hands as if he were erasing my words on a blackboard. "Nonsense. I'm told you had some trouble with locals and that you lived up to expectations."

"I don't like being set up."

"I don't blame you. But I can't say that I'm surprised. You're in West Virginia. This is a primitive state. These people are barely in the twentieth century, let alone the twenty-first."

"I've liked almost everyone I've met here who's actually from the state. The men who tried to lean on me were amateurs, and they were hired. What concerns me more is the explosive device I found in my motel room last night, and the trained sniper who took a shot at me today."

"How on earth did you survive that?"

"He was shooting from an unfamiliar range—about twenty feet."

"That's exactly what I mean. I admire your talent, Mr. Herne. I served myself, you know, but with much less distinction. Ever since I left the Army, I've tried to surround myself with men like you. I don't know that any are actually at your level, but a few are close. Alpha is lucky to have you." Price saw me twitch when he said Alpha's name.

"You know that I left the Army over four years ago, Mr. Price?"

"The Activity is not the kind of place you ever completely quit, is it?" A genuine smile lit his eyes.

"I certainly hope it is." When you're preparing to lie, speak the truth with conviction.

"I'm sorry to have to get down to business so abruptly but it's a very busy day for us, as you know. Since you entered our festival under an assumed name, I'm sure you aren't looking to join our cause, although if I'm wrong I'd love to discuss it with you. I wanted to give you the opportunity to let me know why you're actually here."

I didn't hesitate to answer him. "I'm looking for Heather Hernandez."

"Ah, Anton's girlfriend. She was here for a brief period. I'm afraid that she didn't fit in well. It was Anton's fault. He didn't prepare her. I assure you that I've had a very serious talk with him about it."

"You're saying she's not here now?"

"She hasn't been with us for several days."

"Do you know where she is? Her parents are looking for her."

"I'm afraid I don't know. I'm surprised she hasn't called her parents." Price had just told his first lie. "What's your interest in the girl?"

"She's the daughter of a friend."

"You know Colonel Hernandez?" His voice lost inflection when he said the name. "That surprises me. But then again, I do recall that he served with Alpha. They have a history, don't they?"

I kept my mouth shut. Price stood and extended his hand again.

"If there's nothing more, Mr. Herne, I must move on to other matters. Jay will make sure you get off the grounds safely."

On cue, Ventura returned with four armed men in black turtlenecks.

* * *

We passed the ground floor and kept descending. The guard who'd pressed the button stepped back and I got a peek at the elevator's control panel. The button for level B2 was lit. Trouble. The basement is where you stow things you'd rather forget.

Judging from the pit in my stomach, the elevator was moving at a decent clip, but it was still a few awkward moments before we arrived at the second basement level. We'd be well under the massive structure now, perhaps at bomb-shelter depth. Another bad sign. When the doors finally opened, Ventura stepped out and turned immediately to the right, heading down a hallway. I realized we were walking directly under the conference center auditorium. The hall was Spartan, with concrete floors and white sheetrock walls. Windowless doors lined each side of the hallway at odd intervals. None had nameplates, although there were room numbers above the doors.

Thirty yards down the hall we came to room with a biometric scanner next to the door. Ventura pressed his thumb down and after a few seconds the panel beneath turned green. He pushed the door inwards. I hesitated and one of the guards shoved me roughly across the threshold.

I noticed the thickness of the door first. It was solid steel, the kind you try to avoid at all costs when you're breaching. The doorframe was nearly a foot deep. The inside of the room was lined with gypsum masonry board. My guess was that six or more inches of sound deadening material stood between this room and the hall outside. The room was drab, with dark gray walls and a cement floor painted to match. It would be an easy place to hose out. There was a drain in the floor.

The room had no cameras, phones or desks. A neat array of tools, most of which I recognized, hung from pegs above a steel workbench against the near wall. A car battery and jumper cables sat in front of a wooden chair bolted to the cement floor. Another wooden chair sat in front of a galvanized steel basin, the kind you use to water cattle. The basin had a semicircle cut into it, like you'd see in a beauty parlor sink where they wash hair. The back legs of the wooden chair were set into steel lined recesses in the floor, so that the chair could be fully tilted back without sliding forward or toppling over. A pitcher and three buckets of water sat next to the chair. Several washcloths lay over the arm. The only good news—if you could call it that—was that the chair didn't have built-in arm restraints.

As I stared at it, the guards took care of that. The two bigger guys each grabbed an arm. The third guard slipped thick plastic flexicuffs over my wrists while the fourth guard stood back four feet with his sidearm drawn. They did a good job securing me. The flexicuffs were tight enough that my hands were already numb when they sat me down on the wooden chair, draping my arms over the seatback like a slipknot. Then they cuffed my ankles to the chair using the steel handcuffs that were already attached to iron eyelets on each chair leg. When they were done, two of the guards left.

They left the A-team behind. One of the guards looked like a professional wrestler, while the other was about my size and build. The big guy had his blond hair cut in a flattop like Howie Long. The second guard had a dimple on his chin and smelled like Old Spice.

I looked at Ventura.

"I take it you have more questions?"

"Just a few."

19

Forget any quaint notions you have about torture. Nobody bears the pain gracefully. The process of breaking someone is straightforward. Interrogators inflict extreme, unrelenting pain. The pain is either physical, psychological or both. They interrupt this pain at odd intervals to ask questions. Then they repeat the process.

Within the pantheon of interrogation techniques, waterboarding holds a special place. It was first widely practiced in the fifteenth century during the Spanish Inquisition. The Jesuits believed that the sensation of drowning had spiritual significance. It was used by Dutch traders in the Thirty Years War, by the Japanese in World War II and by the Khmer Rouge in Cambodia in the seventies. And yes, we did it, too—in the Spanish-American War and again not too long ago. Waterboarding is inexpensive, quick and it's not messy. Done properly, it leaves no permanent physical injuries or visible marks.

I've been burned with cigarettes, amped with electricity and cut, poked and prodded in places too awful to mention. I've been kept awake, standing on a chair until my legs would no longer hold me. Yet waterboarding is the only form of torture that has convinced me every single time that I'm about to die, regardless of what my brain says. Unlike the cigarettes and the shock treatment, I'd only ever been waterboarded in training—during SERE indoctrination at Camp Mackall. That was bad enough. This time, there wasn't a doctor standing by, and the men who were waterboarding me had been trying to kill me for the better part of three days.

They didn't bother questioning me first. That showed they knew what they were about, because it's when most detainees create an establishing story. It's a lot harder to keep your lies straight when you're gasping for air, wondering why you haven't drowned.

Let's dispense with another fallacy—the one about staying silent under torture. You don't. Nobody does. Everyone talks. The best way to subvert an interrogation isn't to clam up. Instead, you do the opposite. You tell so many different versions of your story that the truth is impossible to sort out. You divine whatever it is that the interrogator wants to hear and you tell it to them as many different ways as you can. You invent, blur and remix the details. And the key—the real key—is to keep doing that until the bitter end, when you start to want them to kill you just so it can all be over, when you're no longer glad you're still alive after each time they've tried to drown you; when you consider just swallowing enough of the water leaking through the cloth to drown and be done with it.

Until the waterboarding started, Flattop and Old Spice reminded me of nothing more than Army MPs—thugs with badges. But they knew what they were doing. They positioned the basin so that when Flattop tilted the chair back, my neck hit the cradle at such an angle that no amount of struggling would knock me from my seat. Old Spice put the damp washcloth over my face, covering my eyes, nose and mouth, then slowly poured water on the cloth from two feet as you're supposed to. He kept the bursts of simulated drowning to twenty seconds, then let me breathe. I tried to make it easy for them to impress their boss. After the first ten seconds, I struggled, screamed, blubbered and externalized every other awful thing I was experiencing to make sure that Ventura was getting the show he wanted. He didn't strike me as a professional, and amateurs are dangerous when they hold your life in their hands.

The questions started after the third dousing. I kept screaming for a moment after the water stopped dripping and I was pulled upright.

"Why are you here? Who sent you undercover? What do you know?"

Everything was a variation of those three questions. I had answers. Lots of them. I was looking for the girl, hidden nukes, buried gold. The FBI, CIA, NSA, Homeland Security, even the Parks Service had sent me. I'd found nothing, the key, evidence, everything. At one point I may have yelled "It's not safe. They'll recognize you!" I saw the mounting disgust in Ventura's eyes as we continued the dance. I didn't know anything, but my cowardice was making his job harder— that's what he thought.

My mind was getting foggier, and I kept spinning the truth around in circles so I wouldn't recognize it. I started to worry about hypoxia, about dry drowning. On and on it went until Ventura finally got exasperated. "This is going nowhere," he snapped and stalked out. The guards exchanged a glance, the kind enlisted men share when dealing with an officer who's out of his depth. When Ventura was out of the room, they righted me and took a step back, letting me breathe and clear my mind.

They'd made one mistake. A couple actually, but just one unforgiveable error. They left my watch on. Distorting the detainee's sense of time is a basic part of any interrogation. When they righted me, I twisted around and caught a glimpse of the digital readout on the Timex perched just above the black flexicuffs on my wrist. I saw that my torture had lasted for less than an hour. On the one hand, it made me want to scream. Waterboarding turns you into a blubbering mess in less time than it takes to fry an egg. An hour of it felt like an eternity. I would have guessed they'd been torturing me all afternoon. But then seeing the time also brought me back.

Ten minutes later, Ventura returned, slamming the door shut behind him.

"We're not getting anything useful from him. He's just going to keep spewing garbage. He probably doesn't even know what the truth is now." He eyed me with pity. "I can't believe he's supposed to be some kind of war hero." Then he jerked his head toward the steel basin, now half-full of water.

"Kill him."

20

The two men hesitated, eyeing each other before turning to me. Old Spice stood to my right. For the entire interrogation, he'd been the chief torturer, dripping water onto the washcloth covering my face. He'd been careful to keep the Glock 19 on his right hip angled away from me, safely out of arm's reach. Not trusting that I'd stay restrained showed his professionalism, especially since he'd put the flexicuffs on me himself. That composure slipped for an instant when Ventura told the two men to kill me. When Old Spice turned to face me, he stood a foot closer to me than he should have.

I took that moment to punch him in the crotch. As he doubled over, I tackled him around the waist and used his mass to lever the chair from its moorings. As my momentum bowled him over, the legs came free and I cartwheeled over him with my legs still handcuffed to the chair. I drew the Glock from Old Spice's Serpa holster as we rolled and raised it just as Flattop was pulling his Sig Sauer. I shot the bigger guard three times in the chest, then ducked left to avoid the elbow Old Spice jabbed back toward me. I poked the Glock into the soft fold of skin under Old Spice's chin and fired. A splatter of brains painted the underside of the washbasin. I turned the gun on Ventura as I struggled to extricate myself from the chair and the dead guard. He looked ready to wet his expensive suit.

"Uncuff my legs," I said. When Ventura looked around confused, I clarified. "The keys are there on the workbench."

He fumbled with the keys and the cuffs but finally got them off my feet, releasing me from the chair.

"How did you do that? Your hands were tied. I saw them do it!" He was in shock, I could see. He wouldn't be any use to me until he was calmer.

"I think it's my turn with the questions, now," I said, struggling to my feet. "Why don't you have a seat?" I added as I righted the wooden chair and kicked it over to him. He sat and I walked over to the workbench and chose a pair of shears no doubt intended to remove a pinkie or ring finger. I stopped and stared down Ventura for a second, enjoyed watching the blood drain from his face. Then I snipped the right flexicuff off of my wrist and dropped the shears back on the bench.

I'd gotten my hands free by digging a small object from the artificial latex skin the Activity specialist had attached to my waist. The fake love handles wouldn't have been convincing in a bathing suit, but they felt real enough to survive a pat down. The armorer embedded a lockpick on one side and the device that looked like a girl's barrette on the other. I dug the barrette free of its rubber moorings as soon as I was taped to the chair. When Old Spice was first fiddling with the rag on my face, I opened the barrette and slid the thicker section between the hard plastic and my left wrist.

When I finally had my first opportunity to scream without a rag over my mouth, I snapped the ends of the barrette together. A tiny strip in the middle of the device instantly heated to nearly 1000 degrees and the barrette slid through the hardened plastic of the flexi cuffs like a hot knife through butter. I pulled my hand free, then twisted the cut ends of the restraint apart to keep them from refusing as the plastic cooled. I got a nice burn on my wrist in the process. Then I slipped my hand back inside the cuffs and waited for my moment. It took an eternity to arrive. Having my hands free, knowing that I could fight back should have made the torture easier. It didn't.

I checked Flattop to confirm he was dead. There was no question about Old Spice. I wiped the Glock I'd fired down with a rag, then removed the magazine, cleared the chamber and left the gun sitting on the workbench. I proceeded to wipe down the arms of the chair that Ventura sat in and anything else I thought I might have touched, while he looked at me, unbelieving.

"I think Eric will guess who killed them." The acid in his tone was undercut by his trembling hands.

"I don't imagine he'd bring the police into this particular room," I agreed, "but it never hurts to be careful." Using the rag, I pulled the other wooden chair in the room away from the car battery and sat down facing Ventura.

"I'm glad we have this chance to talk. I need to ask you a few questions."

Ventura crossed his legs nervously before responding. "You think I'm going to talk to you? You must have post-traumatic stress. In two minutes, a security detail is going to bust through that door," he flicked his head backwards, "and you'll be dead two seconds later."

"Mr. Ventura—can I call you Jay?" I didn't wait for an answer. "Jay, you and I both know that this is the one room in this entire building without security cameras or a monitoring system. There's not even a panic button in here, which I have to say was an oversight. If you're still here in another hour or two, someone will come looking for you, but it's certainly not going to happen very soon. I can tell you from experience that nobody likes to deal with dead bodies, whether it's theirs," I jerked my head to the two corpses in the room without looking at them, "or mine. So let's cut the posturing."

"I'm not saying anything."

"You'll talk to me," I said evenly. Ventura's eyes flicked involuntarily to the blood-splattered washbasin behind me.

I shook my head. "I won't do that. You're going to talk to me because it's in your best interest. Because it's the last chance you have to save your own neck."

"From you?" Ventura sounded a little less shaky. He was almost ready to think rationally. "You can kill me but I won't talk to you. You're in the middle of an armed camp, Mr. Herne. You won't leave here alive."

"I see. I'm sorry—you probably still think you captured me, right, Jay?" Ventura looked confused. "You think I believed that the guy who was questioning me near the main stage was just some random dude from Ohio? That the folks on the little tour I joined were really there to take a tour and that the Valkyrie you had lead it was just a tour guide?"

Ventura's eyes widened. "You—you knew and you walked into it anyway?"

I nodded. "You were waiting for me today and the only question was whether you were going to try and kill me immediately or question me first. I won that bet," I said. "Now I'm inside your headquarters in the one room with no cameras and a whole bunch of useful things."

"Why would you take that kind of risk?"

"I'm paying back a debt," I said, and my mind went back to the scene in the Activity's tractor-trailer after Nichols left.

I'd asked her to tell the Activity people outside to give me a couple more minutes. I called Alpha.

"Sir, if you want me to walk into the National Front's compound two hours after the third time they've tried to kill me, you need to level with me. This is the second time I'm asking you, and this isn't a request any more. Please don't expect me to believe this is just about some friend's daughter."

"No, it's not. Not entirely." Alpha paused, weighing his words as I held the secure phone to my ear. "This is compartmentalized information, so please treat it as such. Is your space secure?"

"Everyone's out of the rig at the moment, sir."

"I have no faith in coincidences. When Heather's parents contacted me, I' had just finished reviewing a report on the National Front. The group crossed our radar screen because of some recent incidents in Africa."

"Africa, sir?"

"Yes, beginning in the South Sudan. Bombings targeted at oil fields. We first thought the local Al Qaeda affiliate was responsible."

"Yes?"

"The attack was ineffective. Not the devices themselves, mind you. They destroyed valuable exploration equipment. But the goal of the bombing was apparently to scupper an agreement between the government of South Sudan and a Dutch energy company called Vitol for an oil refinery. The deal went forward."

"So how did you tie this to the National Front?" I asked.

"The Dutch company had video surveillance on their assets. They had some high-end monitoring equipment installed in unusual places. We were already cooperating with them on another operation, and the company asked us to help them identify the terrorists. Four men were involved. We captured two faces and connected them back to their passport photos and eventually back to the National Front."

"They didn't cover themselves well?"

"Not effectively. A month later, South Africa experienced a series of terrorist strikes on their infrastructure. All of the incidents targeted power-generating facilities. The last attempt was directed at a nuclear reactor. It was coordinated with a hacking attack that disabled some of the data systems at the plant. Johannesburg experienced a multi-day blackout as a result. No permanent damage was done to the facility, but the security breach at a nuclear plant alarmed the South Africans, who asked for technical assistance. Using facial recognition, we connected one of the men from the Sudan operation to the incident. He had contractor credentials to the site for the day of the attack. This time the cover documents were more professional. We only identified him because he was already in our database from the South Sudan operation."

"How long ago was this?"

"Just over a month ago, at the beginning of September."

"Any clue what they were up to?" I asked. "Could these guys have been freelancing with some other group unconnected to the National Front?"

"That was our initial assessment. Both men were Special Forces veterans and both had served in Iraq. One of them had worked for Blackwater. Our working assumption was that they were contractors working for another party."

"But something changed that assessment?"

"Not conclusively until last night. When I heard from Miss Hernandez's parents and learned that the FBI had an interest in the protestors, I was already inclined to send someone with a skill set to investigate. Her disappearance, along with an active and highly classified FBI investigation and the headquarters of the National Front in one small corner of West Virginia, seemed like too many coincidences. When we reviewed the design of the device found in your room last night, our explosives people confirmed that the signature is similar to an unexploded device we recovered in South Africa."

"Was either of the guys the FBI arrested this morning involved in the African incidents?"

"We haven't positively identified either man yet, though the tattoos you photographed are consistent with National Front membership."

"So there are still ex-SF guys out there trying to kill me?" I'd been hoping that the sniper and spotter the FBI was holding had rigged the bomb as well.

"Most likely."

"And I'm walking into their compound because?"

"You know the reason, Orion."

"Because neither of us believes that the National Front would try to kill me just to hide a missing girlfriend. Because when men come after you with plastic explosives, they're trying to protect something. Because there's obviously something else going on with the National Front."

"Agreed."

"Agent Nichols just told me that one of the Reclaim people killed Wednesday night—the one who was beaten to death—was an undercover FBI agent. I don't think she was supposed to share that," I hastened to add, realizing that I'd just done the one thing she'd asked me not to. But I knew Alpha well enough to know he wouldn't burn her. "And we know Harmon was at Reclaim too. So somehow the protestors and the mine are connected to the National Front. The FBI could tell us more."

"Senior officials at the FBI are very unhappy with our involvement. They've brought pressure to bear to force me to withdraw you. This has gone all the way up." Which for Alpha meant either the National Security Council or the White House.

"I thought they were impressed that the National Front tried to bomb me and wanted to play ball with us."

"At the field level. But the FBI Director is guarding his territory very zealously."

"Seriously?"

"If you fail to find anything today, we'll certainly be pushed out."

"If the National Front had a hand in the murders on Wednesday, it means that they unmasked an FBI undercover agent with a face nobody knew and a solid back story. We can't assume I'll waltz into the National Front's headquarters and nobody will recognize me, even with a $10,000 makeup job."

"No we can't."

At that moment, I realized that escaping detection wasn't the plan—that it had never been the plan.

"Okay, let's talk about what you really want if I can get in."

21

"I'm still not talking to you," Ventura said, snapping me back to the interrogation room.

"You're hurting my feelings," I said, frowning. "So I'm going to walk out of here. I'll leave you completely untouched, next to your dead colleagues. When they find you, your superiors will take one look and assume you've talked to me. If you're lucky, Price will kill you quickly. Tell me if I'm wrong." I got up and chambered a round in the Sig, tucking it into my waistband. I started toward the door.

Ventura grappled with that, then panicked. "Wait. Wait!"

I stopped walking without turning back.

"I'll need immunity and protection if I talk."

"I'm not the FBI, but they'll give it to you if you cooperate. You're a little fish."

"We'll never get out of here."

"First things first. I didn't work this hard to get inside just to leave so soon. We have some errands to run. Let's start with some basics. How many guards on the grounds?"

"I don't know. Fifty maybe? But they're all armed."

"Who told you to kill me?"

"Price."

"He said 'Kill him when you're done with him'?"

"No, he doesn't work that way. He said 'Escort Herne out personally after you bring him to me.' We all know what that means."

"It sounds like it means you were supposed to walk me to the front gate."

"Don't be naïve. That's what he says when he wants someone brought here."

"Maybe. But it also means that he's keeping his hands clean. So people like you take the fall if anything goes wrong. Where is Price now?"

"I don't know."

"You didn't go up to see him just then?"

"I was standing outside the door."

"You're really a piece of work. Why were you questioning me? What were you supposed to find out?"

"Price wants to know what you know about us."

"Why? What specifically does he think I know?"

"I don't know."

I leaned back in my chair and stared at Ventura.

"No seriously. I don't know. But I think there's something big going on—other than the festival, I mean. A lot of Price's guys have been leaving today."

"Price's guys? Aren't you one of them?"

"No, I'm not. I mean, that's not what I mean. I'm talking about his buddies from the PA—the army guys. They're...like you. But most of them are older."

I stood up and took my jacket from the workbench where they'd left it. I laid it flat on the table. I picked up my Spyderco folding knife and cut a foot-long hole in the rayon lining. I slid a hand inside, fished around for a second and withdrew an envelope. I pulled four pictures from the envelope and handed them to Ventura.

"These men—are they part of it?"

Ventura looked at the pictures and then at me. "Two of them look familiar but I don't know them. The other two I recognize. They're Holser and Klaussen. They were both Eric's Army buddies. They're in the inner circle."

"Then why weren't they the ones questioning me? You're a little green for this kind of work." I said it as a fact.

"I told you they all left today. I run the PR office. I don't usually deal with...this kind of stuff."

"But I bet you jumped on the chance to impress Price with your initiative, right?" I didn't wait for him to answer. I looked away, disgusted. "Did these guys rig the explosives in my hotel room?"

"I don't know anything about that." I watched Ventura's face as he said this. It was the truth.

I slid another photo from the envelope and handed it to Ventura. "Do you recognize this girl?"

"That's Anton's girlfriend. Heather."

"Where did Anton meet her?"

"On his mission. He wouldn't talk about it, but she said they met at a mine—Hobbit?"

"Hobart," I corrected.

"When did she come here?"

"Just a couple of weeks ago."

"Have you seen her here?"

"Yeah, she's around."

"When's the last time you saw her?"

"I dunno. Yesterday, maybe the day before?"

"Does she have a room here?"

"She and Anton share his room in the dorm."

"Where's Anton?"

"He's not here today."

"Where is he?"

"I don't know. Someone goes out on a job, you don't ask questions."

"When did he leave?"

"A couple of days ago. In a rush."

"With the other guys?"

"No, I told you they all left today."

"Did Anton know Price from the Army?"

"No, but he's in the inner circle, too."

"Do you have a car?"

"A truck—an F150."

"Where's it parked?"

"Around back in the lot behind the museum. That's where everyone parks."

"Okay, Jay, you've done well. We're almost done. Now tell me where the security monitoring room is."

"Top floor." I caught the pattern in his face when he said it.

"You're lying. Do that again and you're on your own." He considered that.

"It's on this level, around the other side."

"How many men will be there right now?"

"I have no idea. It's not that big. Maybe two?"

"Where is the server room?"

"Server room?"

"A complex this size has an internal network and its own server. It's always in the basement because it's cheaper to cool and the racks are heavy. This building has a data satellite uplink on the roof and it runs its own servers. So stop screwing with me and tell me where the server room is."

"There's another secure room on this level. That might be it, but I really don't know. I'm not a frigging IT guy, okay?"

"You're going to help me get out of here. We're going to drive your car out the front gate."

He nodded. "Yeah, okay."

I shook my head. "It won't be that easy. The moment you see a guard you're going to change your mind and switch teams again. I have to make sure that doesn't happen."

I grabbed my jacket. I detached a seam from the lining and slid it open. Then I pulled a two-foot orange strip from the enclosure. It looked like very smooth Play-Doh formed to the diameter of a finger. I cut an inch off of the strip and compressed it onto the seat of the chair I'd been sitting on. I slid the chair to the other end of the room, then took off my watch and withdrew a slim stick of metal from the back. I pushed it into the strip. I stepped back across the forty-foot room and turned over a small metal table, then knelt behind it and shielded my eyes. I pressed another button on my wristwatch. There was a small explosion—thunderous within the room but not loud enough to attract attention on other levels. I hoped. The chair fell inwards, split in two. I turned back to Ventura, holding up the rest of the strip where he could see it.

"This is Semtex. They also call it plastic explosive or detcord. You can think of it as a chastity belt. It will help you stay true to your vows. Now drop your trousers," I said as I cut off a longer strip.

22

I followed Ventura out of the interrogation room, glad to be away from the water basin and the dead bodies. I was wearing Old Spice's black turtleneck. His blood added a sharp overtone to the cheap adolescent cologne. Getting it off the guard's corpse was the low point in a day where I'd already been tortured, and it had been impossible to accomplish without getting it soaked in blood and laced with bits of brain matter. But it was still better than Flattop's, which was much too large and had three holes in the chest. I wore a baseball cap with the National Front logo pulled down on my face as low as I dared. Flattop's Sig Sauer was in a holster at my hip with fourteen unfired 9mm Parabellum rounds in the magazine and one in the chamber.

"The room I was thinking of is around the other side." Ventura pointed behind me. "Past the elevators and to the left."

I shook my head. "We need to find the security room first."

Ventura pointed me in the opposite direction. We walked down the hall.

"This seems like a bad idea," he said.

"It's necessary," I said. "Will they recognize you?"

"Yes."

"Is it the same group that wears these?" He glanced back and I tugged at my turtleneck.

"Yup."

"Have you been in this room before?"

"Uh, yes. Not recently, though."

"Describe it to me," I said as we turned the corner.

"I dunno—it's not too big. There are lots of monitors."

"Are there offices or locker rooms connected?"

"No, they're not down here."

"Where?"

"At the back of the first floor—that's where the main security office is. The room down here is just a monitoring room."

"Where is the head of security?"

"His office is on the first level."

"Good," I said. We turned a corner and I caught sight of a very visible security camera mounted above a reinforced steel door with a biometric scanner.

"Tell them you need to review some footage. Make it sound plausible or we're both dead."

Ventura pushed a doorbell button below the scanner. I kept my head down.

"Yeah?" The voice sounded bored.

"I'm questioning someone in the Room. I need to look at some tape of him on the grounds a couple of hours ago."

The door buzzed and Ventura pushed through. I stepped in behind him, pushing him aside as I drew the Sig. Two men were sitting ten feet from us at a control panel in front of a wall full of flat-screen monitors. I saw one of them reaching for an alarm button and pointed the 9mm at his head.

"It's not worth your life," I suggested. On reflection, he agreed. I had Ventura put them in flexicuffs, then I used a roll of duct tape I'd liberated from the Room to bind them to the chairs and blindfold them. Silently, I went to work on the monitors.

"You're going to fuck—" Ventura started before I cuffed him on the back of the head and he shut up. In five minutes I ensured that it would take a half-day of repairs before any of the monitors functioned properly. It took five more minutes to program the phone so it forwarded to the main security office. I wasn't optimistic. We probably had a better chance of getting out of the compound unmolested before we entered the security office. But I needed to disable the monitors to increase the chances that my next stop would go undetected.

* * *

It took me a couple of minutes to defeat the electronic lock on the server room door. We didn't see anyone wandering the corridors in the basement level and I hoped that my luck would hold for a few more moments. I pulled out a special USB drive that I'd removed from the lining of my jacket opposite the Semtex as we stepped inside. It was a modern server room, several times the size of the video monitoring office. Racks of blade servers revealed a much larger operation than I'd have guessed, all housed in a dust free, climate-controlled setting.

The room was cold, so I looked around the edges for offices where the network managers would work. Off the end of the third long row, through a glass window, I saw a desk with an ordinary PC workstation under a bookshelf of technical manuals. The office was empty, though I couldn't tell if that was normal or if the festival had changed things. I quietly opened the door, sat down at the desk, and inserted the thumb drive into a USB socket on the front of the PC. I opened the file from the Windows control panel and started an executable program. After a moment, the light on the drive started flashing and a program screen appeared. After thirty seconds, the program screen disappeared and I pulled the drive from the computer.

"What did you just do?" Ventura asked.

"I'm hoping I just opened a window to let some light into this place," I said.

We left the room and I rewired the entry lock. It wouldn't pass close inspection, but if the Activity tech geniuses were as good as I remembered, the damage was already done.

As the elevator chimed for the main level, I leaned in to Ventura and whispered, "Straight out."

The elevator doors opened and we walked briskly toward the glass doors to the courtyard. I walked two steps behind him as the guard I'd replaced had done. Ventura was exhausted and visibly disheveled. If anyone took a close look at him, I figured the game was up. There were four men sitting in the lounge area drinking coffee and talking football but they didn't even look up as we walked past.

We strolled through the center of the courtyard and around the Spanish fountain at a relaxed pace. I nodded toward the dorm building.

"I want to see Harmon's room." Ventura altered our course without complaint.

Ventura tapped his ID on the lock in front of the dorms and the door clicked open. It was quiet in the middle of the afternoon. A cluster of maroon couches sat in front of beverage stations similar to those in the conference center across the courtyard in the lobby. The room was spotless and had the kind of sterile college dorm look that made it appear perpetually unused. We took the elevator to the third floor.

I used the pick I'd liberated from my waist, along with an improvised shim, to open the door to Anton Harmon's room. There was a security camera at the end of the hall but I knew it was offline. The hall was as quiet as the lobby had been. When the door yielded, I stepped into a small apartment that had the same institutional feeling as the lobby. I took that to mean it had been furnished by the designers of the building rather than by Harmon himself. Nobody was home.

"How does this compare to your place?" I asked Ventura, who was looking around with an expression that told me he'd not been inside before.

"It's bigger," he replied. "I don't have a separate bedroom."

"What does Anton do in this organization?"

"I don't know. He's been gone a lot of the time I've been working here. I started about a year ago. Like I said, he's in the inner circle. He has a lot of closed-door meetings with Price and that gang when he's around."

The apartment had a large tiled living room with a flat panel TV and a well-appointed en suite kitchen. The living room and bedroom shared a balcony that had a nice view of the mountains. With my nose pressed against the glass, I could just see the employee parking lot.

I walked into the bedroom with Ventura trailing behind me. He'd been as submissive as a puppy since we'd left the Room. I'd given him a few chances to jump me but he hadn't taken the bait. The Semtex wrapped around his genitals had tamed him as completely as a full course of electro-shock therapy.

The bedroom was cozy, with just enough space for a queen-sized bed, a couple of nightstands and a long, low dresser. All the pieces were finished in a shiny white lacquered veneer that reminded me of Ikea. On the nightstand farthest from the window there was a picture of Anton and Heather. She was smiling, a genuine smile that started in her eyes. The photo was taken in the meadow where the Reclaim group had set up camp—I recognized the stream. It must have been some time in July or August; the light had that quality it gets when days extend far into the evening. I slid the picture from the frame, folded it and put it into my pants pocket.

I rifled through both nightstands. Her side had a couple of books, including a volume of Walt Whitman and a nonfiction book about food called *The Omnivore's Dilemma*. I'd have bet it was the only copy on the National Front compound. A small polished walnut box held some braided bracelets, a few silver and turquoise necklaces and some modest silver earrings. On his side, there was lubricant, a folding knife and some change. That was it. The dresser was divided longitudinally between his and hers. Her side stocked a week's worth of clean underwear—most of it sensible with the exception of a couple thongs—four pairs of jeans, some hiking pants and a couple of pairs of shorts. In another drawer I found a mix of tops, from tie-dye to some semi-dressy Ann Taylor stuff. The drawers on his side seemed a bit light. It fit with his absence. I stepped back into the hallway and found a sliding closet door concealing a washer and dryer. From his grunt of annoyance, I took it that Ventura didn't have one in his unit. I opened the stacked units in turn, but both were empty.

I stepped into the bathroom and slid open the vanity. It confirmed what I suspected. Heather's toiletries were inside but Anton's shelf was half-empty and his razor was conspicuously missing.

I returned to the kitchen and opened the refrigerator. Divided again, with beer on one side and vegetable juice on the other. On the bottom row on her side, a line of self-injecting needles sat side by side in a precision rank. I pulled one out. They were once-a-day insulin shots for diabetics. Two weeks of injectors sat in the refrigerator, prescribed by a doctor in Beckley. I stepped back and my breath came out cold, in a rush.

23

"She was happy when they first arrived because they didn't have much privacy at that eco-freak place. They were playing house here," Ventura said.

"Did she know what this place was about? Really?"

"No, I don't think she had any idea." Ventura coughed, covering his mouth with the back of his hand. "Price is sort of a control freak. I don't know where Anton met Heather, but I'm pretty sure he wasn't supposed to bring her here. Price went nuts when Anton showed up with her. He reamed Anton pretty good, but there was really nowhere for Heather to go so she stayed."

"Why was Anton dating a Latina? What kind of supremacists are you guys anyway?"

"She's not Hispanic. She wouldn't have lasted here a day if she was. She was adopted. I mean, her mother was her mother, but her father wasn't her father and her real dad was white. She found that out not too long ago and she was pissed. She kept saying 'I can't believe *Papi* lied to me.'" Ventura said 'Papi' with a cartoonish Latin accent. "Imagine thinking you had all that bad blood in you and then one day finding out you'd been lied to your entire life."

I wanted to slap him. Didn't. "Is that why she left home?"

"That's what she told me."

"You knew her? Aside from her being Anton's girlfriend?"

"Anton was pretty busy when he got back. She didn't know anybody here, so I ate lunches with her." I translated that to mean he was hitting on the new girl when her boyfriend was tied up.

"How long did it take her to figure things out?"

Ventura laughed. "Longer than you'd think—maybe until the end of the first week. Anton got her a job working in the kitchen so she wasn't really around the events. He avoided the evening programs too, and took her for walks and stuff. I guess it was romantic at first, but after a few nights she started to catch on."

"And then what?"

"They started fighting. Pretty badly. I live on the next floor up, but I know security got called a couple of times. We have a pretty...*traditional* view of women's roles here, but I think Anton was smacking Heather around and that wasn't okay. Maybe that's why he got sent out on another job."

"So she's been here alone?"

"Yeah for the last week or so."

I saw something in his eyes that looked almost human, which made me hate him more for waterboarding me. "You like her, don't you?"

He just sat there for a moment before he answered, like he was seeing her in the room. "Yeah, I like her. She's...pure. Like nothing has touched her, even with what Anton's done. She's so gentle."

I asked the question that had been digging at me for days. "Why did she take it? Why didn't she just walk away?"

"Her biological dad walked out when she was two or three years old. She said she doesn't give up like that. I think she figures that if someone hits you, it at least shows they care. It's pretty fucked up what parents do to their kids."

* * *

A stone-tiled walkway thirty yards long led to the employee parking lot, which housed over a hundred vehicles. The Harley I'd ridden in on was not one of them, but any thoughts I'd had of riding it out had disappeared in the secret room in the basement under the National Front's conference center. I wasn't getting out of this fortified compound on a cruiser and my best hope of getting out at all was walking three steps in front of me. Alarms could start going off any minute, and if they weren't it was because most of the National Front's security apparatus was tied up managing the music festival. I knew I'd pushed my luck by lingering to search Heather's room, but as far as I was concerned, it was the one promise I'd come to honor. Even though I was leaving with more questions than I arrived with.

Ventura led me to his pickup truck, a full-sized Ford F-150. I felt in my pocket for the key I'd found on the smaller guard and traced the initials molded into the hard plastic. It's always nice to have a backup plan.

In that instant, I almost missed an expression that passed over Ventura's face like a rogue wave on the ocean. His eyes flicked over my shoulder as he faced me with his back to his pickup. I heard a click, the barest sound of a round being chambered in a semi-automatic pistol, and I ducked forward, grabbing Ventura's wrist. I pulled him around in front of me just as three slugs that would have hit me tagged him instead. He wasn't a big guy, and there was an instant where I froze, wondering if the slugs would still end up in my chest. But they were nine-millimeter rounds and probably hollow point at that. The damage they did to Ventura's chest was horrific, but the slugs stayed inside him.

I drew the Sig and fired in one smooth motion, targeting a black-jacketed guard who was firing two-handed from about thirty yards. Three guards were within range and I counted another four approaching. The guy I shot first had the best angle on me and I guessed he'd put the rounds into Ventura. His stance also marked him as the most experienced shooter of the bunch. He was turned sideways to show me the narrowest profile, and much of that was hidden behind a Jeep

Grand Cherokee. My first round took him clean in the forehead. I shot for the head because I assumed he was wearing body armor.

My human shield froze the other two guards within pistol range for a precious second. While they hesitated and weighed the risk of hitting a colleague, I fired first, hitting one man in the neck twice and the other in the forehead. The other guards had thrown themselves behind vehicles by that time and I stepped away from Ventura, letting him slide down against the rear tier of the F-150 as I sprinted past, ducking low. By the time I got around the rear fender, shots were plinking and whining past me, but the guards were moving more cautiously now, fanning out to try to flank me. A parking lot has a lot of good cover from small-caliber pistols, so it quickly became a chess game. A round smashed through the driver's side window of a Jeep Wrangler three feet after I'd darted around it, and another punctured the tire of a big GMC Acadia as I passed. I stole a glance at the row of motorcycles at the back of the employee lot and spotted the one I was looking for, a bright orange Austrian dirt bike.

I was pinned down behind the Acadia when I realized that some of the guards were firing at me from behind Ventura's pickup. They most certainly had checked him for signs of life, which they would not have found. Pulling down my sleeve, I pushed the two odd buttons on the Timex and prayed for a second, trying to recall whether the Activity armorer had told me the range limit for the remote detonator.

The explosion came in two heartbeats: a thump followed by a crash that knocked me down on my backside behind the Acadia. As I was struggling to get up, there was a much bigger blast as the fuel tank on the Ford exploded in sympathy. It knocked me back off my feet. I rolled over a few times just to keep moving then pushed myself up off the ground as my equilibrium returned. I clawed the motorcycle key out of my pocket as I ran unevenly toward it, hoping that nobody on my side of the wreck had recovered quicker than me.

I slid the key into the slot just under the right handlebar of the orange KTM dirt bike, swung my leg over and started it up. As I pushed the bike off of its polished aluminum kickstand, I heard the ping of a slug as it ricocheted off of a big Honda cruiser next to me. I revved the throttle and took off, leaning low over the handlebars as I jumped the curb. I ran the bike flat out for thirty yards until I reached the forest. The ground ran level for about fifty yards into the trees before I hit the edge of the holler and the terrain started to grade up swiftly. I heard the sound of four-stroke ATV engines starting up and the crack of a few more rounds shot in my direction but pushed the bike to keep climbing straight up the hill.

The holler enclosing the National Front compound was over a mile long going north and south, but less than half as wide. As the grade increased to the point where my balance got fuzzy, I took a parallel path, heading further south. I saw the first of the ATVs enter the forest below me. It was a natural forest, not a pine stand, so it had to be rough going for the ATVs, which were wider than the dirt bike. But I wasn't making great time, either, and there were too many leaves on the ground for me to see the terrain well. I needed to find a trail quickly before I hit a tree stump or slid the bike into a ditch. I visualized the satellite images of the compound. The property wasn't fenced all the way around, as the 2500-foot-tall mountains served as a good barrier to intruders. I didn't doubt that a paranoid group like the National Front might have motion detectors or infrared sensors along its perimeter, but that wasn't much of a worry for me at the moment as long as they hadn't set landmines. I needed to find a clear path out of the holler that would let me reach a road where I could take one hand off the bike long enough to use my cell phone to call for help.

After running the KTM cautiously for a hundred yards along the sloped, leafy bank on the side of a ridge, I found a dirt trail headed up the hill that switch-backed just enough to make the grade manageable. I powered up the grade, gaining speed and confidence as I went along. Then I heard engines straight down the hill and realized some of the guards must have taken the path from the bottom; I'd lost most of the lead I'd built up in the forest. I pushed the bike harder, and the small but torque-y 510cc engine responded, pulling me strongly up the hill. Some of the ATVs must have been sporting much larger motors, though, because I could hear the drone of their engines getting closer. I didn't want to let myself slip back into shooting range.

I kept climbing, twisting and turning until I reached the top of the ridge. Then I saw a chest-high barbed wire fence blocking the trail. It was too frail and narrow to show up on the satellite images but sturdy enough to stop the bike, and me with it. I had barely enough time to drop the KTM almost parallel to the ground and slide the back tire out to avoid slamming into the wire. I swore as I heard the ATVs pursuing me draw yet closer. There was no question of cutting the fence; even if I had a wire-cutter, the National Front boys would be on me seconds after I stopped moving. Revving the throttle, I turned the bike south, running parallel to the fence. After sixty yards, I found what I was looking for—a downed tree trunk with its tip stuck in the dirt, rising up four feet toward its splintered stump. I powered the bike up the trunk and pulled on the throttle steadily. When the tree ended I had just enough air to jump the bike over the fence. I skidded in wet leaves when I hit the opposite side of the trail but regained my balance and headed downhill. I alternated between stretches straight down and darting south when the grade got too steep and I felt myself starting to pitch forward. After a half-mile or so I found another trail and started to descend in earnest. I still heard the ATV engines, but they were in the distance, and I relaxed a little, focusing on making the best time I could without losing control of the KTM on the steep, muddy trail.

24

For about three minutes I thought I'd lost them.

I'd followed the trail until it ended in the flats rather abruptly, smacking up against a dirt road that headed south. I kept my bearings and cut across the road, heading due east, and up and over another, much shallower ridge. The trail ended in the backyard of a small farmhouse and I had to swerve as I came out of the woods almost directly into a chicken coop. I bypassed that and plowed through a pumpkin patch, threading through monster vines. The small dirt road running in front of the house looked like an interstate to me.

Then I hit an honest-to-God, asphalt-paved, two-lane road and, praying the map in my mind was still running true, I turned north. I got the little dirt bike up to highway speed for the better part of three miles before I ran into a small residential development. It was about a dozen or so small houses huddled around a church. I turned east at the first major junction, past a red farmhouse onto Beckwith Road, which I remembered was Route 16.

If I wasn't mistaken, I was on the outskirts of Fayetteville. I ran down the road as fast as I dared while I dug a hand into my jacket and retrieved my phone. I cursed myself for not grabbing it earlier, knowing that every moment counted. The folks who were supposed to rescue me were on the wrong side of the compound and in this part of West Virginia, that distance would take an eternity to cross.

In a moment, I got through to the Activity op center.

"You've been busy, Orion." It was Mongoose. He was putting in the same kind of hours as Alpha.

"You could say that. I'm not where I expected to be."

"We have eyes on you now. We lost your beacon after you were detained in the National Front headquarters building. Glad you made it through. We sent video of the firefight in the parking lot to the FBI and they're getting a warrant to enter the compound. That was an impressive explosion, by the way."

"You do not want to know how that happened."

"Your immediate problem is that we're out of position to aid you and there's a convoy of six vehicles closing in on you rapidly from the north. Recommend that you maximize speed, continue into Fayetteville and head south-west on Route 19. The FBI will have a helo with snipers over you in five minutes."

"Roger that. Shit," I said as chunks of pavement flew into the air a dozen feet in front of my bike. I swerved and dropped the phone as I grabbed the handlebar of the KTM in a desperate attempt to avoid crashing. I barely escaped ditching the motorcycle as I jumped the curb just to the right of another line of small explosions. It sounded like a light machine gun—perhaps a squad automatic weapon—firing from the passenger window of a black Cadillac Escalade. I caught this and the sight of five more black Escalades behind the first over my shoulder as I shot off the road, jumped a gulley and plowed down a steep hill toward a stand of trees. I heard the crash of bumpers and bending metal as one of the Escalades tried to copy my maneuver and failed. Then I was in the woods, slowing to thread through trees. Fifty yards further and I was suddenly in the clear again, roaring into cut grass. A child's jungle gym set appeared in front of me. I swerved between two swings then sped through the backyard and cut around the tan ranch house, finding myself on First Avenue. I turned south on the road and weaved through the small residential development as fast as I could, hoping the noise of the bike and my velocity would get someone to call the police. I jogged left, hit Second Avenue then Third, and turned south again.

In three blocks I was back on Beckwith Road. I didn't see my pursuers. Slowing, I considered reversing directions, but with my phone gone I decided to keep heading in the direction Mongoose had suggested. In one block I ran into Route 19, a divided two-lane road that passed for a highway in these parts. I was about to turn right—south-west—when I saw two black Escalades approaching from that direction. Just then I heard the crack of a bullet as a clod of dirt exploded from the shoulder of the road next to me. I could hear more SUVs screaming toward me from Beckwith Road as I pulled into oncoming traffic on Route 19 causing an old Chevy pickup to spin out as he tried to avoid hitting me. I proceeded through the light traffic, mindful that I had a slim lead on the procession of Escalades that had converged from two directions and were now speeding toward me in the correct lane of Route 19.

Southbound traffic cleared for a moment and I was able to speed up, momentarily keeping the line of SUVs from closing in on me. In a quarter of a mile, though, a UPS truck driving alongside a minivan with barely two feet of separation between them nearly forced me off the road. I ran onto the shoulder, spinning the back wheel out briefly as I struggled to regain the road. The black National Front caravan would have been on top of me then, but they were frustrated by another minivan passing a school bus, neither moving much more than thirty miles an hour. Speeding past, I heard the indignant horn of the yellow bus as the Escalades passed it blind on the right shoulder. Another half mile on, as my lead dwindled again, the open road suddenly turned into an unbroken line of traffic. I hopped the median and rode between stopped cars, risking a glance back to see the Escalades making steady progress on the fringe of the road, eliciting many fewer horns than they would have in D.C. They were in firing range, but the National Front guards apparently weren't willing to take low-percentage shots in a crowded space. That gave me some hope. The crowd was getting denser. If I could keep them from physically catching me for two or three minutes longer, the FBI would be overhead and I might just escape.

That seemed like a good plan, anyway, until I spotted the reason for the traffic backup about a hundred yards further on. We were approaching a deep gorge, spanned by a steel arch bridge that looked to be the better part of a mile long. The bridge, dramatically perched above a green, rolling river, was blocked off at both ends. The roadblock must have come as a surprise to some, because half the motorists were turning back on Route 19 while the other half took a narrow road running south along the side of the gorge, parallel to the river.

The sight ticked my memory—what was it? Not the river release for rafting—something else. Bridge Day! Nichols had mentioned it. The Bridge was blocked off for some sort of celebration, but I hadn't asked the details. The festivities were obviously winding down because the line of traffic leaving Fayetteville was as thick as the line in, but moving considerably faster. I pulled ahead, swerved around a white Jetta idling in front of me and reached the roadblock. A trooper standing behind the barricade pointed at me and spoke into his radio when I ignored his warning and dodged the bike around the obstacle. Good. I dipped the KTM off the road then gunned it, evoking a very loud protest from a man in overalls who'd stepped in front of his wife, who was cradling an infant in blue swaddling.

The bridge itself was awash with pedestrians, many of them wearing matching sweatshirts with "Bridge Day" splashed on the front. I wove between them, ignoring the angry looks and pointing fingers, and took time to be grateful that the end of the day was rapidly approaching. If the bridge had been as crowded as it surely must have been at midday, I'd barely have made it across on foot, let alone on a motorcycle. I was a full third of the way across the span, slowly threading the bike by foot between angry pedestrians, when I realized I'd been outfoxed.

A half-dozen men wearing distinctive black turtlenecks and windbreakers with the National Front logo were walking toward me from the far side of the bridge. They hadn't yet drawn weapons but I could see that they were armed. I wondered how they'd gotten ahead of me until I noticed the helicopter they'd landed just inside the barricade.

Two very angry state troopers were handcuffing the pilot, and probably thanking their lucky stars that he hadn't injured anyone. Unfortunately, the troopers hadn't detained the National Front security men who'd piled out, and they hadn't attracted the attention of the other troopers and local police on the bridge. They had noticed me, though, and as I started to turn the KTM around, I spotted three officers with hands on their weapons slowly working their way through the crowd toward me. Behind them were eight more black-clad men, some with hands already disappearing into their jackets.

I realized in an instant that whether I moved forward or backwards, the National Front didn't intend to let me get off the bridge alive. The moment they drew weapons, a bunch of cops and a lot of other innocent people were going to get hurt.

Desperately scanning the scene, I noticed a platform erected in the middle of the bridge, raised above the level of the guardrail. A small crowd gathered nearby with backpacks strapped tightly to their backs and helmets on their heads, looking like they'd prepared for an arduous climb. Just a few yards ahead of me, a woman was holding a similar orange and yellow backpack with two leg loops dangling off of it in her right hand while she chatted with a friend. Suddenly the picture snapped together in my mind. I saw a way out. It was insane, but less so than waiting for more than a dozen armed men to gun me down.

I eased the bike forward and dismounted a couple of steps short of the woman. I tapped her on the shoulder and smiled. "Could you show me how one of these goes on?" I asked.

"Ah, sure," she said, glancing at her companion who shrugged.

I eased the backpack from her hands and she helped me put it on and adjust it. Then I thanked her and, stepping back, swung my leg back over the orange dirt bike.

"Hey wait!" she said. I ignored her and drew the Sig Sauer. She backed away from me.

"FBI—clear a path!" I yelled as I fired two rounds into the air. I holstered the Sig as the reports echoed from the hillside, then I gunned the engine of the bike for a long second. The KTM surged forward as screams erupted and the young, fit crowd scrambled out of my path like a herd of gazelles pursued by a cheetah. I prayed that the confusion would keep the three uniformed officers in my sightline from shooting me.

I aimed the bike straight at the platform, locking my eyes on the staircase. As I closed on the structure, the last couple still standing on the stairs belatedly realized I was headed straight for them and jumped off. I twisted the throttle harder, and the KTM mounted the stairs. The top of the platform was about nine feet wide and four feet deep. When I reached it, I turned sharply, pointed the orange bike straight out toward the river and twisted the throttle. The KTM shot off the side of the bridge and into the air.

That was when I experienced my first moment of doubt. As the bridge disappeared underneath me, while the bike was still soaring upwards, I suddenly wondered if I'd made a horrible, horrible mistake. Then I felt the pull of gravity and every other thought left my head.

I pushed off the KTM and watched the bike fall away from me as I spread my arms and legs out and got my body parallel to the river below me. I noted a green and purple-clad body freefalling a few hundred feet below me, a ways off to one side, and felt a moment of relief as I reached back to find the chute release for the pack I'd strapped on. I'd jumped from perfectly good aircraft in the Army, but I'd never made a base jump. I'd always thought that jumping from a fixed object a few hundred feet tall was a form of temporary insanity that didn't complement my life of frequent involuntary risk. But the New River Bridge looked like it was a thousand feet above the river below, which gave me a little cushion.

Still, I didn't wait. A real BASE jumper would have extended the free fall until the last safe moment, but I didn't. I followed the descent path of the jumper below me while my hand searched for the parachute. I was hoping to find some sort of Velcro opening, but I realized that the pouch with the parachute was held closed by a pin. It took me a precious second to work out the mechanism to release it.

For a sickening moment, I felt nothing. Then the small drogue chute exploded out of the pack like a shot from a cannon. Almost instantly, the main chute caught the air and snatched me upwards. The pack stayed on my back and I had a moment of relief as my downward velocity slowed. Then

I started to twist, and I realized that I was still in trouble. I looked up and checked the parachute. One corner of the rectangular chute was fouled, folded under the rest of the canopy and twisted. I'd seen it before. On a normal jump I'd have been able to clear it. But the three or four seconds it would have taken to straighten it would have put me into the river at a murderous velocity. I was descending too fast, and in a second I'd be out of control, unable to keep myself out of the trees on either side of the river. I looked down, saw the bloom of a parachute below me, and made an instant decision.

I slid the hook knife from the rig's shoulder strap and cut the parachute away from the pack. As I dropped away from the fouled chute, I brought my arms and legs into my body, diving downwards toward the canopy below me. I needed to hit the rectangular chute as it passed underneath me, before it was out of my reach. Calculations were running through my head and I prayed that I was not about to kill two instead of one. When I was just about on top of the purple parachute, I spread-eagled to hit it flat and yelled a warning.

I collapsed the chute, but the pocket of air it held acted like an airbag, arresting my fall without killing me instantly. It felt like hitting a 300 pound nose tackle square in the belly at full speed. I guessed that we were around fifty feet from the water when I hit the chute and maybe ten or twenty feet lower when it collapsed. Then I was wrapped in the parachute, unable to see a thing, plunging toward the river, wondering how deep the water was below me, realizing that the hook knife was no longer in my hand and trying to remember if the little Spyderco knife was still in my pants pocket.

It was just at that moment I realized I was jumping into whitewater.

25

"I'll be back soon. As soon as I can."

"That's a good idea."

"How is she doing today?"

"I just left the hospital. She looks better than yesterday. She's still not talking, but she's much more alert. She's eating solid food now. They took most of the tubes out of her, so there's just a port on her arm now."

"They intubated her?"

"I think it was just for food. There might have been oxygen going into her nose, though."

"I don't think Amelia wants me to come back."

"Why does that surprise you?"

"She thinks Mom doesn't want me there."

"Of course she'd say that."

"You don't think so?"

"You remember the woman we're talking about, right? The old battleaxe? She gets her energy from being angry. You'll perk her right up."

"So she *is* mad at me..."

"Don't be a little girl, Michael. Of course she's angry. Her house was redecorated with bullet holes last year. She watched a man hold a shotgun to her baby daughter's neck. And even worse than those two things, those awful men scratched her hardwood floors by pushing around the furniture. She'll never forgive you for that."

"You're confusing me."

"Don't you get it? That's our mother. That's how she is. If she didn't love you, she wouldn't be pissed off. Of course she wants to see you. She'll just never admit it."

"What about Amelia?"

"Who cares about Amelia? She's got her hands full raising the Chosen One. She's going to order you around as long as you let her. Don't pay attention to her. What's she going to do? Her husband worships you and she can't physically throw you out of Mom's room. Amelia is just like Mom. She's always going to be angry about something. You might as well make it something worth talking about."

"Ginny seemed pretty upset when I left."

"Ginny doesn't like fights. She wants everyone to get along. She was too young to remember what Dad was really like so she still has these fairytale fantasies where we're all a happy family together and Mom is nicer and you never left."

"That's what it always comes back to."

"That's the smartest thing you ever did, Michael—getting out of here. I only got as far as Albany and it's not far enough. If you keep reliving the old family traumas it will eat you alive. Everybody has baggage. Just drop it and make them deal with who you are now."

"So I should come back?"

"If you've been listening."

"It may take me a day or two, but I'll get there," I said.

"Don't wait too long. They say a hurricane is coming. We got clobbered by Irene last year."

"I'll come as soon as I can."

"You're okay, Mikey. Just try to show a little backbone."

"Thanks, Jamie. I...I feel like I never got to know you and now—"

"I was twelve when you left. Now's a better time for me. See ya."

* * *

"Trouble?" Nichols asked as she stepped into the waiting room of a private terminal at Chuck Yeager airport in Charleston, where the FBI helicopter had landed.

"Family stuff," I replied, staring at the phone. Then I looked up, meeting Nichols's eyes. "Wait, shouldn't you be somewhere south of here, breaking up a music festival?"

Nichols winced and shook her head. "We couldn't get a warrant. The National Front lawyers have been swarming federal judges, claiming they were conducting a demonstration today as part of their festival and that the gunfire and explosions we observed were all staged."

"Didn't you have someone else inside?"

"Apparently the National Front people kept all the guests contained in the festival area. We couldn't show that they were lying, not conclusively."

"What about the drone footage?" I asked, rubbing my chin.

"Drone footage?"

"We used a Boeing prototype from an abandoned DOD project they flew in from Ohio—a drone with rotors I think. My guys were supposed to supply your people with video to get the warrant."

"I don't know. I'm not in the loop on that."

"The drone footage would have shown people getting shot and bleeding. And worse."

"Releasing that kind of detailed surveillance video would open a can of worms. Are you sure your DOD friends would have shared that?"

"Maybe not," I admitted. Even if the tech weren't classified, Alpha wouldn't risk a media circus.

"That's not the only problem with a rogue special ops group playing soldier in West Virginia, either." Nichols stopped abruptly when she took a good look at me. "What did they do to you in there, anyway?" I had a towel draped over my shoulders and I was sitting on another one. There was a puddle beneath my feet. "Water torture?"

"Actually, yes, but that's not why I'm wet."

"I heard you jumped a motorcycle off the New River Bridge."

"That's true, but there *was* a parachute involved. Or two."

"You landed safely in the river?"

"More or less." Actually, I'd hit the water like a stone, wondering instantly if my back had broken and gasping from the shock of cold water. I struggled with the feeling that I was about to die hopelessly entangled in the canopy of a purple parachute. I put my hands above me as if praying and pulled through the wet material until it wouldn't yield, then grabbed the knife from my pocket with numb hands and started sawing at it. When I'd just about given up I felt myself being lifted from the water and a few seconds later, the purple blob in front of my eyes parted and I saw the sky and the face of my rescuer.

There were three other people in the small rubber motorboat and one of them was the nineteen-year-old woman I'd nearly killed. I expected her to attack me but instead she hugged me. "Dude that was awesome!" she said. "I saw your motorcycle hit the river. Did you breakaway and nearly bounce?" I just nodded and shivered.

The little rubber boat brought us to a parking lot on the shore where EMTs and local police were waiting for me with similar levels of anticipation. The FBI helicopter arrived on the scene just in time to prevent me from being either hospitalized or arrested.

"What happened to the guys who were shooting at me?"

"The troopers arrested the helicopter pilot for making an unsafe landing, public endangerment and all that. Nobody on the bridge witnessed any shooting other than the shots you fired. Apparently you were legally seconded from state to the FBI today, so there won't be any charges. You're very lucky nobody on the bridge was hurt. They stopped and questioned some of the guys who were following you but they had carry permits for their weapons."

"It figures. I met Eric Price, by the way."

"I want to hear about that conversation. Every word of it."

"I'm happy to oblige, but I really need to find some dry clothes first."

Nichols dropped a duffel bag at my feet. "You're in luck. This is from your military friends. They gave it to me after we spoke this morning."

"Thanks." I looked at my watch. "By the way, how did you get here so soon? It's been less than an hour since I broke out. Were you on another helo?"

Nichols didn't answer, just looked at me steadily.

"They pulled you off the case?"

"I was providing office support for the team until we got the 'no go.'"

"I'm sorry. I think this is my fault."

"Nope, this is just about me. I want to debrief you before my colleagues get here. I want to hear the whole story. Did you get anything useful out of going into the National Front compound other than a BASE jump?"

"I'll answer any question you want if we can do it while you drive. But I'd better change first." I stood, grabbed the duffel and headed to the restroom before she could think to say no.

26

The sky was overcast. Not with an ordinary sort of haze, either, but cloudy like the mountain gods were building statues in the sky. They lit up from above where the moon peeked through. The wind on the ground was brisk, pushing the Suburban gently back and forth as we followed Route 60 west out of Charleston. We listened to the radio for a few minutes as we drove. The hurricane had kissed Florida and was headed up the Atlantic coast, destined for the New York area. We were assured the windy night had nothing to do with the storm. I didn't buy it.

"Where are we headed?" Nichols asked.

"We need to talk with the leader of the Reclaim camp. Her name is Roxanne. Roxanne Chalmers. I was hiking with her this morning. Your people didn't detain her, did they?"

"No. We've had a team on her all day, though. Do you want me to confirm her location?" I nodded and she grabbed a radio to make a quick call. Nichols had a terse dialogue with the dispatcher that was so laced with codes and oblique phrases different from those I'd used that it was impossible to follow. When she put down the handset she spoke again. "She's at the campsite. Why are we visiting her?"

"She's at the center of everything that's happened. It was only when I went to see her that the National Front started trying to kill me. They put someone undercover in her camp. Then you guys put someone else undercover in her camp. I'm pretty sure it was National Front people who staged the bus incident to kill your undercover guy. And there's still the question of why Jason Paul was blackmailing her if the result was that the mine was failing."

"How could you know that? About the mine?"

"My old boss had mixed motives for sending me here. He asked me to come and find the daughter of a friend, but he had the National Front on his radar from the beginning. They caused some trouble overseas." I was treading the narrow line between interagency cooperation and illegally disclosing classified information. But she'd taken a risk on me already. "You obviously know that his organization has been assisting my investigation."

Nichols snorted. "I picked up on that when they invited me into the tractor-trailer they sent for you."

"Right. That's not all of it, either. The, uh, specialty of my former outfit was electronic surveillance and recon. A big part of that is gathering computer information. They did some background work for me on the mine operation."

"They hacked the mine's computers?"

"That would be illegal," I answered, not contradicting her.

"And Hobart is failing?"

"Output was down significantly after the Reclaim group split up and Roxanne took charge in September. Paul told me that he had video of the two other leaders sabotaging his site over the summer. That's apparently what caused the split in the camp—the same one that sent Heather Hernandez running off to CC Farms and then the National Front with Anton Harmon."

"Wait. You're saying the mine did worse *after* they stopped the sabotage?"

"Yes. There would have been some residual effects for a few weeks, but not into this month. So if Paul had video proof and showed it to Roxanne, he wanted something from her. He wasn't trying to get her to back off, because handing the tape over to the authorities would have accomplished that. He obviously wanted something else. But I don't know what it was. It's easy to see what she was getting, though."

"Shutting the mine down?"

"Right."

"What could Paul possibly get out of that?"

"I don't know," I conceded. "That's what I'm hoping we can figure out by talking to Roxanne."

"And how does this relate to the National Front?"

"Another good question. But a bunch of analysts are pouring through a mountain of data right now, trying to figure that out."

"Data?"

"From the National Front."

Nichols kept her eyes on the road, but her grip on the wheel tightened. "That's why you went in there, isn't it?"

"I was looking for the girl. But that was part of it, too. That's what my outfit wanted most, I think."

"Jesus, they were playing you all along. The girl was just an excuse for them to get you to check out the National Front."

"I don't know. I don't think it's that simple. But if you're asking then yes, I feel a little used."

"And you let those National Front guys take you just so you could get inside the building?"

"I didn't blow my own cover. They had me pegged from the moment I walked into the festival tents. Which raises another question."

"Yes?"

"Who else on your end knew I was going in?"

"You think the leak was from the Bureau?"

"It had to be. Think about it. The folks on my side are all soldiers in Virginia."

"But they wanted you to be detained by the National Front people."

I shook my head. "It doesn't work that way. They knew I'd have found a way in, whatever it took. That's what I'm trained for. But it's always in my hands. They would trust me to finish the mission."

"You're not in the Army anymore," she said.

"I'm not saying I'm happy with my old commander. He wasn't upfront with me. But I've known the guy for a long time. There was always a line. He withheld, manipulated, pressured. But he wouldn't have sold me out, and neither would anyone else in that unit. What about the FBI?"

Nichols raised a hand off the wheel, then lowered it. She glanced out the side window, at stands of sycamore and maple flying by. "We haven't made a lot of progress in the last two years. Every time we get a lead, it dries up. Our undercover agent was killed. So I guess it's a fair question. The National Front task force knew you were going in today. That's about a dozen agents—a couple here and the rest in Washington. Plus the Special Agent in Charge in Pittsburgh, and his assistant here in Charleston."

"Do those people know where we're headed right now?"

"No."

"Why?" FBI agents have a pretty strict investigative procedure. They do not chase down leads on their own as a rule.

Nichols glanced at me briefly, making eye contact. "I've pissed some people off in the last twenty-four hours. They weren't happy with me to begin with, and there's a pretty good chance they'll use some of this stuff to end my career. Unless I can get a break in this case. Maybe even then."

"I'm sorry. This is my fault. I don't want to make your life more complicated."

She drove on for a mile in silence and I thought we were done, but then she answered.

"I understood the Navy. I'm not saying it was perfect. It was challenging to be a woman and fly the Super Hornet. But I got how it worked. There are so many objective tests. Fighter pilots are under a microscope. If you do well, handle the pressure, work your ass off and find a way to do whatever they ask you to do, you advance. Not forever, but far enough."

I nodded. She'd been a commissioned officer while I was a non-com, but the story was more or less the same.

"It's been different at the FBI. I was second in my class at Quantico. They told me a smaller field office would give me a better chance to contribute immediately. But it hasn't worked out like that. I understand hazing. I've been there. I know how it goes when you're the junior person. But some of the guys in this office, they think I'm around to make coffee and take notes. Not just for awhile, but forever." Her eyes flicked out her side window again.

"Have they hit you on performance reviews?"

"Yeah. Just low enough to make me look bad."

"Don't you rotate soon?"

"Normally at the three year point—so next spring. I'll work in a bigger office. But as things stand, I'll go in with a reputation."

"For what?"

"Not being a team player. Not being one of the guys."

"Did one of those guys get too friendly?"

"Maybe. I don't know. I've been dealing with that kind of stuff for so long that I don't always notice anymore. I've got defenses. If a guy stands too close I step back. If I get an invitation I don't like, I have an excuse that's fake enough so he knows he stepped across the line. I don't think twice about it. I'm used to guys looking. I figured out a long time ago that I was going to have to work harder than any guy to get taken seriously. But I don't know how to do that in this office."

"Is it a cultural thing? Being in this part of the country, I mean?"

"No, not at all. They're all transplants. The biggest jerk is from California. Local law enforcement and state police, they've been great. They kill you with kindness."

"I guess you can hang on and see how things are on your next assignment, but I get how that's frustrating."

"I thought you might."

"More than you know."

"So what's your story? How does someone who can do what you do end up behind a desk?"

"It's hard to live that life forever. It changes you."

She made a sound in her throat. "What do you do at the State Department?"

"I'm an analyst. I follow weapons transfers around the developing world."

"Do you like it?"

"I'm not bad at my job. I speak a few of the languages. I understand the equipment better than some of the academics."

"But?"

"Part of the problem is that I don't have the PhD. The admiral—the guy who hired me—didn't care. But the new guy is an academic. He doesn't think I belong there."

"And the other part?"

"It's what you said. Part of me can't stand being in an office. I wake up every morning and think 'Oh my God, I'm going to be putting a suit on and getting on the metro every day for the rest of my life.'"

"I have those days, too."

"At least you carry a gun."

"There is that."

27

We sat on boulders near the stream, watching each other in the moonlight. Roxanne must have expected the questions we'd ask because she'd immediately taken us out of earshot of the Reclaim camp.

"It's time, Roxanne. We need the whole story. More people died today. You have to tell us everything."

"I need to read you your Miranda rights. And I'm going to record what you tell us," Nichols said. I exhaled loudly, exasperated, but she ignored me. She pulled a card from inside her jacket pocket and repeated the familiar warnings.

Roxanne looked at me, pleading, but I shook my head. "They'll find out everything soon anyway, Roxanne. If you don't help them, they'll come down harder on you. Just don't lie about anything, even a little thing. Lying to a federal officer is a federal crime." I didn't look at Nichols as I said that.

Roxanne lowered her head slowly and her shoulders jerked convulsively as she started to sob. Nichols and I just sat there silently until she finished and looked up.

I started to ask a question but Nichols pointed to the recorder and shook her head. She withdrew a small notebook computer, flipped it open and told Roxanne that she was going to type Roxanne's statement at the same time she recorded it, and that she'd print it out for Roxanne to sign when they went in to the FBI office. Nichols started with simple questions, asking about dates and events that we already knew. When she had Roxanne in a rhythm, she struck.

"When Jason Paul from Transnational Coal showed you video of your co-members planting explosives to sabotage the operations at the Hobart Mine, did he ask you to do something in return for his silence?"

"Yes."

"Okay, we'll come back to that in a moment. Did Mr. Paul give you any additional reasons to cooperate with him?"

"Yes."

"What did he offer you?"

"He said he'd make sure the mine closed forever."

"What?" Nichols and I looked at each other, startled.

We sat there in silence for a moment, the three of us each wrestling with the implications of the words Roxanne had spoken. Eventually, Nichols repeated her question.

"You're telling me that Jason Paul promised to shut down mining operations at Hobart permanently if you cooperated with him?"

"Yes."

"And what exactly did he want in return?"

"Josh and Amy had to leave the state. He wanted to approve anything we did to slow down the mine in advance after that. And he said he would need other things."

"What things?"

"He didn't say. Not then, anyway."

"How was he going to shut down the mine?"

"He said he had information—damaging information—about the mine owners. Things they had done before he took charge that were illegal. Dumping toxic waste, faked assessments, proof they'd bribed officials. He showed me one report he claimed would bury the mine in litigation for twenty years."

"Why would you believe he would end his own career?"

"I didn't have a choice, did I? I couldn't let Amy and Josh go to jail. But...I believed him, the way he said it. Like it was beneath him to lie to me."

"There was more, wasn't there? He asked you to do something else, didn't he?" Nichols asked. Roxanne hesitated, then nodded. "What else did Paul ask you to do?"

"He called me Wednesday afternoon—the day of the attack—and asked me to make sure our bus left Hobart at 6 and that I wasn't on it. I asked him what was going on. He told me they were going to scare the kids. Said he needed to show his management he was taking things seriously. I said hell no, but he reminded me what would happen if I didn't cooperate. He also told me the kids would fight if I was there and someone might get hurt. He said nobody was going to listen to me if I tried to blow the whistle."

"Did you really believe that?"

"No," she said and started crying again. Nichols just waited and let the tears exhaust themselves before she continued. Roxanne talked for nearly an hour. Nothing she said was new, but Nichols went through all the details to make sure she extracted everything Roxanne had to offer. Then Nichols put cuffs on her and we walked her back to the Suburban. Nobody saw us leaving the camp in the dead of the night.

* * *

"You like her, don't you?" Nichols said as we stood in the cool, damp air after she'd put Roxanne, handcuffed, into the back of her Suburban.

"What she's done...it's horrible. But, yeah, I do."

"Why? She's responsible for two deaths."

"She is, but she doesn't think like we do. It's not about people for her. I think she would have done anything to stop that mine."

"Then why feel bad for her? She walked into this with her eyes open." Nichols's voice was softer than I'd heard it. Barely a whisper.

"This girl I'm looking for—Heather. Her father left her when she was three. Her stepdad and her mom didn't try to find her when she stopped writing over the summer. Her friends here at Reclaim knew that Harmon was bad news, but they did nothing. Her roommate at CC Farms knew what kind of guy Harmon was, but she didn't do anything, either. There was even a guy who had a crush on her at the National Front compound who knew Harmon was abusing her, but he never stood up for Heather. Roxanne...she let Heather down, too. She let all those kids on the bus down. But at least she has the decency to be ashamed for it. I think she may be the only one."

Nichols put a hand on my shoulder. It was just for a second, and her touch was light, but it made an imprint. Then we got back into the Chevy and headed back to Charleston.

28

Nichols kept me out of custody again that night. Assistant Special Agent in Charge Daniel Levisay had a full head of steam when he intercepted us in front of the FBI Resident Agency in Charleston. He was the local man in charge, down the chain of command from the Pittsburgh field office. He was also Nichols's boss.

Levisay handcuffed me on the spot, marched me inside his Spartan office and sat me down forcibly on a plain wooden chair in front of his desk. Nichols had moved to intercept him but I shook my head quickly. Levisay was a bit plumper than I expected for an FBI agent, with a shiny bald head, a smooth baby face and narrow eyes. He lapsed unconsciously into the third person while he was yelling at me—a finely tuned mix of threat and remonstrance. He talked to me as he would have to a five-year-old, speaking slower when he used large words. He assumed I had no idea how serious an offence shooting people or starting a forest fire might be. He vowed that I would spend the rest of my life in jail when the FBI got into the National Front compound and gathered forensic evidence of my crimes there, though we both knew any traces of evidence were long gone. But still he pushed on, openly speculating on what other federal crimes I might have committed.

Then the phone on his desk beeped. His assistant on the intercom said "It's the Director, sir." She said it that way, with a capital 'D.' Levisay froze. Looked at me for a second wondering if he should shoo me out of his office. But I was handcuffed and he didn't have time. He picked up the phone. He said the words "Yes, sir" and sat up straight in his chair, then listened for five minutes before he put it down gently on the cradle. All the blood had run out of his face. He got up slowly, walked around the desk and uncuffed me, returned to his chair and, looking at me carefully said, "I would like to personally apologize for my behavior. The FBI appreciates your cooperation and the personal risks you have taken to uncover the truth behind the murders of the activists. We value interagency cooperation and would like to extend you the full support of this office in your efforts here in West Virginia. Please let me know what we can do to help you." The apology must have taken two years off of his life, but Levisay looked scared.

"The Director. You mean the Director of the FBI?" I knew the answer but I wanted to hear him say it.

"Yes. The Director of the FBI."

"I'm going to need an empty office and a phone right now. Then I need Agent Nichols's undivided time. And you might want to keep the team you assembled to go into the National Front compound this afternoon on alert. You're about to get a warrant to arrest Jason Paul from Transnational Mining."

I turned and walked out of his office without glancing back at him. Then I got on the phone to the Activity. An hour later, as I was hanging up, I saw Nichols walk by the office and waved her in.

"I understand that I have you to thank?" I smiled.

She shrugged. "One of the guys in the trailer gave me a card with a number to call if I needed help. I figured it was time to make that call. You just broke a high profile multiple homicide wide open. I faxed over a copy of Roxanne's signed confession. I figured that would give your boss enough leverage to fix things on this end."

"He certainly did. Agent Levisay just got a call from the Director of the FBI."

Nichols smiled. "I am so very sorry I was not in the room when that happened."

"You really are." I motioned her to a chair. "The guys have been chewing on data all afternoon. I told them about Paul's play to shut down the mine."

"What did they think?"

"They've found a connection between him and the National Front. He has a separate Gmail account he uses to communicate directly with Eric Price. He was careful with it but he apparently accessed it once from his work computer, so they were able to identify and access it. Most of it is innocuous stuff, but there's definitely a connection between Paul and the National Front."

"It's good to have confirmation. It makes more sense."

"Yeah," I agreed, "it fills out the picture a little better. But Paul seems like more of an opportunist than a race warrior. He hooked up to the National Front through the PA."

"That fits."

"They're looking into Paul's personal records to try to find a motive. But they haven't broken into the National Front's system yet and there are terabytes of data, so it's a big project. They might have something by the morning."

"Do you think whatever he's doing is just about him and not the National Front?"

"No, I don't think so. Price must have sent Anton Harmon to Reclaim. And Harmon had to be there to help Paul with something. Maybe he was there to unmask the FBI undercover agent. What if they were tipped off about that by someone here?"

"I'm not biting on that yet, but it's a possibility," Nichols conceded.

I remembered something Alpha had told me. "The reason my unit was onto the National Front was energy. Maybe there's a connection. Some National Front guys were sabotaging power infrastructure in Africa."

"Africa? Why on earth would they do that?"

"It didn't make a lot of sense. They first assumed these guys were just freelancing—that it had nothing to do with the National Front itself. But when we found the device in my room last night, it had the same signature. Ninety percent chance the same maker who pulled one of the African jobs built it. So we have to wonder."

"Because now they're intentionally shutting down an enormous coal mine..."

"Right. It's not an exact parallel, but I wouldn't want to call it a coincidence either. I'll make sure our guys look at that, too."

"What about the girl?"

I put a hand behind my neck, massaging stiff tendons. "It's a cold trail. She hasn't logged on to her e-mail account since Wednesday. I got into her room in the National Front dormitory—the one she shares with Harmon. All her things were there. And there was a couple week's supply of insulin in the fridge."

"So the message she sent her mom was false?"

"Or she was trying to say something else."

"What?"

"She said she was going to run out on Monday. But she had plenty of insulin. So maybe the message wasn't about insulin, but about Monday."

"And what's going to happen then?"

"A hurricane is going to hit. Beyond that, it's a very good question."

29

I woke to a burst of light in my eyes and the old question on my lips: *Where am I?*

A shaft of sunlight stabbed through a gap in the cloudbank over the Dunbar section of Charleston and pierced an east-facing window in the guest bedroom of the small house that Special Agent Nichols rented. It disappeared as soon as it arrived, leaving the sky an unbroken blanket of gray. I looked at the wind-up clock on the nightstand and saw that it was six a.m.

The night before, we'd eaten a quick dinner at the only diner still serving in Charleston near midnight. Then Nichols asked where I was staying. I told her to drop me at any motel, but she offered her guest room instead. Nichols's place was a small, immaculately kept green Victorian. She'd painted and decorated the rooms—something I had never managed in any of the four apartments I'd lived in since moving off-base after my first few years in the Army. I had never hung so much as a poster on a wall until I was attending Georgetown. I'd never used an appliance other than the refrigerator, the toaster and a microwave.

A picture of Nichols with a tall guy who looked like he might be an Abercrombie & Fitch model sat on the kitchen counter, staring into the dining room. I hadn't asked her about it—I just thanked her for her hospitality after she showed me the room and fell asleep a few seconds after I hit the bed. I'd forgotten the toll that being shot at takes on you, the adrenaline deficit that exhausts the body. Not to mention the physical toll of being tortured and then jumping off a bridge. Or maybe the aftereffects of this kind of stuff were getting worse since I passed thirty.

I left the house, glad for the Blackhawk shell I'd discovered in the large duffel Nichols had passed on from the Activity. It was drizzling outside; a cold haze hung over the street, highlighting how close the mercury was to freezing temperatures. An electronic weather station sitting near the door revealed 90% humidity at 40 degrees as I left for my run.

I returned forty minutes later with coffee and muffins from Dunkin Donuts. Nichols had pulled on a wool turtleneck and jeans and was reading e-mail on her laptop. I handed her a coffee and the bag of muffins, then headed straight for the shower.

When I was clean, I dug through the duffel until I found the encrypted satellite phone I knew would be there. I perched myself against the window in the guest bedroom and called Alpha. A half-hour later, I emerged with the phone in my hand. Nichols was sitting at the counter with a newspaper open and one foot up on a chair, eating a muffin.

"I'm putting you on speaker. Special Agent Nichols of the FBI is here with me," I said.

"Nice to meet you, Agent Nichols. Your assistance has been invaluable," Alpha said.

"You boys sure can throw some weight," she replied. "Thanks for including me on this call. I have to tell you, though; I'm confused by your involvement in this case. I thought Mr. Herne was here on a personal errand to find a missing woman. I don't understand why the Army is getting into the middle of a missing persons case." I'd never heard someone talk to Alpha that way, but it was a fair question.

"Mr. Herne's trip started as a private investigation, but matters changed when we discovered that someone from our community left an explosive device in his motel room."

"You're certain about that?"

"We are. After he notified us, we were able to retrieve the device from the West Virginia State Police before they disposed of it. Our experts confirm that the bomb-maker was trained in the special operations community. Several men connected to the National Front fit this profile."

"That's true."

"Yesterday, the National Security Council authorized my command to liaise with the Bureau in an advisory capacity. Based on some of the new information we're looking at now, we may need to expand the relationship."

"New information?"

"Last night, I told Agent Nichols that you linked Jason Paul to the National Front," I interrupted.

"Good. In the interim we've been analyzing Mr. Paul's e-mail. We're also working to gain access to information on the National Front."

"Working?" I asked. Getting the Activity's hacking program installed on an inside computer usually compromises the network immediately.

"The security protocols on the National Front's network are top drawer. The server you got us into was nearly a closed-loop system," Mongoose piped up. "They almost caught us right at the beginning. We're working a plan to break through, but we're still at least half a day away."

"We'll never be able to use any of what you've found in court." Nichols stood and paced away from the phone, turned back.

"The Reclaim leader's confession gives you the proof you need to arrest Mr. Paul and seize his hard drives. We can show you how to connect him to the National Front. Once you document the connection between Mr. Paul and the National Front, you'll be able to obtain a warrant to search their headquarters. But our concern is prevention, not prosecution, Agent Nichols. The National Front is responsible for several bombings overseas. We need to ensure they're not planning domestic terrorism."

"I mentioned the African activity to Special Agent Nichols, sir, but you might want to brief her."

"There was an attack on oil fields in the South Sudan. A few months later, a team infiltrated and sabotaged two South African power plants. We were able to connect the attacks to members of the National Front."

"You think they're planning something here?" Nichols asked.

"Possibly. Mr. Herne has a strong opinion on that."

"They have to be up to something significant, sir, or they wouldn't have been trying so hard to kill me. When they... *questioned* me yesterday, they were trying to find out what I knew of their plans. Which suggests that they have plans."

"I think Michael is right," Nichols said, glancing at me and quickly looking away. "Eric Price is a megalomaniac. He's been growing his organization by leaps and bounds. We know the National Front has sold arms and drugs to finance operations. Price will do just about anything to expand his influence."

"Mr. Herne told you that we found an e-mail account Mr. Paul used to communicate with Mr. Price. There are some recent exchanges. The language is oblique, but it may support the idea that something significant is planned very soon."

"They also tracked down Heather's insulin prescription," I told Nichols. "She had it refilled last week before she wrote her mother. So we're wondering if Heather was trying to tell her mom that something bad was going to happen tomorrow."

"Like what?" Nichols asked.

"We know that Paul promised Roxanne he was going to blow the whistle on his own mine. That would make no sense unless there was something in it for the National Front," I offered.

"Such as?"

"The National Front was trying to compromise the energy supply chain in Africa. Maybe that was just a trial run. What if they're trying to put some kind of a crimp into coal production back home?"

"To what end?" The question came from Alpha.

"It could be financial. Half of electric power in the U.S. is generated by coal, right? Anything that threatened coal supply would drive up the price of other fossil fuels."

"Would shutting down one mine really have that effect?" Alpha asked. It was a question for his staff, and after a moment of keys clicking, one of them responded.

"No. The largest mines are in Wyoming, not West Virginia. They're exponentially larger than Hobart. And there's a larger one in West Virginia, too—an underground mine." I didn't know the man speaking, but he sounded like an analyst.

I remembered something Roxanne had told me earlier. "Wait, didn't Paul work at a big coal mine in Wyoming?" I searched my memory for the name. "North Antelope?"

There was silence on the other end of the line again. Then the same analyst spoke, with some excitement in his voice. "He actually worked at the two largest mines in Wyoming— the North Antelope Rochelle Mine and Big Thunder. Together they produce one hundred and eighty million short tons of coal every year. If you combine those with the two biggest mines in West Virginia—Hobart and Gilroy—you have twenty percent of the national output of coal."

"Gilroy Mine?" I asked. "Have you found any reference to that?"

More clicking. This time Mongoose chimed in. "There was a mention of Uncle Gilroy in one of Paul's e-mails last week."

"In the theoretical case that you were able to disable that percentage of coal output in the U.S., what effect would that have on oil prices?" Alpha asked.

"Oil is a huge, globally-driven market, so it's hard to say," the first analyst answered. "But if you look at natural gas, things get interesting. The supply was stable for a long time. Then a few years ago, someone figured out how to inject pressurized chemicals into shale and extract natural gas that was impossible to drill for previously. It's not as easy or cheap to transport as oil, so the market is more local. The U.S. has huge deposits. Now there's a drilling boom and the price is at historic lows."

"You're talking about fracking, right?"

"Hydraulic Fracturing," the analyst corrected me.

"And what would happen to the price of natural gas if the coal supply was threatened?"

"It would go through the roof."

Nichols's phone rang, shattering the silence on both ends of the line. She stepped out of the room.

"We know that Paul can disable the Hobart mine by releasing documents. But how would he shutter the other three?"

"Perhaps there are some clues in the attack on the oilfield that we can uncover," Alpha said. The line went mute for a moment and I imagined the man issuing a terse string of orders to a roomful of analysts and surveillance experts.

"We're going to figure that out," Alpha said when he returned to the call a few moments later. "And we'll contact the Gilroy mine. It's in West Virginia, but some distance from Charleston. Perhaps..."

Nichols burst back into the room. "We've got an arrest warrant for Jason Paul and a search warrant for his house and office. Do you want to come along?"

Alpha answered for me. "Go. We have more work to do on our end, anyway."

30

Jason Paul's house was across the river from Nichols's place—over the South Side Bridge in the Kanawha section of Charleston. The city is built mostly on the flatlands where the smaller Elk River meets the Kanawha, but the tonier houses are up in the surrounding hills. Paul's was on Newton Road, in the thick of old Charleston money. It was a Tudor trying very hard to look like an English country estate.

Paul's mansion had three sections—the main house and two wings. The central section was a large, conventional pre-war Tudor. The wings were much more recent additions. They might have been framed out with steel, and looked to be single-story with vaulted ceilings and vast expanses of glass. The living spaces inside must have been pretty impressive, but the place was a hodgepodge from the outside. The property sat at the end of Newton Road, on the plateau atop a hill overlooking Charleston. The driveway was long and stately, with a line of elms planted on either side that evoked an antebellum plantation. The driveway ended in a large circle. The island formed by the circle had a waist-high hedge maze landscaped into it. It looked like a real puzzler for a cocker spaniel.

A Maserati coupe and a Range Rover sat in the circle along with a dozen FBI vehicles. State police cars lined the rest of the driveway. An FBI SWAT team was milling about outside the house, wearing green military-style uniforms with body armor and carrying assault rifles. I had a hard time seeing Paul wielding anything more threatening than a birding shotgun, but you never can tell about people.

We parked at the end of the long line of official vehicles, more than a football field's distance from the house. As soon as Agent Nichols stepped out of the Suburban, Agent Levisay started walking toward us. I realized he'd been waiting.

"Your status has really risen," I whispered to Nichols.

"Sure. It's me. It's not your boss. I believe that."

Nichols was right. When we reached him, Levisay ignored her and held his hand out to greet me. It was clammy and cold, just about the same temperature as the chill air. "Both vehicles registered to Mr. Paul are here," he said, turning toward the house and putting his hand on my shoulder. "I understand that the man is single. We're going to knock on the door now."

"Have you tracked his cell phone?" I asked.

Levisay nodded. "It's inside. Wait here and we'll bring you in when we clear the house. Special Agent Nichols, please continue to accompany Mr. Herne." Levisay did not even glance in Nichols's direction as he spoke.

Nichols kept cool but I saw a tendon ripple in her jaw.

"You just know that man is constipated," I said when Levisay was out of earshot. Nichols coughed to avoid laughing.

We watched as the helmeted FBI assault team approached the house. Levisay had a vest on under his FBI windbreaker, but his bald dome was exposed to the elements. It was drizzling, and a bit colder on the hilltop than down in the city.

"There's something that still doesn't make sense to me," Nichols said as we watched Agent Levisay ring the doorbell, then pound on the door.

"What's that?" I asked, distracted.

"Why did Jason Paul blackmail Roxanne?"

"To get her to cooperate."

"But what did he actually need from her? A bus route? There's nothing she gave him he couldn't have done for himself. He could have found a simpler way to keep her off the bus. Why would he risk involving her?"

Nichols had a point. It was a loose thread in the narrative.

"You're right—it doesn't make sense. And I still don't understand why the National Front sent Anton Harmon to infiltrate Reclaim."

Nobody had come to the door and Agent Levisay was still pounding. He sent someone to retrieve an electronic bullhorn from his Suburban.

"Exactly. What would it buy them?"

"Why did you guys send an FBI agent into Reclaim?"

"I called someone about that this morning. A friend who talked to me off the record. We sent our guy in because we knew the National Front had put someone undercover at Reclaim and nobody understood why."

"So your guy was in there because the National Front showed an interest?"

"Right."

"But your guy was still there six weeks after Harmon left."

"That's true—so?"

"He must have discovered something that made it worth staying undercover."

"Okay."

"But that leaves us about the same place where we started. We don't know why the National Front put Harmon in."

"Unless..." Nichols said.

"Yes?"

"Harmon was an ordnance expert in the military—he was the guy who knew about bombs, right?"

"In Special Forces you train in a specialty. That was his."

"What if he's the one who persuaded the two Reclaim leaders to sabotage the dragline? And rigged the charge himself. It makes more sense than two environmental activists successfully sabotaging a multi-million dollar piece of equipment. Do you know how big that rig is? You could put four Suburbans in the bucket."

At the door, Levisay was getting impatient. He held up one finger and then pointed at the entry specialist, who was carrying a sledgehammer that looked like it could take the door down with one stroke.

"But why would the National Front want to risk involving Reclaim?" I asked.

"Let's say that the National Front isn't actually sabotaging Antelope Valley and Big Thunder. Those are strip mines that use tons of explosives ever year as a matter of course. How on earth would you slow them down? If you could only stop Hobart and Gilroy, how would that work? Instead of cutting off 20% of the coal supply, they would only be affecting 2%. So how do you move the price if you're only stopping 2% of the supply? You do it like Sadam Hussein did when he invaded Kuwait. You convince everyone else that the first 2% is just the beginning."

"How would you do that?"

"What if the National Front convinced everyone that environmental terrorists were targeting coal mines? If they did something really newsworthy? Then they wouldn't have to hit so many mines to have the same effect. Not if it was terrorism."

"Leaking a bunch of documents wouldn't do that," I agreed.

"What if the terrorists exposed the documents like a WikiLeaks thing? And then bombed a second mine. Gilroy, for instance? That's underground, so it would be more vulnerable. Then the trail would eventually lead back to Reclaim—and there would be video proof that they had already used explosives at Hobart."

"But how does this help if Paul is in custody? Wouldn't he talk to keep himself out of jail?" I asked. "He doesn't strike me as the type to sacrifice himself for the team."

A helmeted FBI SWAT agent had his face pressed against mirrored glass, peering into one of the picture windows on the east wing of the house. Then he turned toward the main entrance, cupping his hands around his mouth. "There's a man tied to a chair in here. He's facing away from the window, but it could be our guy," he yelled. Suddenly, the pieces in my head snapped into place.

I saw Agent Levisay motion to the breach specialist, who raised the sledgehammer parallel to his waist and behind him, like a baseball batter with a low swing.

"Wait! Stop! Stop," I yelled as the man swung at the door. I was too far away. If Levisay or the breacher heard me, they took no notice. The sledgehammer hit the door just above the lock and started to swing open. I tackled Nichols and we hit the ground just as a fireball exploded from the house, sending a wave of heat and force that leveled everything in its path.

31

The helicopter carried us swiftly northwards under cloud cover. Special Agent Nichols sat next to me, her face still a shade paler than it had been in the morning. We both wore headsets but neither of us had said a word since the helicopter lifted from its launch pad near the end of the runway at Chuck Yeager airport.

I didn't blame her. We'd both served in combat, but her experience at 10,000 feet had been less intimate than mine. I would have bet she'd never seen an IED cut through a convoy, or the aftermath of a suicide bomber in a crowded marketplace. She'd probably never had to look at the lifeless eyes of the children that terrorists had used as human shields. Still, seeing carnage on home soil shook me up, too. We were almost a hundred yards from the house when the bomb triggered, and it felt like we were copper beaten against a hot anvil. It would take days to make sense of everything in and around the house. And most of the FBI field agents in West Virginia were either hospitalized or dead.

Minutes after the blast, television news stations and print journalists received e-mails claiming responsibility for the explosion along with a link to a series of documents that tied Transnational Coal to a large number of environmental offenses. Many of them had Jason Paul's name on them. The group behind the blast called itself Coal-Free Dawn. I didn't doubt that the e-mails would somehow trace back to Roxanne and Reclaim.

In the chaos following the blast, we got caught up giving first aid to the FBI agents and State Police officers who'd survived the detonation. There was already an ambulance on site, but the injuries overwhelmed the two EMTs. It was a gruesome business; all the pieces of the house, from the glass picture windows to the cement foundation, had become shrapnel. We ended up helping the EMTs by tying tourniquets and dressing wounds. It took over an hour for enough medical personnel to arrive to allow us to leave the scene. By the time we boarded the FBI helicopter, the morning was almost done. I only hoped we weren't already too late.

"I have a call for you from Washington, sir. I can transfer it through to your headset." The pilot's voice startled me, pulling me away from my thoughts. I wasn't used to hearing anyone call me 'sir.'

"You're headed to the Gilroy mine?" It was Alpha.

"It's not far from the Ohio and Pennsylvania borders, but we'll be there in under an hour. We have two men from the state police bomb squad with us," I said, eyeing the men in jump seats facing me. There was also a Malinois, a remarkably calm Belgian Shepherd strapped between them, looking about with an intelligent expression. "Sir, what can you tell us about the mine?"

"There are almost eight hundred men working at Gilroy mine, most of them underground. They're evacuating the mine right now and local police are sealing off the three entry portals."

"Have you figured out how they could disable the mine? If we don't have a good idea..." I trailed off. The mine was small on the surface but enormous underground—the mirror opposite of Hobart.

"Coal mining releases pockets of methane gas and a great deal of coal dust. Both are highly flammable," said the analyst who'd spoken earlier. "Even a modestly-sized explosive device set off anywhere in an underground coal mine would be catastrophic. The worst mine accident in history happened in Monongah, West Virginia in 1907. Workers mishandled a small amount of dynamite and 500 miners died. So really, any explosive charge set off inside the mine near the coal seams could be devastating. If you wanted to be sure to maximize the damage, however, you'd want to set it up near a seam where methane gas is being released."

"You said they're evacuating the mine?"

"Yes, that's correct."

"Do they have anyone checking the miners? We need to know if there are any outsiders there—replacement workers, inspectors, journalists, anyone."

"We asked the foreman not to let anyone leave. The county sheriff is at the mine with four deputies. They're holding the miners on the site for now. The State Police should be arriving about an hour after you. They'll process the miners."

"How deep is this mine?" Nichols asked.

"Nearly three thousand feet."

"Is there any way we can get down to the active coal seams without using the elevator?" I asked.

"No. This is a shaft mine with a central elevator, so even after you drive in, there's only one way to get down and back up."

"Great," I said. "That's just great."

32

"You folks aren't planning on carrying firearms into the mine, are ya?" Earl Jones, the mine superintendent, asked the moment he stepped into his office. He eyed the .45 caliber automatic I was strapping to my leg as he spoke. Jones was a small, wiry man with thick, wavy gray hair and a voice like crushed gravel.

Nichols, the two bomb squad agents, Cody the Malinois and I had been gearing up in Jones's office as we waited for him to arrive from one of the mine portals. The four of us exchanged a look.

He pulled a map down in front of the white board behind his desk. "You pull the trigger once down there and you could collapse the whole mine without help from any damn terrorists."

"We won't use weapons underground. We understand the risks," I assured Mr. Jones.

"So why carry 'em?" he asked bluntly. He saw he wasn't getting anywhere and moved on. "I'm sorry to keep you waiting, but we're doing a headcount as our workers surface. We initiated an emergency recall for all of our underground personnel when we got word of the terrorist threat, but it takes some of our miners two hours to get topside." He glanced at the four of us. "I have to say, I was expecting a few more people. Four of you won't be able to cover much territory down below."

"In two hours you'll have more help than you know what to do with," I said. "But we can't wait that long. We have a credible threat of sabotage against your mine. We believe the attack is planned for tomorrow, but we have no idea when. If the terrorists are using explosives, they may have already placed them."

Jones looked skeptical but didn't argue. I judged him as a man with a good deal of common sense. A brunette in a blue suit with her hair in a tight bun stepped into the room and handed Jones a folder.

"You wanted to know who's been in the mine in the last few days? Other than employees?"

"We should also look at employees you hired in the past six months as well as any who used to work for Transnational Coal. But the visitor log is a good start."

"We've only had three outside groups visit in the past two weeks. Some inspectors, a class from WV State and a PBS film crew."

"Did you know any of the visitors personally?"

"No, but the inspectors were from the Mine Safety and Health Administration. That's a federal agency and it was a scheduled inspection."

"What about the other groups. When were they here?"

"The students were here on Wednesday. The film crew was here on Friday."

"Where did they go?"

"The students went through the Epply portal. I don't know where they went from there but the man who guided them is topside now so I can ask him. The film crew...let me see...they used the Foley Portal because they wanted to see a longwall setup with robotic equipment. And their guide—oh, that's odd." Four heads jerked up.

"They were taken down by a relatively new supervisor. Jeb McFarland. He called in sick today."

"How long has McFarland been with you?"

"Three, maybe four months. I'll pull his file."

"Is it normal for a new miner to give a tour?"

"It's not. It's usually my deputy or me. I'll have to find out what happened."

"It makes the film crew a good candidate for us. Would anyone else here have seen them before they went down?"

"Yes."

"Give me your fax number and I'll have some photos faxed over. If we can match anyone we'll have a better idea where to look." Earl gave me the number and walked out of the office to tell his secretary to bring in the fax. I stepped outside and pulled out the satphone to call the operations center for the Activity to have the photos sent over. I would have had them e-mailed but Earl's computer didn't look like it was capable of displaying a photograph. Earl was back in five minutes. He handed me one of the faxed pages.

"Your boys sent over six shots. I haven't talked to my deputy yet but the Foley Creek foreman rode down on the lift with the film people and he thinks he remembers this one—one of the cameramen. Hard to be sure, though." The photo was grainy, and it was a surveillance photo, not a mug shot. But the man in the picture had a sickle shaped scar under his right eye that would be hard to miss. A marking in the corner of the photo told me that it was one of the men the Activity had identified in South Africa. I realized I should have asked for the photos earlier.

"I recognize him," I said. I'd seen the man the previous afternoon in the National Front's employee parking lot. He'd been shooting at me. He was a good shot, and I killed him while I was escaping.

Nichols grabbed the photo from Jones and turned to me. "Can your boss connect this man to an act of terrorism?"

"For the FISA court?"

"Yes."

"I think so."

"Mr. Jones, I'm going to need to take a statement from your foreman right now. Then I need a phone and a fax." Jones motioned to his assistant, who was perched in the doorway, and asked her to help Nichols; the two women disappeared. If Nichols could get an eyewitness statement confirming that a known terrorist was inside the Gilroy mine, she might be able to get a FISA warrant to give the FBI legal access to the e-mails from the National Front that the Activity had already accessed with PRISM. That in turn could give us enough evidence to get a warrant to search the National Front compound. I was ready to go back there and knock down every door until I found Heather Hernandez.

"I asked my deputy why McFarland gave the tour. Apparently they asked for him by name. They said he'd taken them around at Stony Creek, the last mine he worked. Plus he had ten years as a foreman there before he was laid off, so he was qualified."

"Who owns the Stony Creek mine?"

"Transnational."

"Do you have security cameras here?"

"Yessir."

"Would you have footage of this film crew?"

"There's a camera on each elevator. I think we keep about a week's worth of video on a DVR in the security office."

"Let's take a look."

* * *

Six of us jammed into the security trailer around a thirteen-inch black and white screen as the guard zipped through hours of footage of miners coming and going down the platform of the mine shaft elevator. The tension was palpable and I had the strong sense of time slipping away from us. But given the size of the mine, we had no choice. We could wander around for days underground without finding anything unless we were sure about where we were heading.

The security guy finally found what we were looking for. The PBS film crew was made up of six men, mostly big guys. I recognized the one from the National Front parking lot. I turned to Tim Quigley, the sergeant from the West Virginia State Police bomb squad.

"What do you think?" I asked as we watched the video. We watched the men enter and exit the elevator, after skipping through most of the footage of them standing in place in between.

"They're avoiding the camera," he observed—and he was right. The men had their heads down, turned away from the camera.

"Look at their gear. Can you guess how many devices they might be carrying with them?"

Quigley shrugged and ran a hand over his close-shaved head. "Hard to say. Looks like they have two camera bags plus the cameras. They could be hiding something in the cameras. If not, and depending on the explosives they're using and the design of the devices, they could easily have three or four complete devices. Less if they had to conceal the devices within the bags."

We both looked over to Jones. "We always check bags to see what visitors are bringing down into the mine. Can't tell you how many lighters we've confiscated."

"Maybe two or three devices, then. But don't hold me to that."

* * *

Back in his office, Jones turned to the map he'd rolled down from the wall. It was a cutaway view of the mine, showing different layers of activity.

"Here are the three portals—Epply, Foley and Glassy. Between Epply and Glassy is nearly four miles. In total, the mine spans across surface territory that's twenty miles long in some places. We've been working this mine for going on sixty years and there are over two hundred miles of tunnels in total here, not counting those that have been filled in. So the first thing to realize is the scale of what you're looking at. This isn't like visiting a paper plant and inspecting a couple of big buildings. This mine is more like the New York City subway system."

I looked at Nichols and saw anticipation warring with futility.

"The film crew went through the Foley Creek Portal. They were planning to see the Kitaniny Seam. That's our most productive seam at the moment—a forty-foot seam that we found two years ago 2600 feet down—a half-mile under the surface of the Earth."

Earl looked at the four of us seriously. "How many of you have visited a working mine before?" Not one of us twitched. Earl shook his head in disgust.

"I know the picture you have in your mind. A bunch of men with pickaxes on their shoulders riding in a little car down a roller-coaster chute, right? That's not hardly the situation here, boys." Nichols cleared her throat. "Excuse me, ma'am," he corrected himself.

"The Kitaniny seam is a longwall operation. We're using a piece of highly automated equipment that extracts and transports coal on its own without any assistance. We also have a few older continuous mining machines in operation on that line, but they're nearly a thousand feet shallower."

"If you were going to place a device to do the maximum damage to the mine, where would you put it?" I asked.

"Well, I can tell you where mines have had the worst damage from accidents. When mines lose elevator shafts, it limits our access to the rest of the damage. The Foley Creek portal has a passenger elevator and a coal elevator sharing the same shaft. The second area we worry about is the ventilation system. We set up ventilation lines along all of the working seams and in the main tunnels to evacuate methane from the mining environment. There are four conduits with aboveground motors that power the fans. We have to be extra careful around the ventilation because that's where the greatest concentration of flammable gases build up. Finally, there's the seam itself. We've had some issues recently with larger pockets of methane being released there. We had a fatal accident not eight months ago because of that."

"Is that something that other mines would know about?"

"Yes, it's all public. You can find a copy of the report on the Internet."

"Okay, I guess that gives us some places to start," I said.

"We'll need a guide," Nichols interjected. It was a statement, not a question.

"I'm responsible for safety in this mine. If someone put something in there, it's my fault."

"Thank you, Mr. Jones. We can use your help."

"I'll take you to the locker room now. We'll give each of you a suit to put on over your uniforms. You'll be glad when you see how much dust you pick up. You're going to get hardhats with headlamps, a methane detector and a self-rescue breathing unit. You'll also have a locator and a token for emergencies."

"You should activate all of the locators before we go under so the state police know where we are in the mine," Quigley suggested.

"That's a good idea. I'll explain how to use the breathing and safety equipment and some of the precautions that you need to take. Please listen carefully. You can't afford to make mistakes underground."

33

I'm not prone to claustrophobia. I can spend an hour inside a submerged wreck sucking on a re-breather without getting jitters or a whole day buried under mud, sticks and leaves in a gilly suit in the jungle. But when the elevator began to descend down the mineshaft, I felt the weight of the entire mountain pressing down on me. There's something fundamentally wrong with descending straight down beneath the earth's surface. On a primal level, you know that you're trapped, at the mercy of immense geologic forces held at bay by imperfect human technology. The explosives we were looking for might have been part of it, too.

The elevator ride was shorter than I expected, just a few minutes. In that time, we'd traveled down a distance that was twice the length of the Empire State Building. The car was quite large—big enough to hold twenty or thirty miners with ease. When we got out, though, it was all blackness save the faint glow of low-wattage lighting.

Sergeant Quigley didn't waste any time when we got out of the elevator. He motioned to Walters—the second bomb squad guy—who leaned down and talked to Cody before giving him a pat. The dog set off around the elevator at a brisk trot with Walters and Quigley close behind. Jones motioned to us to wait and hurried after them with a worried look on his face. Nichols and I looked around to get our bearings.

The ceiling was set low, a few inches shorter than me, and it was irregular. There were steel posts driven into the roof, supporting plates I assumed kept the whole thing from falling in on us. Given the near absence of light, I would have put numerous gashes in my skull without the helmet. Nichols could just stand but I had to hunch over. Nichols and I were staring at a large, low-slung vehicle with big wheels when we heard the dog bark. In a moment, Jones appeared and motioned to us. "They found something."

We followed him through a side tunnel past the large coal elevator. The car was sitting idle at the bottom of the shaft. Quigley, Walters and Cody were behind the elevator.

"Take a look." Quigley motioned to us. I peered over Walters's shoulder. The dog was sniffing at one of the enormous steel girders anchoring the elevator. An orange box sprouting yellow wires connected to four bricks of high explosive.

"Can you deactivate that?" Nichols asked.

"It's already done," Quigley said. "This is a commercial rig. They've just attached a timing device to a Lorica Electronic blasting system. They set the charges to amplify the damage to the elevator rail systems and collapse the shaft."

"This is very visible." I turned to Jones. "Shouldn't you have spotted it?"

"Nobody would be back here unless we were doing work on the elevator." Jones was staring at the blasting setup with a look of incomprehension.

"What are you going to do?" I asked Quigley as Walters withdrew a hard plastic Pelikan case from his gear bag and handed it to him.

"We'll leave the high explosive here for now. It's stable on its own. The guys who come after us will have disposal containers with them. But I'm removing the blasting caps. We don't want them anywhere near the Semtex." Quigley gingerly removed the caps from each block of high explosive, unwired them from the blasting system, wrapped them up in non-conductive insulator and put them into the hard case.

"The timer," I asked Quigley after he'd finished securing the blasting caps, "when was it set to go?"

"In two and a half hours." Silence. Nichols gave me a significant look and I was pretty sure we were having the same thought. We'd guessed wrong. Right about the mine but wrong about the day.

"You better tell the people up top not to send anyone else down after us," Nichols said to Jones. When she said it, any thoughts of cutting bait and hauling ass out of the mine dissipated. Jones looked shaken but he just nodded and walked over to the call box wired up at the bottom of the elevator.

* * *

"That dog handled himself pretty well on the helicopter," I said to Quigley as we rumbled through the mineshaft, sprawled in the uncomfortable, low-slung electric vehicle called a mantrip. If the elevator ride down to the bottom of the mine was quick, the journey to the Kitaniny seam was not—it would take nearly forty minutes in the subterranean people mover. Cody, having received a treat for sniffing out a bomb, was sitting happily next to Quigley, his tongue hanging out and his nose poked cautiously from the side of the vehicle.

"He's a veteran," Quigley said.

"Literally?"

"You bet. Iraq—two tours. He was a combat dog. Walters was his handler. He adopted Cody when he retired and trained him to be a sniffer. Cody is happiest when he's working," he said, scratching the dog under his chin.

"You served there, too?" I asked. Quigley handled himself like he'd seen a few things before.

"Yes. Three tours. We've met before, you know."

I squinted harder through the gloom. "I'm sorry—I'm pretty good with faces but I don't remember you." I'm told I have an eidetic memory. I don't know if that's true, but when I see something it usually sticks.

"I was wearing a blast suit at the time. In Fallujah."

"I was there more than once."

"This was in April 2004. I was an EOD specialist with the Second Infantry, Second Battalion. We were sent to help an A-team raiding a small munitions factory. The hadjis booby-trapped the entire place, bricked up the overhead entrances and blew a bunch of our guys to hell. We were trying to disarm some of the devices on a side door to give another assault team a way through when we came under heavy fire and got pinned down. It was just two of us in blast suits with six dead soldiers piled up around us. We called in and our Lieutenant said they were sending help. We sat there for nearly two hours, into the night, with these guys plinking at us every few minutes like we were squirrels in the vegetable patch. Without the blast suits, we both would have been dead.

"Eventually the shooting stopped—but not all at once. It got lighter and lighter for a while and then we noticed that nobody was shooting at us anymore. We had just started to work on the door we'd been trying to get through again when it swung open. A guy in black walked through and said, 'It's clear.' Then he took off his helmet and ran his hand through his hair. It was the same color as the uniform. I won't ever forget that face, even with the black paint. It was yours. You didn't say anything else; you just walked off.

"When we went into the building we found some tricky shit they'd left for us—all disabled. And about a dozen insurgents, all dead, some of them without a bullet hole in them or a drop of blood spilled anywhere. I remember asking the Lieutenant if he'd seen the rest of your team. I figured you were Special Forces or something. He just shook his head. 'That was a recon guy from one of the ghost JSOC units,' he said. 'They sent him in alone. As far as you're concerned, he was never there.' They gave us bronze stars for that action, but we didn't do a goddamn thing to earn them."

I didn't say anything and I don't think he expected me to. We both had particular skills, and he'd found a good way to use his after he left the service.

"So Mr. Herne, if you want to know why me and Walters are willing to take a trip into hell with a civilian to find explosives that may detonate before we reach them when nobody's life is at risk, it isn't because some politician told us to. It's because I know your character, I owe you and that's all that matters."

Quigley's words should have made me feel good, but I was distracted by a stronger sensation. I had a tingle in the middle of my spine, like an itch I couldn't scratch. It was the same feeling of being yanked around that I'd had since I first stepped in West Virginia. Like someone smarter than me was pulling the strings and I was one step behind.

34

"We've got another one." Walters's voice came from the darkness.

Nichols and I rounded a corner to find Quigley and Walters crouched over another orange box with three yellow leads snaking out of it. Jones was shining a battery-powered lamp on it while nervously checking methane levels on a handheld detector.

It had been slow going after the rush of finding the initial device so close to the bottom of the elevator shaft. If you've never been in a mine, you have no idea what darkness really is. The night sky is full of light, even when it's overcast. Even night vision goggles don't work in a mine because there is no light to amplify, only inky darkness. The narrow cone of a headlamp defines your world underground, and you're reminded of its limitations every time you stumble on uneven floor or bump your head against the irregular, low ceiling. We had to stay within earshot of one another because communications devices work poorly underground.

I had briefly entertained the idea of bringing goggles down in the mine anyway, for the infrared, but they wouldn't have helped. Infrared might have helped me see Nichols, Quigley and the others, but it would have done no good at all with the regularly spaced steel pillars holding the unnatural roof of the mine aloft.

We scouted a half-dozen different junctions of the ventilation system as we made our way to the idled mining machine on the Kitaniny seam. As we walked, Jones explained the basics of how the mine functioned. Long wall mining has been around since the late 17th century. The idea is simple: you cut coal out of the earth and let the roof collapse in on itself. The trick is to make sure that the seam doesn't collapse on you, by placing roof supports where you're mining. Now everything is automated, including the removal of the coal. On the new systems, the ceiling is held up by hydraulic lifts that are part of the automated face conveyer system mining the coal.

The Kitaniny seam was a big one—three hundred meters wide and nearly four miles long. The AFC was about a third of the way through it, so we had to travel along an access tunnel that had been cut alongside the seam. The vent for the gas and dust ran along the entire length of the tunnel, at moments intersecting with other vents running up or down to other seams. We stopped at each of these to let Cody sniff for explosives. It was painstaking work.

All of us were nervous because we were past our fail-safe time—the point when we'd need to turn back if we wanted to get topside before the first device would have detonated.

"What's the timer set for?" I asked.

"Same as the other one. Under an hour from now."

"Now we're committed."

Quigley didn't answer. He and Walters worked quickly to disarm the device and secure the blasting caps. As with the other charge it wasn't hidden, just set up where miners making their way to the active seam wouldn't accidentally stumble across it. We were moving again in ten minutes, and Jones stopped the mantrip after another ten minutes of travel.

"The AFC is about a hundred yards from here." He pointed.

"How far has it moved since that camera crew was here on Friday?" I asked.

"That's why I stopped. The AFC would have been right around here on Friday when the film crew visited. There were two shifts, but we discovered a binder in the seam during the second shift. Some kind of clay or shale and it's the devil to get out. We had to stop work to let the geologist evaluate it."

Nichols grabbed me as Quigley and Walters followed Cody toward the mining machine.

"Doesn't this strike you as a little too easy? Two devices almost in plain sight, set up so that a six-year-old could disarm them?"

"They weren't expecting anybody to be looking."

"I don't buy that. These guys are professionals. There have been at least two shift changes in this mine since they left. You think the elevators don't get inspected regularly when they're three thousand feet underground?"

"You think they're decoys? How would that make sense? They'd search this place high and low for anything else once they found them."

"I'm saying that it was too easy finding and disarming them if the men who did this are as experienced as we think."

It was a disturbing thought, but it made sense.

* * *

"Got you, you bastard!" Quigley said as he shone a hand-held light at a third explosive device, looking much like the other two.

"That's the beam stage loader," Jones explained. "This is the end of the cutting line. The shearer there," he pointed to an enormous piece of equipment over ten feet in diameter that looked like twin pizza cutting wheels with spikes protruding from the edges every foot or so, "moves along the AFC, shearing coal from the wall. The coal drops onto the conveyer and gets pulled down to the end of the line where it hits the beam stage loader. It turns the coal 90 degrees and drops it onto the main conveyer. The conveyer takes the coal all the way back to the coal elevator, where it's compacted and taken to the surface."

"Why would they put a device here rather than on the AFC itself?" I asked.

"I don't know too much about explosives, but the shearer makes a lot of noise and vibrations. And there are always at least two miners supervising it."

"Wouldn't they see something going on here, too?"

"Maybe. That would depend on how long it took to set up the bomb. The shearer takes a little while to get from one end of the seam to the other. They wouldn't see that back there unless they were servicing the machine, I think." I could tell that Jones was wondering if there was another man on his crew he couldn't trust.

"We've only got twenty minutes left on this one," Walters said as he reached for one of the blasting caps protruding from a block of plastic explosive. Something in my mind tripped, like tumblers lining up on a bank safe.

I dove at Walters, tackling him before his hand inched past the bright orange control box. Cody snarled and pulled me down by the arm. There was an awkward moment with the three of us piled up, both Walters and I trying to avoid tumbling into the device itself and the dog's growl echoing through the silent tunnels. Then Walters called Cody off and Nichols pulled me off of Walters. I felt bruises developing on my arm where the dog took hold of me, but he hadn't broken the skin.

Quigley had figured it out by the time Walters and I disengaged. He leaned in toward the device and pulled a light from his belt. "Turn off your headlamps," he said. When the rest of us complied, he clicked on the small light. Its four red led bulbs illuminated a narrow section of the commercial detonator. As he slowly moved them across the face, there was a stray gleam, an unexpected reflection of the light. He stopped and inspected closer then swore softly. "Son of a bitch." Turning the light slightly, he pointed to a monofilament strand the width of a mosquito's wing. "How did you know?" he asked me.

"I didn't. She did." I inclined my head to Nichols. "She figured out that the first two were decoys."

35

"There's a second device behind this one. They've got it rigged to go if the timer attached to the commercial explosive is disabled. What's our time?" Quigley asked. Quigley was on his knees on an antistatic pad he'd laid in front of the device. Walters was on the other side, flat on his back, looking up.

"Eighteen minutes," Nichols said.

Walters swore. "There's not enough time. There are two fully autonomous devices here, and I think both of them are booby-trapped and cross-connected."

"What if you had three sets of hands?" I asked.

"How long has it been since you disarmed an explosive device?" Walters asked.

"You don't want to ask me that."

"It doesn't matter," Quigley interjected. "It's the only way. We'll never make it out of here in time. And I for damn sure don't want to run to a safe room right now, hope we survive and try to live down here for a week while they dig us out.

Agent Nichols and Mr. Jones can hand us tools. Walters, you're on the primary and I'm on the hidden device. We'll do this step by step. Herne, you stand above me and do exactly what I tell you."

"Okay."

There's a game called Operation my sister Amelia bought for twenty-five cents at the Goodwill when I was six that we played obsessively one winter. It's a battery-powered board with a cartoon version of the human body on it. Each turn you draw a card and have to remove some bone or organ from the body. Each one of these—or at least the half of them that our game still had—sits in a recessed well with metal sides. You use metal-edged tweezers plugged into the board to do the surgery. If you touch the sides when you're operating, the game buzzes and a light comes on. We never had the rules so I don't even know how it was scored, but Amelia was great at getting inside my head to make me flinch. This time the stakes were dangerously—fatally—higher.

I spent nearly a decade in the Army, all but the first two years during wartime. I've seen a lot of explosive devices. I set some of them myself, but most of them were IEDs I discovered and marked. I disarmed my share, and some were tricky. But as far as explosives go, I'm more like a backyard chef or the guy who mods his Mitsubishi Evo than a real expert. I was looking at a device that was out of my league. We worked quietly, furiously for fifteen minutes. Then Walters came around to the backside of the loader with a hard plastic case that he'd been toting around in a gear sack. He opened it up and started assembling a tripod while Quigley explained.

"We've taken down the trip wires, the motion sensors and disabled the commercial device. But now we're at the tricky part and we only have about three minutes left. Do you see these blasting caps? They're not commercial, but I think there's a commercial cap inside. The outer layer is a hypergolic failsafe. If we remove the wire to the blasting cap from the power source, a small charge will dissolve a membrane in the sleeve surrounding the blasting cap that's currently separating two chemicals. Think shells and hydrochloric acid in middle school chem class, but about a thousand times more explosive."

"How do you disable that?" I asked as Walters completed the tripod and began mounting what looked like an oddly-formed telescopic rifle site on an articulating metal arm extending from the end of the tripod.

Quigley gestured to the tripod. "It's called a recoilless EOD disrupter. We shoot a water jet at the cap at a very high velocity. It knocks out the initiator and stops any chemical reaction."

"And it will disable the chemicals in the outer sleeve and the blasting cap inside?" Nichols asked.

Quigley shook his head as he knelt in front of the device. "That's the theory, but honest to God, I have no idea. I've never seen a design like this before. But this is our best shot." He looked at the timer and then at Jones. "Is there a safe room within sixty seconds of here?"

Jones shook his head. "It'd take at least five minutes to get to the closest shelter, even on the mantrip."

Quigley turned back to his work and finished positioning the disrupter. He looked up before he triggered it. "If I'm wrong, it's been good working with you all."

36

"We've matched both of the National Front men we identified in Africa with video records from the mine," Alpha told me as I sat on a hill overlooking Earl Jones's office, talking on an encrypted satellite phone. The signal was a lot better with a clear line of sight to the southern horizon. In the compound near the mine portal, officers from the State Bomb Squad stood alongside a dozen FBI agents flown in from Pittsburgh. Nichols and Quigley briefed them.

"So that gives us a definitive connection to the National Front?"

"Not definitive. But it should be enough for the FBI to obtain a search warrant for the National Front compound."

"I'm glad to hear that, sir. We won't find Heather unless we can get back in there."

"Based on your reconnaissance, do you believe that you can find her?"

I hesitated for a moment because I'd already answered this question for Alpha the day before, when Nichols had first given me the gear bag containing the satphone after I'd taken my involuntary motorcycle ride off the bridge. I reconsidered what I'd seen in the apartment Heather shared with Anton Harmon.

"I can't be sure, especially with someone her age. She could have stuffed a few essentials into a daypack and taken off. But she left a lot of insulin in the fridge. Apparently Harmon beat her pretty badly some time in the last few days. If she left the compound with visible bruises after that, she'd be gone for good. I think she would have taken all of her insulin. So if I have to guess, I'd say she's still there."

"Her parents were comforted to hear that she hasn't run out of insulin."

"That's the part that worries me, sir. If she was really sending a coded message about these devices, she could be in trouble."

"I agree."

"What about the mines in Wyoming, sir?"

"No progress. The mining equipment has been carefully inspected and it hasn't been tampered with. The FBI is doing a sweep of the sites, but they're enormous. We also have a conceptual problem understanding how those particular mines could be sabotaged. Surface mining as it is practiced in the western states involves blasting holes in the earth using a tremendous amount of explosives. Those mines routinely employ charges hundreds of times larger than what you found in the Gilroy mine today. The draglines are very specialized, expensive pieces of equipment, so disabling them would have an economic impact on the mines. But no evidence of tampering has been found. It's very difficult to see another way that this type of a mining operation could be impeded. Our theory of an attack on these Wyoming mines may be wrong."

"Then it's just a document release on the Hobart mine and the explosive devices we found here?"

"So it appears."

Neither Alpha nor I were entirely settled with that.

"With the immediate terrorist threat passed, I would appreciate it if you could refocus your efforts on locating Miss Hernandez."

"I'll do that, sir. But I also need to get back to work."

"Very few in Foggy Bottom are going to work tomorrow, Orion. The State Department is limiting non-essential personnel to help ease the rush hour in preparation for Hurricane Sandy, which is expected to make landfall some time in the evening. I'd advise you to stay put for the time being. There's no sense stepping into a hurricane."

But that was exactly what I was doing.

37

We sat in the back of a long, narrow restaurant with oak floors, a series of round mirrors and green-hued walls studded with modern artwork. I was staring at a pizza that had marinated pulled pork, caramelized onions, pineapple and jalapeños with the sort of distrust I normally reserve for the tap water in Pakistan. I was raised on a narrow set of staples: meatloaf, mac & cheese, hot dogs, that kind of thing. I've struggled with food ever since. During my years overseas I learned to eat lots of other things, from kebab to curry, but to me it was just like putting a sixty-pound ruck on my back— part of the job. A tentative nibble of the slice I'd been served confirmed my visual analysis. The place was called Pies & Pints and I couldn't blame them for my food issues. Nichols, Quigley and Walters had already wolfed down most of the colorful pizza.

"You've been run off the road, hit, kicked, bitten, tortured, shot at, rode off a bridge and nearly blown up in a mine, but you still haven't found that girl you came looking for?" Nichols said evenly as she reached for another slice.

"I've had better weekends," I admitted.

"Hell no you haven't," Walters grunted. Laughs all around.

"I found the apartment she's staying in on the compound. I understand that there's enough evidence now to tie the National Front to the Gilroy bombs. When is the FBI going to get into that compound?"

Nichols shook her head. "Everything's a mess right now. Six agents from my office are dead and a dozen are in the hospital. And now they're saying that this hurricane is going to turn into some kind of superstorm in the Northeast. Pittsburgh is our managing field office. They flew in a forensic team today to investigate the blast at Mr. Paul's house and sent an explosives unit to Gilroy, but we're not getting any more help until after the storm. I think the Bureau is redeploying a lot of agents to East Coast cities right now. We're on hold until this storm passes."

"That's ridiculous. The National Front will erase every trace of what they're doing."

"Don't you think they've already done that? They know we'll get a warrant soon. They've known that since you escaped yesterday. Anything that can be erased already has been. If there's a case to be made against them, we'll have to get someone to talk."

"Okay, fair point," I conceded.

"Are your people still watching the compound?" Nichols asked.

I looked at Walters and Quigley before I answered. My status was still a gray area as far as they were concerned. But they must also know that the governor had personally interceded with their bosses, so it was obvious that I had someone backing me. And they'd kept me from getting buried under a mountain, after all.

"Yes, they have eyes on, but they haven't seen anything helpful yet. They're not in a position to track the principals." The Activity was watching the National Front compound with drones, so they knew which cars were coming and going. It was possible to track individuals, but they didn't have detailed enough visual profiles of the National Front leaders to maintain that level of surveillance.

"That's frustrating," Walters said, "because they're bona-fide terrorists, that's for sure. What kind of West Virginian would want to kill miners, for God's sake?"

"Eric Price and Jason Paul are both out-of-staters." I found myself echoing Roxanne's words. It was true of her, too.

"Figures," Quigley grunted.

"I'm still a little surprised they killed Paul," Nichols said, fiddling with a piece of crust. "It's a terrible way to cover their tracks."

"Maybe they plan to pin it on the eco-terrorists?"

"No way. That wouldn't fly. They needed Paul to furnish the evidence to connect the dots to Reclaim. And this kind of murder looks a lot more like a gangland hit than the work of some radical lefty group. Besides, when you kill FBI agents, you're guaranteed to trigger the kind of investigation that's going to uncover the truth."

"That's a good point. These guys are professionals. They could have arranged for a heart attack or a traffic accident for Paul if they really wanted him out of the way."

"You met Jason Paul the other day. Did he strike you as a committed racist?" Nichols asked.

"No, but that's what you told me to expect, right? The MO of the new National Front is dentists and accountants for racial purity, that sort of thing. But still...he seemed more like an opportunist than anything. He might have some of the prejudices of the National Front folks, but he doesn't seem like the kind of guy who joins an extremist group. On the other hand, the PA has a lot of political pull. I can see why he'd want to be part of that. But it's still hard to imagine him putting anyone else's agenda in front of his own."

"So what if he was playing his own game? Joining the PA and helping the National Front, but all the while making his own side bets?" Nichols tapped fingers on the table.

"But if they didn't kill him...wait...are you thinking what I'm thinking? He faked his own death?"

Nichols nodded. "Either that or the National Front faked it to give him a way out. Listen, I bet they're still working the scene. Do you want to take a look?"

"I do."

"Mind if we tag along?" Quigley asked and glanced at Walters, who nodded.

"Don't you guys have somewhere better to be on a Sunday night?" I asked.

"My boy is already down for the night. And if there's anything I can do to get the sonofabitches who planted those bombs, I'm in," Quigley answered. Walters nodded to say that was enough commentary.

"You guys can come if you bring the dog," Nichols said as she dropped three twenties on the table and stood up. I got a feeling that this particular restaurant didn't welcome mutts, but after taking a look at the police uniforms and the FBI windbreaker, the hostess had decided not to press the point. With a wistful look at the uneaten pizza, Cody followed us out. We'd been huddling in the back of the restaurant and the place was now more than half full. I couldn't tell if the stares we got were from the dog, the uniforms or the coal dust that blackened our faces. Probably all three.

"What about the boyfriend?" Nichols asked as we walked outside.

"Harmon? What about him?"

"Did you find him?"

"No, he was gone. Sent away after he beat Heather up."

"Away out of town?"

"I don't know, but I understand he left the compound."

"Did you track his credit cards?"

"What?"

"If he's not spending cash, it's an easy way to get a fix on him."

I pressed the heel of my hand against the side of my forehead. "It honestly never occurred to me."

"You're not much of an investigator." Nichols smiled.

"Most of the people I've hunted never used plastic. I have no idea how you'd track a credit card in Yemen, anyway."

"Here in the US, people use them reflexively. Sometimes even when they don't mean to."

The rain was coming down cold and I turned my face up toward the night sky to let it wash some of the dust off my face as we piled into Nichols's Suburban.

38

Quigley and Walters formed their opinions of the scene at Jason Paul's house without me. When we arrived, they were let through immediately, but Nichols was unsuccessful in getting me in. She argued that I'd been on the scene as a guest of the FBI when the crime took place, but the Bureau's lead forensic investigator from Pittsburgh was having none of it. So I waited just outside the yellow tape while the three of them scoured the scene. It seemed like the more tenured the agent, the less interested he was in cooperating with outsiders.

The house had a big divot taken out of it, like Paul Bunyan had whacked it with a monumental four-iron. The fire crew must have arrived pretty quickly because two of the wings were still standing. But the central structure, the oldest part where I remembered a very solid double oak door with brass fittings, was just a pile of scorched rubble.

"They've got part of the device," Walters said when the three of them met me back outside the security perimeter.

Cody had stayed outside with me, perhaps understanding that the smell of soot and ash would overwhelm his sensitive nose. "It's the kind of rig they'd use for a mountaintop removal operation. Not that different from what we saw underground at Gilroy, but a different brand. They overdid it on the explosives, though. They damn near blew the hell out of this neighborhood. This house is heated with natural gas and the explosion tore into the basement. Came pretty close to the burner and the gas lines."

"DNA evidence?"

"They'll find some, but it's going to be hard to know where it came from. The body was very nearly vaporized. I'm not sure if they're going to be able to distinguish DNA from the body from anything else that would already have been in that room. And you can forget dental records."

"So we don't know if it was actually Paul in that chair?"

"Not with any certainty."

"And what do you think happened here?"

Quigley weighed his words. "We'll never know who died here from the evidence at the scene. Since it's Paul's house and the FBI was coming to arrest him here and an agent saw a man tied to a chair before the device exploded, the county coroner will issue a death certificate for Mr. Paul. If I was trying to fake my own death, this is how I would have done it."

"What do you think?" I asked Nichols.

"The only forensic trail that's going to lead anywhere is financial," she said. "If we assume he set this up in order to disappear, we'll want to look for offshore accounts, aliases, and a way that he might have used them to make a bet on energy futures."

I sat down on the granite stoop, about the only part of the main house that was still intact. In my head I stepped back to the beginning and put myself in Paul's place. It's a trick I learned overseas. Not from the army, actually, but from an Arab man I spent an afternoon with while waiting for the sun to set in Yemen. When I traveled in the Middle East, I habitually carried a small chess set with me. Most men in the region played, and it was an excellent way to stay alert while I passed time.

This particular Yemeni asked if we might reverse the board for a moment in the middle of a game, when I'd unexpectedly put his king into check. When I asked why he said, "You must always think of the board from the position of your opponent." After he'd had a chance to peer from behind my pawns, he laughed as he tipped over his king. "The best players can see both sides of the board in their minds. Not I."

As I played through events from Paul's perspective, I saw a break—a flaw in the pattern. I opened my eyes to see Quigley and Nichols staring down at me.

"Let's say Paul did kill himself and that the FBI never caught on. The National Front would still have known that he was running his own game. They'd obviously know that they didn't kill him, either. And they've got the kind of men who could track him down wherever he went. So why take the risk? Paul could have just holed up on the National Front compound for the time being. If the scheme gets blown, he could always make a run for it later."

"But we were already coming to arrest him," Nichols pointed out.

"Good point. But that's only because Paul screwed up when he blackmailed the Reclaim leader, Roxanne. Now you guys have her in custody and she's going to testify that he was complicit in the sabotage against his own mine."

"Which would be a good reason for the National Front to want to kill him before he flipped and pointed it back to them."

"But what if his disappearance was part of the plan from the beginning? He was always going to be the weak link. If the Bureau brought him in, you'd eventually uncover his connection to the National Front."

"Unless we weren't looking for it," Nichols said.

"Right. If what looks like a hit job at first glance quickly starts to look like a disappearing act by Jason Paul, that changes the story, doesn't it? Imagine that you find a bunch of financial bets that Paul made against his own company and his own industry. He makes a quick score, converts his off-shore accounts to bearer bonds or something and disappears while the FBI is still trying to figure out whether he's dead or not."

"Then it would look like this whole business was a get-rich scheme Paul cooked up on his own. The tapes and everything else would prove that he was trying to implicate Reclaim. And Roxanne could testify that Paul had blackmailed her."

"That makes sense. But what does the National Front get out of this?"

Nichols answered quickly. "They're much more sophisticated in their financial dealings. They have the ability to get thousands of individuals to place bets for them. They might not even need to. If you buy the shares of a company right before it takes off and make a windfall, there will be an investigation. But natural gas futures are widely held. If the price spiked, so many people would make a killing that the National Front could get lost in the shuffle."

"But this leaves some open questions, doesn't it?"

"Right. For instance, why has the National Front been trying to kill you? Why is the girl important? Were they afraid she'd warn someone about the Gilroy mine?"

"Harmon certainly would have known the plan, so it's possible," I suggested. "But in the note she wrote to her mother last week, Heather said she was going to run out of insulin tomorrow, not today. She was specific about the day. Gilroy was clearly timed for today. So what if she was trying to warn us about something else?"

"What?"

"I don't know, but it might still involve energy. We don't know why the National Front would want to sabotage power stations in South Africa. How does that help them blow up a coal mine? They already know how mines work."

"Yeah, I agree. We're still missing something."

"So you folks think the whole business today was some scheme to blow up energy prices?" Quigley asked.

"Not oil but maybe natural gas or coal."

"Shutting down a coupl'a mines in West Virginia wouldn't do that. Production out west's way bigger than here these days."

"Right, that's what the analyst told us," I agreed. "At first we thought they might try to sabotage Wyoming surface mines where Paul worked previously, but that seems unlikely."

"And your analysts think a terrorist strike on Gilroy would have a big effect on prices?"

"They don't know. Maybe, because it's hard to tell with terrorism. But it's not certain. Commodities analysts know that it's not too difficult to mess with an underground mine. But surface mines use blasting to get at the ore, and they're enormous. They're not so vulnerable to terrorism. We can't see how you'd threaten them."

"Oh that's easy," Walters said. All three of us swiveled toward him.

"Easy?" I asked.

"A dirty bomb." Walters crossed his arms when he said it. I looked around, suddenly concerned we were being overhead. But the cops manning the tape were swarmed with reporters.

"How would these guys possibly get hold of the materials to make a nuke?" Nichols asked.

"I didn't say a nuclear weapon, I said a dirty bomb. For a dirty bomb, you don't need weapons grade uranium or plutonium, just highly radioactive material. The bomb itself is conventional, but it spreads out the radiation pretty widely."

"I thought the whole idea was discredited," I said, trying to recall what I'd heard from the WMD briefings during the Iraq war.

"As a way to kill people, it sucks. You never get high enough radiation levels to do much damage. Conventional weapons like a fuel-air bomb work much better. But if you're trying to turn a working mine into a superfund site, you couldn't do much better. If you took the kind of charges we saw yesterday and upsized them for the kind of demolition work they do at surface mines, then packed a bunch of radioactive material around it, you'd create about a century's worth of EPA litigation in a heartbeat. Nobody would be able to touch that coal in our lifetime."

"Is there any chance that one of the power plants the National Front targeted in South Africa was nuclear?" Nichols asked, straightening up.

"I'd better find out."

39

Alpha reached me on the tarmac of Chuck Yeager airport, which had temporarily re-opened to allow a single government plane to land. "I just spoke with the South Africans. You may find this interesting. The reactor that experienced the incursion last month does not create weapons grade plutonium as a byproduct. The spent fuel rods from that facility primarily contain thorium and reactor grade plutonium. Shortly after the security breach, the database that tracks inventory at the nuclear waste facility co-located with the reactor became corrupted.

"A manual count was ordered, and it appears from the existing paper records that two fuel rods might be missing. But there was a gap of some weeks in the physical paperwork, so that was thought to be the source of the discrepancy. Because the rods in question did not contain weapons grade plutonium, this was not reported to international agencies."

It was a few hours to midnight and the West Virginia governor had declared a state of emergency. An exhausted flight controller told me that Charleston was expecting a foot or more of snow and blizzard conditions overnight. The rain had picked up and the wind was gusting heavily.

"Could they have gotten radioactive material out of the country and into the U.S. undetected?"

"It would have been difficult, but not impossible. The control rods are not as large as you might think. Breaking them down would be hazardous but not complex. Major airports and ports in both South Africa and the United States have radiologic detection equipment. But there are thousands of private airports in both countries. We've observed jets taking off from South Africa under visual flight rules, flying to Namibia and then diverting to international routes from there. It could have been done."

"I thought the South African incidents were intended to cripple the power industry?"

"It appears so. A technician who performed an inspection ahead of schedule because she was about to go on vacation found a device that would have exploded and triggered a containment leak and a major nuclear crisis. Stealing some commercial-grade spent fuel is a minor crime by comparison."

"Do we have enough evidence to make this scenario plausible?"

"We have another new piece of information," Alpha responded. "We sent over Mr. Harmon's photo to the South Africans and asked them to check it against their plant records. There was a visual match—he had been issued a contractor pass for that day. We're cross-matching photos of all the other visitors at the facility on that day with National Front members. We'll send photos and profiles to your device in the next twenty minutes."

"One of Heather's friends—her roommate at the commune—mentioned Harmon had taken a trip while the two of them were together."

"Given his familiarity with the Hobart mine, it's a cause for concern. But if a radiologic device is anywhere near that mine, they'll find it."

I heard the squeak of rubber as a jet touched down and then the whine of engines reversing before a Gulfstream appeared. The cold, driving rain beat against the fuselage of the executive jet. We were just a few degrees away from snow. I jumped back into the Suburban with Nichols and we drove onto the runway, followed by two other black Chevys with flashing lights. As the doorway to the plane opened and the staircase dropped down, I had my first glimpse of one of the specialists who had made it to Charleston less than two hours from the moment I first called Alpha.

There's just one agency that deals with radiologic threats in the U.S.: NEST, the Nuclear Emergency Support Team. I didn't see how we could call them in with unsupported speculation. But when I spoke with Alpha and laid out our suppositions, he had no qualms. He notified NEST immediately, then contacted the South Africans.

The NEST team mobilized from Andrews Air Force Base so quickly that we had to leave the crime scene at Jason Paul's house abruptly to prepare for their arrival. Nichols liberated two extra Suburbans from the FBI carpool and Quigley called in the State Police SWAT unit to meet us at the mine entrance. A team of eight rumpled looking men and women filed from the jet. I greeted the man at the front of the line, a thin, graying scientist with rain-splattered, steel-rimmed glasses and a firm handshake.

"I'm Michael Herne. It's my fault that you're getting wet. This could be a false alarm."

"Dr. William Harris. Call me Bill," he said as he shook my hand. His voice rose as the Gulfstream's engine powered back up and the plane glided off toward a hangar. "Don't worry, Mr. Herne—most of what we do is chase down false alarms. But the last time we found a functioning radiologic device, the woman who called us in said the exact same thing."

"We found explosives set in an underground mine today a few hundred miles north of here. We've tied them to the guy running a surface mine about twenty miles from here," I said as I looked at the rest of his team. They were male and female, young and old. They all carried various backpacks and pieces of luggage that I'd been told contained testing equipment rather than personal essentials. They looked a little like an American tour group preparing for a safari.

"And you think he's concocted a radiologic device?"

"We think he—or a group he's been associated with—plans to scare the markets by disrupting the country's coal supply."

"How?"

"He's affiliated with a group that may have stolen spent fuel rods from a reactor. If he did set a device, there's a good chance it's at his own mine—the largest surface mine in the state and the second largest mine overall. The biggest one is the underground site where we found the conventional explosives."

"That seems a little self-destructive. Blowing up his own mine, I mean."

"He wasn't going to keep the job for long. We think he faked his own death this morning."

"You've had quite a day," Harris said. I exchanged a glance with Nichols.

"This group has been very aggressive in trying to keep us out of their business. Is your team armed?"

"Heavens no! We're scientists. We like to be attached at the hip to law enforcement. We'll rely on you for security," Harris said, glancing at Special Agent Nichols.

"There's a state SWAT team meeting us on site. How do you need to conduct your search?"

"We can do it from vehicles if we drive slowly. The trick is separating the signature of a radiologic device from background radiation, which may be especially difficult in a mine. But we have lots of experience with doing our job in difficult conditions and this isn't the worst we've seen."

"I'm sorry to bring you out here in this weather. I'm afraid it's about to get a lot worse."

"I work in a lab without windows all day. I love getting out in bracing weather like this."

I smiled. "I think we're going to get along just fine, Dr. Harris. Did you bring something for me?"

"Ah, yes, the courier almost missed our departure, in fact. We have several bags for you. Heavy ones."

"They always are."

40

A shot rang out, shattering the silence of wind and rapidly falling snow. I didn't see the muzzle flash; I'd been looking too far north as I scanned the ridgeline. Nichols tapped my shoulder. "Eleven o'clock at 1600 yards," she said. I pivoted slowly and adjusted the infrared scope. I found what I was looking for: the glowing white silhouette of a prone man with a sniper rifle, the barrel still hot. As I adjusted the scope again for the range and calculated the effect of the wind, another shot rang out. Sirens wailed and the Hobart mine exploded into activity.

We'd met the State Police a quarter mile from the main mine entrance. The command staff rode in a purple and blue recreational vehicle functioning as a mobile command communications center. A dozen cruisers and two armored trucks accompanied them. Nichols had wrangled a warrant to search the mine and its offices, but Colonel Smith—the gray-haired, green-clad head of the State Police—didn't ask to see it. After five years in which not a life had been lost, the West Virginia State Police had two troopers killed in August, when a detained suspect produced a hidden weapon in the back of the car.

Now four of his men had perished at Jason Paul's mansion, and a dozen more had been wounded. The troopers were hungry for blood. Surrounded by tragedy in the face of a rapidly building blizzard, they had lost interest in the niceties of criminal procedure. If we had asked them to level the mine offices with bulldozers, they would have done it.

The task of searching the mine for an explosive device in a snowstorm was compounded by the mine's size. The Hobart mine sprawled over an area ten miles wide by five miles long. The entire site was sunken below the surrounding topography and shielded by ridgelines. Five roads entered the mine, not counting the main entrance, but in practice four of them ended at cliffs several hundred feet above the mine site. The roads had disappeared as surely as the mountains they'd once scaled.

We spread topographic maps on a planning table inside the purple RV and pored over them with Nichols, Dr. Harris, Colonel Smith and Sergeant Ogletree from the West Virginia Special Response team—as the state SWAT team was called—along with Quigley and Walters.

Dr. Harris confirmed that the most likely place to plant a device would be near the active mining activity, where the conventional explosive would stir up enough dust to allow the thorium, plutonium and depleted uranium from the control rods to disperse as widely as possible. That put our primary search area under a sheer wall shaped like a horseshoe that ran up some 300 feet above the mine. I'd seen the site twice in the daylight—once from the inside and once from above—and I was worried.

I ran the math in my head again, to make sure I'd lined the shot up right. I relaxed, slowed my heart rate, held my breath and then gently, smoothly squeezed the trigger of the rifle. The big Barrett—an M107A1 if it matters—punched against my shoulder. It was a lighter punch and less of a bang than I remembered because this was a new model, and suppressed at that. But it still made a big noise when it fired and I held myself absolutely still under the thermal blanket that Nichols had pulled over us. The blaring sirens of the cruisers helped to cover the sound of my counter-fire, but anyone near enough to the bullet would still hear the supersonic whine.

"Got him! I mean, *hit*," Nichols corrected herself. "Next target one o'clock, 1900 yards."

When we looked at the mine site, Colonel Smith, Sergeant Ogletree and I saw the same thing: a shooting gallery. We hoped Harmon had planted the device and left—or better yet, that we were really on a wild goose chase and there was nothing to find. But if it had been me and I really wanted the thing to go off, I would have put snipers up on top of the ridge overlooking the mine. They could bring any search to a dead standstill for hours, and remotely trigger the device when they were forced to retreat.

And that's exactly what they'd done.

It took me longer to find the second target. He was better dug in and I couldn't see his entire body with the thermal scope—just his head and the silhouette of the gun barrel. I wouldn't even have spotted the gun barrel if it hadn't been warm because he'd just fired it. I switched between monochrome and color display on the FLIR scope. Nineteen hundred yards is over a mile, and the wind was gusty and unpredictable. Several inches of snow had already drifted onto the heat-reflective blanket we were under and without the thermal scope I couldn't see much past ten feet.

"Miss! Say eighteen inches to the right," Nichols hissed. My second shot went wide. But it was close enough so that the shooter felt the round impact the ground next to him and realized he was in my sights. He rolled, jumped to his feet and started to run. "Hammer, we have a target on the move in sector three." Nichols spoke over the State Police radio, about the only communications device that functioned reliably in the hills.

We'd divided the horseshoe-shaped ridgeline around the mine into eight sectors. The rapid response teams had cut around the mine and were waiting to comb the woods as we identified the shooters. To conduct the search at ground level, we paired the NEST scientists with State Police cruisers and sent them in through the main entrance. They started with lights flashing but no sirens, so we'd hear if someone started shooting. And someone did.

Sergeant Quigley took one of the FBI Suburbans in through the main entrance and Dr. Harris rode with him. Nichols and I followed the rapid response teams around the perimeter of the mine, cutting off-road to avoid the half-hour it would have taken to connect the main roads. We stopped pretty quickly, choosing a spot on the extreme southern end of the site, nearly at the beginning of the cliff wall. It made for some long shots to the opposite canyon wall, but gave us a wide field of vision. We had parked the Suburban at the base of the hill and stripped down quickly, donning the white camouflage artic combat uniforms I'd asked Alpha to send along with my care package. I averted my eyes when I caught a flash of a sports bra and remembered briefly that Nichols was unmistakably a woman. We sorted and divided the rest of our gear before scrambling up the hill and settling in before signaling the others to proceed.

"Third target, 2300 yards, two o'clock. Check that, third and fourth targets."

I might make a shot like that in a competition, or on a nice day at the range. But the odds weren't good with the wind picking up and snow pelting us and melting off the barrel of the Barrett. I went through the routine anyway, calculating how much the round would drop, guessing at the wind, calming myself and holding my breath before I squeezed again.

"Unbelievable! Hit! On the shooter. Spotter is on the move." Nichols put a hand on my shoulder as she said it.

I didn't wait, chambered another round and sent it flying toward the second man. He was bent over the shooter for a second, then sprang to his feet.

"Miss. Two feet left. Spotter is moving away from the hill." A pause. "Hammer, we have another target moving in sector...ah, sector 5." An instant after Nichols said the word, a mound of snow erupted just in front of us, temporarily blinding me. I rolled over Nichols with the rifle as a second round struck where I'd lain. I reached my feet and grabbed Nichols's hand, pulling her behind me. She sprang forward as a third round puffed behind her, the crack of the rifle following it. I ducked behind an old oak and pulled the rifle back to my shoulder. She settled next to me and was back on her infrared binoculars.

"I think I've got him," she said after a moment. "He's thirty yards north of the third shooter. Say three o'clock."

I dropped to the ground and took aim at the fourth shooter. I went through the calculations quickly but I knew that in these conditions, the shot was a Hail Mary.

"Miss. Four feet to the right. Target is up and moving." Nichols relayed the last man's location to the SWAT team. I raised my scope and watched. I briefly got a bead on the man again, but he was darting and weaving. The Barrett rounds can penetrate the steel plating on an armored car, so I didn't want to take the chance of hitting a state trooper when the shooter was heading right for them.

Nichols and I must both have been tracking the man because I heard her gasp as I saw a streak of light flash onto my scope. Then suddenly the man was down, wrestling with a ball of light.

"What was that?" Nichols asked.

"Unless I'm mistaken, that was Officer Cody."

41

Nichols and I had done our part.

Even though I'd missed half my shots, we'd spotted five men. The three I hadn't hit fled straight into the SWAT drag-net. I watched through the scope as a swarm of white bodies appeared along the ridgeline. There might have been more than five National Front guys dug in out there, but any soldier with half a brain would have turned tail by now given the combination of counter-sniper fire and mop-up teams.

"We've got three in custody now," Nichols said, "and two confirmed kills."

"Good."

"Do you think it worked?"

"We'll have to wait a little longer to know."

We held our breath. Whoever had put the snipers on the ridge wanted the dirty bomb to detonate, but didn't want to be anywhere nearby when it did. Instead of setting it on a timer and leaving, he'd left snipers to protect the device. That only made sense if one of the snipers had a remote detonator to trigger the device when they were pulling out. They'd figured the authorities would turn cautious when they started shooting and that it would bog things down for hours. That's not what happened.

One of the pieces of equipment I'd requested from Alpha was a high-power signal jammer. We were hoping they'd constructed the dirty bomb with a commercial rig, because we could jam that part of the radio spectrum effectively. If they had military-spec equipment, Nichols and I might be covered in radioactive dust very soon. We waited for what seemed like an eternity. The snow was coming down harder every minute. It was cold—absurdly so for a place that had been eighty degrees a couple of days earlier. I tugged at the sleeve of my jacket and peered at my watch. It was past midnight. Nichols crept back toward the edge of the cliff and grabbed the thermal blanket. She shook it off once. It had a hole in it. She pulled it over us and we crouched close, waiting. I pulled the rifle back up and kept my eye on the scope. There were patrol cars slowly moving around the mine site, trying not to get stuck in the snow, sand and muck.

Then Nichols put a hand to her ear, listening intently.

"They found something."

* * *

"This would have done the job quite nicely," Dr. Harris said. They'd already disassembled the device by the time we got there, and separated the radioactive material from the high explosives, blasting caps and assembly. Harris had just pulled the headgear off of a radiation suit and motioned us to join him after taking a radiation reading. He showed me the trigger mechanism.

"Does this look familiar?"

"Sure enough. It's rigged the same as at Gilroy." Walters answered for me. I looked down at Cody, who was sitting alertly at Walters's side, as if he hadn't just taken down a veteran sniper.

"They over-engineered this device. There was enough plastic explosive to send a dust cloud over Charleston with the prevailing winds. I doubt it would have killed anyone, but you could be sure there'd be a lot of cancer ten or twelve years from now..."

"That's a cheery thought."

We walked away from the NEST team and drove back to the mine entrance. We'd just gotten out of the Suburban when one of the SWAT vans approached the pool of cruisers parked around the purple RV. Sergeant Ogletree hopped out.

"That was some damn fine shooting. What the hell was that, two thousand yards?"

"Twenty-three hundred," Nichols said.

"I was Marine recon and I've never seen anything like it—not in these conditions."

"It was a lucky shot," I said. I saw from his face that I would never convince him, but I was telling the truth. It was amazing I'd hit anything at all with the wind swirling and gusting to forty miles per hour. I changed the subject. "Did you get them?"

Ogletree nodded. "Three alive and two dead. Even had a bomb dog take down one dirtbag."

"I'd like to see them."

"The live ones aren't talking," Ogletree said, "and we've got someone from the U.S. Attorney's office here now so we have to play it by the book." This he added with some regret.

"I just want to take a look at them. I'm looking for one man in particular."

"Ah, gotcha. Hang on," Ogletree said as he spoke into the radio he'd clipped to his vest. "Okay, the live ones are in the back of our MRAP and the meat wagon is coming around with the other two."

We walked around to the back of the armored vehicle and Ogletree pounded on the back. The doors swung open and another black-helmeted trooper swung down.

"Haul 'em out for inspection," Ogletree said to the trooper. Two more state troopers carefully brought out the three men. A man in a hooded raincoat over a suit scrambled after them. He interposed himself between the prisoners and us.

"I'm Assistant U.S. Attorney Mark Sweeder," the suit said. "These men have invoked their Fifth Amendment rights and asked for their attorneys, and I'm afraid I'll have to direct you not to question them until he arrives." From my perspective, Sweeder looked to be about nineteen years old, but I had to assume he'd finished law school.

Sweeder addressed Nichols. She pulled out her I.D. "Special Agent Sabrina Nichols, FBI. I'm invoking the public safety exception to Miranda—New York v. Quarles. The Nuclear Emergency Search Team just defused a radiologic weapon one mile down that road. Do I have your attention, Assistant U.S. Attorney Sweeder?" she snapped as Sweeder looked down the road that led past the mine office into the mine.

"Yes, ma'am, er, yes Special Agent Nichols," he said. The boy lost about two inches during the exchange.

"We will interrogate these men at length, but first we need to attempt to identify them. Sergeant, can you please give us a good look?"

"Yes, ma'am," Ogletree replied, snapping to attention. He barely concealed a grin. The state troopers stood the three men up and hit them with the floodlight from one of the cruisers. I stepped closer. They'd lined the perps up by height. The first guy was 5'10 or so, thin and had dark hair and a bushy beard. He wouldn't meet my eyes. The second was my height with sandy brown hair and a mustache. He kept his gaze straight ahead as well. The last guy was a true Aryan specimen: 6'2", blond with the strapping kind of good looks you imagine all Swedes must have until you visit that country.

"Daniel Lee Stewart. Marine Scout Sniper, 2004-2008. Twenty-five confirmed kills. Bronze Star, Unit commendation, Purple Heart. Dishonorable discharge after court-martial trial for raping an Iraqi woman in a mosque. Was he firing an M-14?"

"Yes he was," Ogletree answered. Unlike the other two, Stewart had his eyes on me. He was angry.

"You very nearly got me, Corporal. That was a hell of a shot in this weather."

Silence.

"Agent Nichols, I recognize Corporal Stewart because he is one of our video stars from Africa. He was part of the team that infiltrated the Koeberg nuclear power station, set an explosive device and apparently stole control rods."

Stewart looked surprised. It only lasted a second, just a minor facial twitch, but I knew I had him. In fact, I was bluffing. I knew his face and background from the profiles of National Front members I'd reviewed that morning. But he wasn't one of the faces they'd matched from the reactor. He's the man I would have taken on that job, though, so I guessed, and I could tell that I was right.

"Let's look at the bodies," I said as one of the Surburbans pulled around. The State Trooper inside popped the trunk and Ogletree gingerly zipped open the bag. "Gotta be careful, here. This boy is not all in one piece. That cannon of yours nearly cut him in half."

This one I recognized. Bobby Glenn. He had served with the 82nd Airborne. He was one of the saboteurs the Activity had spotted in Africa. The last body was another stranger.

I was turning back toward Nichols when I saw Colonel Smith over her shoulder. He had his hat on and he'd straightened his tie.

"I have some bad news. I gather you haven't been told. The first shot hit Sergeant Quigley. I know he was with you today at the Gilroy mine. They just pronounced him dead on arrival at Charleston General. There were two more troopers hit and they still have a fighting chance. I want to thank you for helping us stop these lunatics. It's a shame we couldn't have brought all the terrorists in like that," he said, glancing at the body bags.

My fists clenched involuntarily. I swallowed. I looked at Nichols and saw a reflection of what I was feeling. I remembered that Quigley had mentioned having a young boy and felt myself retreating, growing cold around the heart. Nichols and I stood silent for a moment. I realized for the first time that she'd known all the FBI agents who'd been killed earlier in the day— and perhaps their spouses and kids, too. I met her eyes.

"None of these guys is Anton Harmon," I said.

"Where does that leave us?" Nichols asked.

"With unfinished business."

42

MONDAY

I remember a particular helicopter ride in the Hindu Kush. It was at the beginning of the fighting season, the last year that I was with the Activity, in the Nuristan province of Afghanistan. There'd been a heavy firefight that day. The Taliban had ambushed a Special Forces team trying to extract one of their leaders. At they end they'd identified their man but had to withdraw with heavy casualties. I was sent in alone that night to finish the job. It was just past winter, in the tallest mountains in the world, in a specially modified helicopter flying at the extreme limit of its operating ceiling. Riding any helicopter in those mountains felt like being the little white ball in a table tennis match, but that one was worse. There are some times you just know that an aircraft has given everything it has but it's still not enough, that your life depends on how severe the next burst of wind shear is and whether it slams you into the mountain.

When Colonel Paine pulled the nose of the Gulfstream off the runway in Charleston, I had that feeling again. As the aircraft powered off the white strip, a huge snowy fist slammed into us and we were suddenly staring at the ground. The stall warning went off as the fierce blast of wind pushed us downward.

We'd figured it out in the Suburban, as we crawled back from the Hobart mine toward Charleston and the blizzard got steadily worse around us.

"Anton Harmon was at the Gilroy mine yesterday and Hobart today, right?" Nichols asked, her eyes fixed on the road ahead as she drove with complete confidence in zero visibility conditions.

"Definitely at Gilroy. If he was at Hobart, he left before we arrived."

"Why did they leave snipers guarding that device?"

"To keep us from getting to it."

"No, I mean why didn't they just put it on a timer and set it to detonate as soon as they were a safe distance away? Why risk sending men to guard it? What's the point of that? Now we can connect the device to the National Front."

"What do you want to bet that those men end up swearing that Jason Paul hired them? This could be part of making him the fall guy."

"So if the National Front was so keen on making sure the dirty bomb wasn't defused before it detonated that they were willing to leave snipers to guard it, why didn't Harmon stick around?"

"Maybe he isn't suicide squad material?"

"Or maybe he had something bigger to do. And maybe that's part of the reason for the snipers...to give Harmon time to do something else."

"Go on..."

"Didn't you say that the woman you're looking for sent an e-mail to her mother last week?"

"Right. That's why I came here to begin with."

"And in the message she says she'll run out of insulin on Monday, right?"

"Yes."

"Not Sunday?"

"No, it was Monday."

"So if that message was a warning, then it wasn't about what happened today. It's about what's happening tomorrow."

"It's already tomorrow. I mean it's after midnight now. It's Monday."

"Right, but all the explosives at Gilroy were set to go off on Sunday. Even the dirty bomb at Hobart was set to go off before midnight."

"So?"

"So maybe there's another part to the plan. One that Anton has to finish himself."

I chewed on that for a minute. "Anton has an electrical engineering background. I think they said he was a civil engineer."

"Okay..."

"So I wonder where he was actually working before he went fulltime undercover for the National Front."

"Why don't we ask your magic 8-ball?"

"He'll love that you called him that," I said and pulled out the satellite phone. Alpha was still awake and at the tactical operations center. He had the answer in five minutes.

"Mr. Harmon was sentenced to three years for sexual misconduct and battery. He had relations with a seventeen-year-old girl and assaulted her when she tried to end the relationship. But he spent two of those years on work release in Illinois."

"And what was he doing?"

"He was working in a power plant." Alpha sounded angry, undoubtedly unhappy that the analysts at the Activity hadn't asked the same question about Harmon's background.

But I wasn't angry at all. The last puzzle piece slid into place. Suddenly it all fit together. I put the phone on speaker so Nichols could hear.

"Sir, I think I know what the National Front is trying to accomplish. It's more than just raising funds. I think I know why they infiltrated the power plants in Africa."

"Blackmail of some kind?"

"No. The National Front has been building political influence for the past ten years. Part of their strength is that they're not partisans, at least not in a conventional sense. They focus on minutiae—small, technical, local issues—and they give money to both Democrats and Republicans. They mask their real motivations behind a bunch of political action committees. And they've avoided national politics because that would tip their hand. But right now a black president is running for re-election. And I'm told the vote will be close."

"You think they're trying to tip the election?"

"They wouldn't do anything that revealed their role because it could backfire with voters. That's why it's too dangerous for them to get involved with big national elections on the political level, right? Too many questions," Nichols chimed in. She knew where I was going.

"Right. But if you know the election is in the middle of a busy hurricane season, then..."

"Power outages," Nichols said.

"Right. A blackout. A huge, messy, utter blackout like the one we had on the East Coast back in 2003."

"Which makes everything that happened in Africa a trial run," Nichols concluded.

"Pennsylvania is a swing state in this election," Alpha said.

"Right. And if you handled it right—if you hacked the grid, you could ensure that some kind of isolated power problem turned into a widespread outage just as a storm hits."

"But they couldn't have known that a storm would hit so close to the election," Alpha pointed out.

"Maybe that wasn't part of the original plan. A messy blackout could have hurt the administration regardless of the circumstances. But they had to be thinking about hurricanes. The eastern seaboard has something like a 50% chance of being hit by a hurricane every year," I argued. "So maybe they wait for a hurricane but decide that they're going create a power outage within a week of the election even if there's no storm. And then along comes Sandy and all their prayers are answered. A massive power outage that makes hurricane relief and recovery harder would make the administration look incompetent right before the election."

"But if it was shown to be the work of terrorists, it might have the opposite effect."

"Maybe. But short of us wandering into the middle of this whole scheme looking for Heather, what are the odds that it gets uncovered in the next forty-eight hours? After that it's academic."

"Good point."

"Sir, do you have any information from the National Front servers?"

"Our cryptographers have full access, but they're working through a tremendous amount of data. A good deal of information was deleted, but we apparently have the ability to recover some of it. Now that we have something specific to look for, we might move quicker."

"Did you check Anton's credit cards?" Nichols asked.

"I believe we ran a check. Hold the line."

Nichols and I rode in silence for a half-hour with the line open before Alpha returned. I could tell he was excited because he spoke more precisely.

"We have something. There is a single credit card charge from Mr. Harmon's personal credit card about two hours ago from a gas station in Mechanicsburg, Pennsylvania. We also crosschecked power plants in that area against the National Front information we've decrypted and found schematics for a coal-fired plant near Reading. Homeland Security is speaking with management at the plant right now."

"They'll have called everyone available in to work by now, right? And security will be high. If Harmon went there, I bet he's already on the payroll."

"We can work with the plant manager to identify him."

"Do that but don't have them approach him. Right now he still thinks he's in the clear and this plan only works if it goes undetected. If he gets an idea that we're on to him, he may do something unpredictable."

"We can get a team there in two and a half hours," Alpha said.

"Sir, with your permission I'd like to finish this. Special Agent Nichols and I can track down Harmon."

"I thought you were stranded in the middle of a snowstorm?"

"Agent Nichols is driving us through that, sir. If you can get us a plane, we can get to the airport."

"Actually, there's a government Gulfstream G650 fueled and sitting in a hangar at Chuck Yeager airport right now," Nichols said, loud enough for Alpha to hear.

"I can get you that plane," Alpha said, "but the pilots may not be willing to fly in this weather."

"Let us handle that end," Nichols said.

"I'll see what I can do."

Alpha made good but was right about the pilots. There were two of them. The Gulfstream's captain was a civilian government employee and the co-pilot was uniformed military—an air force Colonel. As far as Captain Malisse was concerned, a non-nuclear emergency didn't make his list of priorities. He wasn't about to take the plane out of the hanger in a blizzard, let alone fly it. He had a civil servant's "you can't fire me" attitude about the orders he'd received from Washington. As far as he was concerned, he was the man on the spot, the plane was his and it wasn't going anywhere if he didn't think it was safe.

Nichols saw it differently. She started with national security and used progressively stronger language until she actually pulled a pair of handcuffs from her belt. The Captain, a tall thin man with slicked back hair, turned and walked out of the hanger. The uniformed officer, Colonel Christian Paine, didn't move.

"Colonel Paine, will you fly us out of here?"

"I'll fly you through the goddamn hurricane if you want, but it's a two-pilot aircraft."

"I'll be your co-pilot," Nichols said.

"Are you rated on a G650?" Paine challenged her.

"Nobody is, other than the two of you," she responded. "This jet isn't supposed to exist yet. I thought the first delivery was going to be next month to some billionaire."

Paine smiled. "Tell me more."

"I'm rated on the 550 and current," she said. I looked at her quizzically. Her expression said *long story, don't ask.*

"There are important differences, but you'll do. Are you gonna cover my ass when Captain Malice complains?"

"I'll take care of that," I said.

"You'd better. Or I'll be grounded."

Which was exactly how it was looking as the earth approached us in a rush just seconds after takeoff.

Paine and Nichols had worked side by side on the electronic navigation systems; quickly running through the checklist and filing an instrument flight plan as the plane rolled to the runway. I sat in the jump seat behind the two pilots and watched as a plow finished a sweep of the runway that cleared four inches of snow from the tarmac.

Then we took off. It was a surreal experience. I've been on small jets before, but most of my time in aircraft has been in helicopters and big, ponderous troop transports. The Gulfstream was a rocket. Until it wasn't.

We'd been flying into the wind to take off, but it must have shifted direction, because the bottom seemed to fall out from underneath us and the stall warning went off. We were less than two thousand feet in the air and we lost half that altitude in a few seconds. Paine and Nichols stayed calm, though, and suddenly the plane started ascending again.

We left the snow behind in West Virginia. But some time after we'd left the Hobart Mine, Hurricane Sandy had made its anticipated left turn back toward the continental United States. Instead of a hurricane, we'd soon be dealing with a superstorm. It was still sixteen hours before the storm made landfall but already a driving rain and high winds were lashing the seaboard. Even inland, the weather was disturbed. We touched down on the 7,000-foot runway at Lancaster Airport. The power plant was about halfway between the airport and the town of Reading. As the Gulfstream engines powered down, Nichols flashed me a brilliant smile. She looked alive in a way I hadn't seen her in the three days I'd known her.

"You enjoyed that flight, didn't you?" I asked, shaking my head.

"It never gets old," she replied, patting the aluminum skin of the Gulfstream as we walked down the staircase toward the cascade flashing lights surrounding the runway.

Paine stayed in the plane and kept one engine running, ready to set off again quickly if necessary.

"Are you going to vote for him?" she asked me, shifting topics as walked down the stairs onto the runway. I understood the question. The majority of military guys vote Republican. But we were risking our lives to save the political future of a Democrat.

"It doesn't matter. I don't much care one way or another. I've met politicians and they all sound pretty much the same to me. But I'm not going to let a bunch of supremacists rig the election. And electoral fraud isn't the worst part. You know what happens when there's a long blackout? People die, especially seniors. Hospital patients get sicker instead of having surgery. It's harder to clean things up and ordinary, hardworking people suffer. I'll be damned if I'm going to let that happen."

Nichols smiled again. I guess I passed the test.

43

"The men you're looking for aren't here," Mort Anderson, the plant manager of the Lime Rock Generating Station, told me the minute we'd cleared security. He must have seen the look in our eyes because he quickly added, "They left less than an hour ago. One of them had a family emergency and the other guy was his ride. They were only on shift for four hours."

We could have passed them on the road from the airport, I realized.

"Wait, men? More than one?"

"Yes, two men from the list." Anderson looked at us as if he'd need to spell the big words out. "Isn't that what you were expecting?"

Both Nichols and I started to speak at once but Anderson held up his hands to forestall us. "I'm sorry, but the call I received from Washington was very specific: I was not to do anything but figure out if any of our employees matched your head shots. So I had to sit down with my security director and the head of HR and match entry records and badge numbers to photos without alerting anyone else. That took two hours. This request came at the worst damn time for us, too. There are incidents from Long Island to North Carolina right now and it looks like we're going to have a bunch of blackouts in New Jersey in a matter of hours."

"We understand, Mr. Anderson," Nichols said. She'd pulled an FBI windbreaker on in the Gulfstream after we landed. "Did they explain what those men were here to do?"

Anderson nodded vigorously. "Ruin my career! Turn the next month into a living nightmare! Yes, I understand. The men we identified—Harmon and Greenwalder—"

"Greenwald," I corrected. He was one of the National Front men who'd taken part in the South African plant sabotage.

"Whatever. They were contract engineers. They've been here about a half dozen times in the last year, always together. We've isolated the section of the plant they were assigned to today and we're inspecting it carefully. If they sabotaged something, we'll find it. Given the concerns about the integrity of our software, we're also about to reboot the mainframe and restore our operating system from a backup. Do you know what that involves? This is a twenty-seven-hundred megawatt facility. Do you know what happens when we go offline for an hour? Do you understand how complicated that is for the grid, especially right now?"

"We understand what will happen if eight states go dark during a hurricane, Mr. Anderson. We believe that any damage these men did to this facility would have to look like an accident, or it wouldn't accomplish their goals. We'll leave you to your business but we need to see if we can identify the vehicle that Harmon and Greenwald are driving." Nichols understood that there was nothing we could do at the power plant. If the men had set something up to fail, it would have to be subtle enough to look like an accident when it caused the blackout. I hoped Anderson and his crew were up to the job of figuring it out. I was pretty sure they'd have plenty of help very soon.

"If you catch them, bring them here and we'll fry them for you," Anderson said, stopping at a door just thirty yards or so from the main entrance. He knocked before tapping his security pass against the gray pad and entered when the lock disengaged.

"This is Eddie Capella from HR and Jill Seeley. Jill is our security director. Jill, these FBI agents need to get a visual of the gate entrance for badges..." he paused to look down at his clipboard, "55327 and 56134. Subcontractor is Webb Engineering, names are Anton Harmon and Alexi Greenwald."

"The guys we just identified?" Jill asked.

"The same."

Jill stood and walked over to a printer, pushing her head to the side with the heel of her hand to stretch her neck. She came back with two pieces of heavy photo paper and handed them to Nichols. I looked over her shoulder to see pictures of Harmon in a Mustang with stripes on the hood at the guard gate and the back end of the same vehicle on its way out. The time stamp on the second photo showed that he had almost an hour on us.

"I figured this would be the next thing you people asked for when we realized these guys left the facility. Unless I'm mistaken that's a 2009 Mustang Shelby GT500. West Virginia plate number G23 569. That car's a scorcher, but I wouldn't want to be driving it in this weather."

"Thanks very much. This is impressive." Nichols shook Jill's hand.

"I hope you catch the sonofabitch," Anderson said. He was edging back to the door, clearly anxious to get back to his task.

"Pennsylvania has highway cameras all over the state. You can even access them on the web. The state can grab you the last location of a specific vehicle if you have a plate number. There won't be too much traffic right now," Jill said and leaned down to grab a pen. She scribbled a name and number on a post-it and handed it to Nichols. "My ex works for the highway authority. Tell him the check is late."

44

"We've got a hit," Nichols said as we boarded the Gulfstream. She had her cellphone pressed to her ear. "The Mustang is on Interstate 76 heading west. He was six miles east of Harrisburg ten minutes ago."

"Speed?"

"They're calculating. We need to get airborne and get ahead of him."

We touched down at the Somerset County airport about 120 miles east of the Lime Rock plant twenty minutes later. Paine had left one of the Gulfstream's engines running, and he stayed in the cockpit chatting with the nervous airport manager for our entire absence. I strapped into the jumpseat directly behind Paine and Nichols as they ran through the last steps of the preflight check while we rolled onto the runway. Our departure was less dramatic than the escape from West Virginia, but the flight was just as nauseating. By the time we were in the air, the air traffic controller was clearing us for a flight plan to Somerset airport some 120 miles to the east.

Some math geniuses with the Pennsylvania State Police had pegged the Mustang's speed at 72 miles per hour, which was aggressive for the weather conditions even though the speed limit on that stretch of road was 70. State police set up a roadblock two miles from the airport, and on our request an all-wheel drive Ford Taurus Police Interceptor stood empty alongside the tarmac in Somerset with an escort of three fully-manned cruisers. We had just ten minutes to make the roadblock. There was already a line of traffic on the westbound lane of the highway when we arrived.

"I'm Captain Lee, from Troop K." The police commander introduced himself when we hopped out. "If your suspect is on this road, we'll get him."

"How far back does this jam extend?" I asked.

"Two miles right now. It's building, but nothing like it would be without this weather."

"How long until it backs up far enough for traffic to start bailing at the last exit?" Nichols asked.

He shook his head. "That's twenty miles. Unless we're running this until rush hour in the morning, it won't be half that long. Especially with the hurricane coming."

"We need a snare," I said. Both Nichols and Captain Lee looked at me oddly.

"A snare?"

"A tempting diversion to trap him with. This guy," I said, speaking loudly over the rain, the sound of sirens and police loudspeakers, "has been trained in evasion. Once he sees the roadblock, he'll find a way to take off. If we don't channel him, we could get a bunch of people hurt. What we need is to leave him an escape route that we can control. Somewhere we can take him down safely."

"What are you thinking?"

"Do you have any gated service roads on this highway? Something that leads off to a rural area that isn't built up and doesn't have a lot of connecting roads?"

Lee nodded vigorously. "There's one about a mile and a half east of here, at the intersection with Huckleberry Highway. Troopers use it. The only way he'll be able to go from there is north, and the only town near there is Shanksville, which has a population of around 200."

"Send a cruiser through there right now," I said, getting into the Taurus on the passenger's side, "and have him leave the gate unlocked and a hair open. Let's get on the other side. I want three or four miles to run him down. He's not going off-road in that Mustang."

"Okay, follow me," Captain Lee said. His eyes were dilating a bit and his skin was flushed. "I'll take you the back way and we'll figure out the plan while we drive."

I let Nichols drive because I understood the difference between a good pursuit driver and a naval aviator. Her instincts were a lot better at high speeds.

"Is this a good idea?" she asked as we peeled away.

"If you try to take a man like Harmon down in a crowd like this, he's going to blow something up, I guarantee you."

"Because that's what you'd do?" she asked.

"No, not here. Not with civilians around. But I'm not him."

45

Waiting is always a letdown after you've raced hard to get somewhere. That's when doubt creeps in. What if they don't come this way? What if we've read the whole situation wrong? But I had some confidence in our plan. One vehicle had already escaped through the hole we'd created—an impatient trucker hauling cupcakes. We let him go. The Activity had managed to retask a satellite and get eyes on the highway and they identified the distinctive striped top of the Mustang just as it reached the traffic backup a half-mile from the gated exit we'd unlocked.

Nichols and I sat in the cruiser just a few hundred yards from the off-ramp. We had the Taurus pulled back on a dirt road beside a red horse trailer in the shadow of a ramshackle farm building. We were staring at a tiny cemetery on the other side of the road with fifty or so unadorned headstones silently bearing the rain. It was past dawn, but the pallor of the sky was unrelieved by direct sunlight. The State Police Captain was parked next to us and a series of units blocked off three side streets in the next mile of road that weren't dead ends. I was thankful we were in farmland.

"Do you think they'll take this route?"

I lifted my hands. "I would. They can't be sure the road-block is for them but they must know they're caught if it is. An interstate with a full median and guardrails doesn't give a sports car a lot of options. When they see the gate open at the trooper exit, they'll wonder if it's a trap. But really, what choice do they have? Getting onto a country road at least gives them a chance of escape."

"And why are we giving them a better chance to get away?"

"We've got two very dangerous men in that car. They're armed and they've spent the better part of the last three days trying to blow things up. If they realize they're caught, they may decide that death by cop is a better option than being sent to prison as white supremacist terrorists. A lot of people could get hurt."

"Is this personal?" Nichols took her eyes off the road to look at me. "Do you want to be the one to take Harmon down?"

"I do, but not for the reason you think. Most of these state guys have never seen men like him and Greenwald." Alpha had forwarded highlights from Greenwald's file to me. He'd spent six years on SEAL Team Two.

The police radio in the center column crackled just then. "Suspects turning off of I-76. I repeat: we have a red Mustang exiting the interstate onto Huckleberry, copy."

Nichols picked up the radio. "This is Special Agent Nichols with the FBI. Please stay dark until we light him up. If you stop this vehicle, DO NOT APPROACH. We have two suspects who are interstate fugitives and both will be armed and dangerous."

Ten seconds later the Mustang screamed by.

The driver saw us. I knew he would. Two state police cruisers sitting off the road just after dawn stick out, even when they're trying to be inconspicuous. The moment he spotted us, he put his accelerator to the floor. The Mustang made a sound like God's own trumpet and left two black streaks on the damp pavement as it peeled off. I couldn't see inside the car to tell who was driving, as the windows were tinted far beyond the 35% allowed in West Virginia. The front windshield was almost entirely reflective, and I caught a glimpse of swirling clouds where the driver's head should have been.

Nichols gunned the Taurus and we swung out onto the road behind the Mustang as it receded into the distance. I found the switch for the siren and the lights and flicked them on. Behind us I heard Captain Lee's cruiser follow suit. The modified Taurus picked up speed smoothly, and soon we were up over a hundred miles an hour. Small intersections flew by, and the lights of State Police cruisers blocking the side roads seemed to bend along with the Doppler shift of the sirens as we passed.

I glanced down to the speedometer, something that Nichols certainly wouldn't risk. We were pushing 130mph and the Mustang was still pulling away from us. Red brick farmhouses rushed by in a blur. Cows in a field stood alongside tremendous round bails of hay saturated with wind-driven water. Even with four-wheel drive, the speed felt perilous. The roads were still damp. Swirling winds threatened to push us into a ditch. Even a substantial puddle could send us into the next county as we plowed straight down the middle of the two-lane road. In the distance, we watched the Mustang blaze through the intersection with Corner Stone Road. It was the one we'd been worried about because it led to the only major cluster of inhabited buildings in the area: the small town of Shanksville. The police had managed to get two John Deer tractors and a cruiser in front of that intersection, and the driver could only have made it past them by running into a fallow field, which would have been a ballsy move with a $60,000 Mustang.

We weren't losing any more ground to the Mustang as we crossed Corner Stone, which meant that he was going as fast as he dared. I was relived to see that the troopers had managed to close off the next few small roads leading to subdivisions around Lake Stonycreek with a combination of cruisers and more commandeered farm equipment. Three miles further down the road, the Mustang hit the first trap.

The goal was to slow him down, and the staties had managed to pull campers across Huckleberry and the eastbound side of Lincoln Highway. Other than turning back straight into us, the Mustang's only choice was a sharp turn left to head west on Lincoln. He must have slowed down to sixty or so to make the turn, but he still slid the rear out and slammed into a vintage aluminum Airstream camper with the back end of the Mustang. That cost him a rear quarter panel and precious seconds, and we'd nearly caught up as he cleared the intersection.

Nichols managed to put the Taurus into a masterful drift right through the turn, clearing the broad side of the crumpled aluminum camper by inches. Four wheels bit as we pressed forward on Lincoln Highway, passing a red barn posing as a country market and a battered colonial advertising BBQ. Just as the Mustang's driver tamed its wandering rear axle and started to pull away from us again we saw a puff of smoke, and the red-striped hot-rod started spinning.

46

Hitting spike strips at high speeds can create the kind of accident most people only see in Formula One racing. The Mustang didn't give us that kind of show, though, because we'd slowed him down at the turn. But the momentum the speeding car carried was still impressive. It spun three times then rolled over, doing a complete turn over its roof before finding its wheels again. The car ended up facing us from the oncoming lane of traffic, with the trunk busted up against a wooden power line pole and the rest of the car pressed against a guardrail.

We narrowly avoided the same fate. The trooper who'd dropped the spike strip was just a hair slow in retrieving it. Nichols hit the brakes as soon as the red Mustang hit the spikes, and swerved as she saw the trooper trying to gather in the strips in a hurry. We still grazed the strip with our right rear tire and it blew out, but Nichols worked with the stability control system and anti-lock brakes to keep us from hitting the Mustang head-on.

I heard the pop of pistol fire just as I noticed holes sprouting in the windshield of the Taurus. Three rounds in a fairly tight group had struck the driver's side.

The driver's door started to swing open and Nichols, who had ducked down when the windshield was struck, plowed the Taurus right into the Mustang, pushing the car backward, smacking the opening door with our steel brush guard and pinning the Mustang to a side rail. I jerked against my seatbelt as the Taurus came to an abrupt stop, then I was out the door. Pulling myself up with one hand on the roof and another on the door, I popped onto the hood of the cruiser and leapt onto the crumpled roof of the Mustang, trying to land on the somewhat intact c-pillar.

As I hit the roof, a man slid from the passenger window. He was tall and broad shouldered, and when he started running he moved with some grace. The man sprinted through waist high scrub brush toward a stand of chest-high saplings. Beyond them was a vast open field.

"I've got the runner," I yelled to Nichols.

I hit the ground in stride and closed the distance between us in thirty yards. I was good for a 4.4 forty in high school and I've only lost a tenth or two since I hit thirty. When he heard my footsteps, the driver half-turned with a Browning Hi-Power semiautomatic pistol, and I juked as he fired twice at me. He took off in a different direction, but had to thread his way through the saplings. I took an angle on him, and caught him about a dozen yards further on, when he started to turn again with the Browning.

I planted my face in the side of his ribcage and wrapped him up, ducking underneath his gun arm as I brought him down. It felt just as good as hitting a scrambling quarterback in high school. He met the wet grass face-first, the air coming out of him in a rush.

His left elbow jabbed back toward my face and as I moved to avoid it, he hit me in the bridge of the nose with the back of his head. My ears rang and I jerked back, then realized he was trying to free enough space to roll and bring the Browning to bear on me. So I slammed my forehead between his shoulder blades and pushed him forward as he tried to rise, grabbing his gun arm at the elbow and pinning it back to the ground.

He rolled left, and I let go of his arm. I splayed my legs out to stop him from pulling me under him and brought my freed hand down on his elbow like a hammer. It was bent at an awkward angle as he tried to twist the Browning to fire at me, and I felt something snap when I hit it. His grip relaxed for an instant and I pulled the automatic from his grasp and rolled away. He started to rise, but thought better of it when he heard Nichols and Captain Lee shout. Nichols had a Glock 23 pointed at the man's chest and Lee was wielding a shotgun. He dropped back to his knees and I got a look at his face. It was Greenwald.

"Did you get Harmon?" I asked Nichols as I stood. I cleared the chamber of the Browning and ejected the magazine, handing them to one of the troopers who'd followed Captain Lee. Two more troopers moved in quickly, cuffing Greenwald and professionally searching him.

Nichols shook her head. "There was nobody else in the car."

"What?"

"It was empty."

"How did he get out? Did we confirm that both of them left together?"

"I'll call the plant right now but I remember the manager—what was his name?"

"Anderson. Mort Anderson," I prompted.

"Right, I remember him saying that the guard had checked both men out together in a Mustang."

"We need to look at a map," I said to Captain Lee.

"I've got one in the cruiser."

An FBI helicopter had braved the weather and was landing a dozen yards down the road from the Mustang and the state police cruisers. It was Hostage Rescue. Alpha had sent the cavalry, after all.

"Be careful with Greenwald," I told Captain Lee as we walked back toward his car. "He's dangerous."

"This field has seen worse," he replied. I stopped and looked back toward the vast expanse of grass and then at Captain Lee, a question on my face.

"We're just outside of Shanksville. United Airlines Flight 93 crashed in this field on 9/11, about a mile south of here. If you look at that semicircular road, the memorial is just north of it. When the plane hit, they'd just about finished reclaiming the ground."

Nichols and I looked mutely over the vast green space that spread out as the land gently fell below us. Even Greenwald stopped struggling with the troopers.

"Reclaiming it?" I asked.

"Didn't you know? This used to be a strip mine."

47

"Okay, boys, we've found your train." The pilot's voice came through the comm system on the Blackhawk.

It was good news. The train's GPS locator had been disabled an hour earlier, and it was running through the rainstorm twenty miles per hour above the track speed. Traveling at nearly seventy miles an hour, the mile-long freight train was near its theoretical maximum speed, less than twenty miles from its destination.

We'd been flying two thousand feet up, in a UH-60 Blackhawk moving at top speed to intercept the train, all the while buffeted by winds and pelting rain. The hurricane was still eight hours from landfall, but its brawny presence was tangible in the wind. The clouds were lying low and moving fast, not settling long enough to become fog. Nichols was as calm and collected a passenger as she had been co-piloting the Gulfstream. She'd spent the better part of an hour trying to convince the Hostage Rescue team commander to let her jump onto the train when we found it. Gatto wasn't buying it. The famously bald Kip Gatolewicz had been the Master Chief of DEVGRU before a brief and unsatisfying stint in the private sector pushed him back to the government. His wife had prevailed on him to find a stateside job, though she was less than thrilled when that job was leading one of the assault squads of the FBI's elite Hostage Rescue team. Gatto and I knew each other from the old days, which was a good thing. I don't think he'd have let me on his helicopter otherwise, regardless of his orders from Washington.

The argument between Nichols and Gatto ended abruptly with the pilot's announcement. I looked out the window to the cabin door as the pilot banked the helo. The train briefly appeared between the clouds. Two orange engines pulled 118 tanker cars full of crude oil extracted from tar sands in Canada. It was just minutes from crossing over into New Jersey from Pennsylvania.

Gatto made his way forward to speak with the pilot then came back and knelt down in front of me. "Okay, Orion, I have orders to put you on top of that train. I don't know how the fuck you managed to get clearance, but you're first on the deck. The plan was to put you down with three of my guys on a fast-rope but that's not going to work. We've got driving rain and fifty-five knot winds. The only way you're getting on that train is to jump, you read me?"

"Yes, chief."

"I'm going to try to get three of my guys down after you. One is going to help you get your man and the other two will uncouple the tanker cars from the engine. This train will take two miles to stop at this speed. If my guys can't uncouple the cars and you can't stop that engine, you're going to have to find a way to get the fuck off, because it's coming off the rails."

"The track doesn't run straight into the refinery, does it? Can't we just lock the switch to keep it on the main line?"

"It's an electronic switch and the control center has been disabled by a cyber-attack. There are three other failsafe measures that keep these trains from derailing inside a refinery. Do you wanna bet these dirtbags haven't found a way around them, either? We've fucking gamed this exact goddamn scenario before, but not during a hurricane. If this train blows inside that refinery it's going to barbecue the whole fucking state of New Jersey."

"I read you, Master Chief."

"Be goddamn careful because nobody trains for this kind of shit. There's rain and wind and two moving objects. This is more like landing a bird on a carrier than jumping into some field in North-fucking-Carolina. I can't let your partner leave this helo because it will end my cushy life in the government, but she could be more qualified for this than you, do you read me?"

"Loud and clear, Master Chief."

"Okay, get ready. Sit your ass down as soon as we open the bay door and watch me for the jump signal."

Then it was hand signals as the other men adjusted their helmets and gear.

Jumping from a helicopter onto a moving train in a hurricane was already a worst-case scenario. The helo pilot had to match speed with a train moving seventy miles an hour and maintain a straight and level course while gale-force winds buffeted the Blackhawk.

When we dropped down closer to the train, though, I spotted another problem. No coal cars. In fact, there was hardly a flat surface to be found. An open-top car would have at least ensured that I wasn't going to fall off the speeding train. But this train was made up of just one thing: an endless procession of oil tankers. The tankers looked like grain silos tipped onto their sides with narrow, 30-inch walkways slapped on top. Low iron rails on either side of the walkways made jumping onto them in the wet impossible.

That just left the engines, which were situated butt-to-butt so the front engine faced forward and the second engine faced backwards. Each engine was about forty feet long. There was a dome over the engineer cabin. Behind it, a ten-foot stretch of flat grated decking was joined to several irregular sections with odd angles and protuberances. The helo pulled down over the flat section of the second engine.

I got the signal when the pilot was as close to the surface of the locomotive as he could manage—about seven feet between microbursts of turbulence. I gave the thumbs up to Gatto, focused on a spot near the center line of the second engine and jumped.

* * *

We'd been stumped at first, looking at the state map by the roadside in Pennsylvania. Greenwald could have let Harmon off anywhere along the route from the power plant to the road-block and it may have just been to pick up another car. But none of us believed that. For one thing, the Shelby Mustang was registered to Harmon and a man like that doesn't give up the keys to his ride without a good reason. It suggested that Harmon didn't want his car anywhere near where he was heading.

Captain Lee, Nichols and I leaned over the map, shouting ourselves hoarse in the wind and the rain. The Blackhawk carrying Gatto and the rest of the Hostage Rescue team landed while we were still crouched over it with flashlights, two troopers holding ponchos over our heads to keep it from getting soaked. We all thought Harmon was up to something else, but nobody had any idea what it might be.

Nichols had the breakthrough. "Do you remember exactly what Heather's e-mail to her mother said—the exact wording?" she asked me.

"Yes. It said, 'Mommy I miss you. I'm going to run out of insulin and gas for my car on Monday and I wont be able to get more. Can you please help me? Sorry about things. Tell Dad I miss him. Love you. H.'"

"She said she's going to run out of gas, not just insulin."

"And we know she wasn't going to run out of insulin."

"And then she says she won't be able to get more."

"Gas or insulin?"

"Exactly!"

"There's something else I just realized," I said. "In the note she says 'Dad' but I was told she called her father 'Papi.'"

"Why didn't her parents notice that?"

"Maybe they did. Maybe that's part of the reason they asked for help."

"What do you think the part about gas means?"

"Maybe she's saying there won't be any more gas available after Monday?"

"It could be. Could the National Front sabotage a refinery?"

"There's no way Harmon has been working at a power plant and a refinery for the last year," I pointed out, "so it would have to be terrorism. If they blew up a refinery, it wouldn't look like an accident."

"Unless you ran a train into it," Gatto said. We turned to him as he poked a finger toward New Jersey. "The oil that supplies East Coast refineries used to come in from overseas by tanker. Not anymore. Now it comes overland from Canadian tar sands. A lot of it travels by train. A train full of crude oil at full speed is a big goddamn bomb. And if it derails in a refinery, it could look like an accident because shit like this happens when engineers get drunk. There wouldn't be any evidence left to find after the explosion, anyway."

A call to D.C. revealed that an oil tanker train had passed through Harrisburg less than an hour earlier, on its way to a refinery in Greenwich Township in New Jersey, across the river, just south of Philadelphia International Airport. The FBI contacted the rail company, which confirmed they'd lost contact with the train after a massive network failure had disabled their control center. We sprinted for the helicopter. Alpha had already greased the skids with Hostage Rescue. The sensible thing would have been to board the train from a vehicle driving alongside it, but the terrain didn't lend itself to that kind of solution, and we couldn't get the right kind of truck into position quickly. Given the speed the train was running, it probably wouldn't have worked, anyway.

* * *

I hit the top of the engine and immediately lost my footing. I sprawled with my arms and legs wide and managed to get a gloved hand into the metallic grate I'd landed on before my whole body went over the side. For a few seconds the outcome was uncertain as the rain and wind beat at me and my legs slid off the train and started to pull the rest of me with them. Then I got another hand around and latched it onto the grate. I pulled myself back onto the train and clipped a carabineer into the decking. The other end was attached to my belt by a six-foot nylon strap. Then I looked up to the Blackhawk and waved the next man down.

Things started to go south the moment he released from the helicopter. A burst of wind knocked the Blackhawk toward him and the side of the bird hit him in the back of the head. His Kevlar helmet kept him from being killed instantly, but he pitched forward, nearly missing the train altogether. As he flew past I managed to get a hand through the harness of his assault rifle, an M4. His momentum would have carried me off the train but for the carabineer rigged to my belt. He was dangling off the train from a gun strap as I heaved him back. We both collapsed onto the deck of the engine. I pulled a glove off and checked his pulse. He was alive and breathing, but unconscious.

Gatto was yelling in my ear, but I didn't hear him until I had the operator secured to the deck with two more straps crisscrossed across his torso to the grating.

"Orion, Copperhead, what is your status?" he said for the third time.

"Read you, Dogpatch. Copperhead is down but alive and secure."

Gatto said something unintelligible through the comm, perhaps cursing in a language we didn't share.

Then I heard gunfire.

The Blackhawk veered off immediately, disappearing into the storm that pressed against the train. I leaned over the right edge of the engine and saw the muzzle flash of a rifle from the open door of the lead locomotive. A few seconds later, the Blackhawk pulled back into view. It was ahead of the train and off to the starboard side. A fusillade of small arms fire streamed toward the train. It was smart positioning, because the doors to the engineer's cabin faced back toward the rear of the train. The HRT snipers were trying to avoid hitting the train controls while forcing Harmon to step out of the cabin to return fire.

I unhooked myself and gained my feet, then sprinted forward as fast as I dared. While the Blackhawk continued to engage Harmon, I reached the end of the second engine and took the four-foot leap to the first train. That's when the steel trestle bridge appeared in front of me.

A yardarm of some kind swung loose from a girder on the bridge, skimming just feet above the top of the locomotive. I landed on the front engine and immediately hopped back into the air, just before the steel beam hit me in the knees. I landed again and narrowly kept my balance. I dropped to my knees and scrambled forward, keeping a careful eye on the bridge as it whizzed by.

The Blackhawk peeled off as I got to within a few feet of the crew cab of the lead locomotive. There was a walkway on either side of the engine and both of them led to identical doors to the cabin. I attached another strap with carabineers to the top of the engine and slid down over the left side, unhooking myself when I'd gained the walkway with a hand on the railing.

I crept forward along the gangway. I stopped a few feet short of the door and tapped my comm.

"Dogpatch this is Orion. Go on three."

"Roger, Orion. Three, two, one...go."

A burst of gunfire erupted from the Blackhawk. I climbed two stairs and stepped up to the door to the cabin. I peeked through its glass window.

The first thing I saw was a body, slumped back in a seat. For an instant I thought Gatto's shooters had hit Harmon. But it was one of the train crew, probably the conductor. He was a slight man with large ears and a neat little bullet hole through the side of his head.

Peering around, I spotted the train engineer. The cabin was divided into two compartments that gave each crewmember a parallel but separate view of the track ahead. There were fewer controls on my side, so the engineer's station had to be on the other side. It looked like the engineer was secured to his chair with duct tape, although at least one of his arms was free.

Then Harmon leaned forward and I caught a glimpse of him. He had his back to me and was peering out the other train door, holding a short-barreled M4 carbine out in front of him. He was searching the sky for the Blackhawk. This time he'd be gunning for the tail rotor or the rotor housing. At close range he could bring the helo down and kill the entire crew if he hit it.

"Rifle out the door and hands behind your neck, fingers interlaced," I shouted as I stepped inside the train compartment.

Without hesitating, Harmon ducked through the door he'd been holding open with surprising speed, and the shot I fired missed the back of his head by an inch or two.

I darted after him, just catching the engineer's door with the edge of my foot before it slammed shut. I sprung through the door and juked left as the barrel of Harmon's rifle turned toward me. I stepped on top of the railing, perilously close to the edge of the bridge, then pushed off and launched myself into Harmon, switching the Kimber into my left hand and bringing my gloved right hand down on the top of the receiver of the M4, where the scope would have been if he'd attached one. I pushed the rifle down and away from me as I slammed my elbow into the side of his throat.

Harmon dropped the rifle, then ducked and hit me in the chest with his shoulder. He followed up with an elbow shot to my ribcage. Then he slid a hand around my waist and tried to hip-toss me off the train. I stepped my right foot in front of Harmon's left to block the throw and clung to him as he tried to shoulder me straight off the train instead. My head slipped back for a fraction of a second before I saw a steel beam whizzing by and pulled it back. I slammed my helmet into Harmon's forehead and speared the tips of my gloved fingers toward his Adam's apple when he pulled a knife with his left hand and slashed out, snagging it on one of the pouches on the front of the ammo vest I was wearing. I grabbed his wrist and stepped back while twisting, pulling him off balance by the knife arm. Then I torqued the wrist and slammed it to the ground. He dropped the knife as his wrist broke, and I jabbed the .45 into the soft spot between his collarbone and his Adam's apple.

"Where's Heather?" I asked him.

"Heather? Seriously? You're on a train that's about to derail and that's what you're focused on? They were right about you. You're a goddamn pit bull."

I didn't answer him, just tightened my grip around his broken wrist.

"You're never going to find her. You'll never see her. She's gone," he said.

Then he lunged toward me, arcing his free right hand toward the elbow of my gun hand.

At point blank range, the Kimber bucked twice in rapid succession.

FIVE DAYS LATER – SATURDAY

"That was beautiful. Sad but beautiful," Nichols said as we walked toward our cars. It was a cold, gusty afternoon at the Donel Kinnard Memorial State Veterans Cemetery. They'd just buried Tim Quigley.

"It was. You've been to a few of these?"

"A few. You've probably been to a few more."

"Yeah, I have." Dozens.

"How's your mom doing?" she asked.

"She's recovering. They have her in physical therapy. They think she'll be able to speak and function normally, but it will take a while. The left side of her body is weak right now."

"You made it back home?"

I nodded. "I rented a car in Camden and drove straight through to Conestoga. I got there just before Sandy made landfall. My mom was still in the hospital so I stayed at the house with my sister Ginny. We lost a tree and a few shingles, and the sump pump failed so the basement flooded. We had our hands full for a couple of days...I appreciate the advice by the way. I'm not sure if I would have been as quick to go back if you hadn't encouraged me."

"I'm glad it worked out."

"They're all crazy. Ginny tries to please everybody, Jamie says whatever comes to her mind and Amelia hates me. But it's a family."

"Every family is dysfunctional in its own way." Nichols smiled. "Are you sure you don't want to stop for a late lunch before you head home?"

"I've got an appointment."

"About the girl?"

I nodded.

"I heard about that," she said.

"You free for dinner?" I asked.

"Sure. Gourmet pizza?"

I made a face. Nichols laughed.

"So where do things stand with the National Front?" I asked.

"It'll take months to work our way through all the data. They tried to destroy all their computer records, but we miraculously found an intact copy of the entire dataset on one of their secondary systems."

"It's funny how those kinds of slipups happen." She caught my eye; it was obvious she knew it was no accident at all.

"But they're done regardless."

"Too much bad publicity?"

Nichols stopped. "I thought you already heard this."

"What?"

"They're broke. They must have bet everything on the energy scheme. We think it was all supposed to be invested by Jason Paul, because he would be dead at the end, right? But the investments never got made and the cash disappeared. Right now the National Front can't even afford to pay their lawyers."

"So Eric Price is headed to jail?"

"We hope so, but it will be a long process. He was very careful not to get his hands dirty. We're hoping to flip someone in the National Front. That may be the only way that we get him."

"That's disturbing," I said.

"Washington is livid."

"What about Jason Paul? Did you figure out if he's dead or alive?"

Nichols shook her head. "We haven't, at least not conclusively. But there's a huge amount of money missing, so we think he faked his death. He must have been planning this for a long time because he really did disappear without a trace."

"And he's the one responsible for all the agents who were lost."

"We'll find him. Whatever it takes."

"What about you? Do you know what's next?"

"It's hard to say. I'm going to be decorated for our actions. There's been a lot of publicity. The Bureau and the West Virginia State Police have been showered with praise. It's amazing, though, that your name hasn't surfaced in a single article."

"My old boss is an expert at keeping a low profile. It sounds like you were about to say 'but'?"

"But I didn't do things the Bureau way. I've been told that in no uncertain terms."

"That's ridiculous. You stopped half the country from going dark. I wouldn't have put things together on my own nearly as quickly as you did."

"I doubt that." Nichols smiled.

"I may have—I mean I have—I think..." I stumbled. Nichols cocked her head and I composed myself. "I don't know how you're going to react to this, but I talked to a friend at the Bureau in D.C. His name is Dan Menetti. He's just been put in charge of the Counterterrorism division. I gather it's been a mess there, but he has a pretty broad mandate to turn things around. He'd like to talk to you if you're interested."

Nichols stopped abruptly. "Am I interested? Seriously? Do you think I'm an idiot or something?"

"I wasn't sure how you'd feel about me pulling strings for you."

"I'm not twelve. I appreciate help from my friends."

"So we're friends?" I asked.

She patted me on the cheek as we reached her Suburban. "Play your cards right and some day we might even be good friends. See you tonight."

* * *

The sun hung low over the horizon and the afternoon air bit crisply. I stood with Alpha beneath the shade of an old oak on the National Front compound. We were in the back yard of the family mansion on the far end of the property.

"I thought you'd want to see this, sir. This is where Heather is buried."

"Are you certain?"

"We won't know conclusively until they get her out of the ground but I think so, yes. The FBI had cadaver dogs all over the compound for a few days before someone thought to check the family house. The earth right here has been dug up within the past two weeks. They used ground-penetrating radar yesterday to confirm that the remains of an adult human female are buried here. A bunch of men died last week over at the compound, but she would have been the only woman. I held off the medical examiner because I thought you'd want to come here first. Heather's mother will come tomorrow if she's recognizable enough to identify. Unless you want to spare her that."

Alpha looked at me, raised his eyebrows.

"Heather *is* your daughter, after all," I said.

He exhaled slowly and completely. "Was it obvious?"

"It was a lot to ask for a friend's child, so I wondered. I guess I was thrown off at first by her last name. But when I met Eric Price, he said something about you and Colonel Hernandez in a way that made me wonder if you'd had a falling out. Then one of the National Front people told me Heather's biological father had left when she was young and Colonel Hernandez was her step-dad. Heather found out about you recently, I take it?"

Alpha nodded. "We had lunch two weeks before she left home to join Reclaim. I hadn't seen her since she was three. Her mother remarried quickly. Hernandez was a friend but we didn't speak after he started seeing my ex-wife. Then I was deployed overseas for a number of years. Heather's mother persuaded me to sign the legal papers allowing Hernandez to adopt her. Did Harmon kill her?"

"I don't know. He didn't tell me at the end, but he may have. You'll have to wait for the medical examiner to tell you exactly how she died. I'd bet she was killed because of the warning she sent to her parents. Heather was brave. And whether Harmon killed her or not, it was his fault. He never should have brought her here."

We stood there in silence for a while before I turned to leave. Then Alpha started to speak.

"You helped avert a catastrophe. Given the gas shortages in New Jersey right now, you can imagine how much worse things would have been if the refinery had been damaged."

"The aftermath of the hurricane seems pretty awful as it is."

"I know you've had some...difficulties...with your job at State. The right people know what you did here. I've taken steps to ensure you're protected."

"Thank you, sir, but it's not necessary. I'd prefer to succeed or fail on my own merits."

Alpha shook his head. "It won't work that way whether I intercede or not."

"Maybe."

"You have another question," he said. His voice was as still as the oaks around us.

"No. The rest is between you and Heather." I turned again to leave, but he continued.

"Heather's mother and I met in high school. We married just before I enlisted. I spent the first two years of my marriage in Vietnam and Laos. Heather was a surprise. Her mother didn't think she could have children by that time. She came along just at the moment my career was starting to accelerate. I was young, ambitious and impulsive. When Heather's mother and I had fights, I got very angry. Once I hit her.

"When she was three, Heather was playing with a bottle of ketchup about an hour before my promotion ceremony to Major. I asked her to put the bottle down. Instead she threw it at me and it spilled on my only dress uniform. I slapped her. Very hard. The look on her face will never leave me. Her mother was just coming down the stairs when I did it. She took Heather up in her arms and walked out the front door. It was more than twenty years before I saw either one of them again."

I looked him straight in the eye for a second, then withdrew. He stood in the lengthening shadows as I drove away.

SOURCES

Master Sergeant Rodney Cox was an invaluable source of information. He read the entire manuscript and reread numerous versions of the action sequences to help me get the technical details right. His contribution of personal time was especially generous considering his rapidly expanding duties at SWCS in Fort Bragg. Thanks also to Captain Steve Gettman at Fort Leavenworth for his insights at the range and creative ideas for *Binder*.

A special thanks to my friends at Blackhawk!/ATK including Chuck Buis and Tim Brandt as well as Matt Rice and Greg Duncan of Blue Herron Communications for their thoughts and recommendations on gear.

Joe Vlasak was kind enough to lend his experience with freight trains.

Walter Harris, whose expertise in systems administration and coding is monopolized by Goldman Sachs during the day, helped me with the details for the National Front's server room. His sideline as a private pilot was also invaluable, although he points out that like Special Agent Nichols, he is not rated on the G650.

My research assistant, Elizabeth Kelley, worked with meteorologists from the National Weather Service in West Virginia to help me understand the bizarre and quickly changing weather that the state experienced in the days leading up to Hurricane Sandy. Elizabeth unearthed significant climate differences between West Virginia locations very near to one another. While I have made some minor changes for dramatic purposes, my intent in this book was to be as true to the actual weather as possible.

Bridge Day in 2012 was on October 20th, not October 27th, so it preceded the storm by more than a full week. I hope that Bridge Day enthusiasts can forgive me rewriting the timeline to put Bridge Day into the narrative. The proximity of the bridge to the other events in this book made it irresistible.

The communes, cults and compounds described in this book are invented. While I did a great deal of research on environmental protest groups, socialist communes and supremacist groups, I created wholly fictional groups and characters for *Binder*. Although there are supremacist groups in the region, no real-life analogue to the National Front exists in terms of methods or organization.

West Virginia is sometimes caricatured in the media, but my personal experience of the state has always been one of unfailing hospitality and kindness. It is one of the most beautiful places in the U.S. While I have set some very bad and desperate events in the state, West Virginia residents should note that outsiders perpetrate most of these acts in the book. This is my reading of the history of the state, as well.

I intentionally limited my descriptions of explosive devices and altered some technical details. Please forgive the inaccuracies but understand their intent.

Thanks again to those others who contributed and cannot be named. Any technical errors that remain in *Binder* are mine alone.

ACKNOWLEDGEMENTS

My indie writer's life started when I realized that I could compare over a dozen editing samples before I picked my dream editor. Rebecca Faith Heyman has been that great collaborator for the past two thrillers. Louise Darvid's painstaking proofreading was called out in several reader reviews of *Operator*, as was Stef Mcdaid's exceptionally clean Kindle conversion, and they've both reprised their roles for *Binder*.

Jothan Cashero brought his keen commercial packaging design skills to the book cover for *Binder*, as he did for *Operator*.

When I was working on my first thriller eighteen years ago, Jo Greenfield, fresh from finishing her M.F.A. at Columbia and publishing a story in the *New Yorker* gave me memorable advice on writing, which I rely on to this day.

A Pubslush campaign helped make this book possible. Thanks to my friends from Staples who supported *Binder*, including the eponymous John McCarthy (from the prologue), Ray Larney, Brad Hurley, Joan Robins Brady and

Heather Belaga McLean. Also thanks to some other friends who also made this book possible: Mike Mills, Connie Greenfield, Paul Koulogeorge, Dan Goldstein, the author Seeley James and Stan Chan. And thanks to my family members—Leslie, Jill, Mom, Sumati, Karina and Courtney—who helped support *Binder*.

Finally, my eternal love and gratitude goes to my wife Michelle, who continues to support my fiction writing as a sideline to teaching and training even when her own two jobs and our two young children make it all seem impossible.

ABOUT THE AUTHOR

After a brief stint as an intelligence analyst, David spent nearly 20 years working with corporate brands. He writes for Forbes, teaches at New York University and loves reading and the outdoors.

Visit David's profile on Forbes

Visit David's Amazon author page

Follow David on Twitter

THE MICHAEL HERNE NOVELS:

Operator

Binder

For more information, please visit www.facebook.com/operatorthenovel

CPSIA information can be obtained
at www.ICGtesting.com
Printed in the USA
LVOW12s0316040516
486574LV00008B/264/P